Reviewers' comments on Stephen Ar

—— On *Astrology, Psychology & the*

"...it's stupendous — just what is need of modern astrology in the face of its e tion and fragmentation by others."

— Kenneth Negus, Ph.D.
Rutgers University

"You have presented so eloquently, so practically, the only new approach to astrology in a generation."

— Dr. Arthur D. Cain

"...a *thinking* book that is warm, practical, beautiful, and holistic without losing sight of the 'real' problems that are the daily concern of man. A student will be safe from the inflexible, unfounded, limited, and limiting cook-book descriptions that are flooding the market. Arroyo's presentation is simply superb."

— Lore Wallace
Astrology Now

—— On *Astrology, Karma & Transformation* ——

"Arroyo's new book reflects a real depth of comprehension and ability to integrate humanistic astrology with Jungian psychology and Eastern philosophy. The simplicity and clarity of his treatment of complex ideas is remarkable; it makes accessible even to the beginner a wealth of understanding...giving meaningful psychological grounding to astrological interpretation."

— Library Journal

"This is straight, clean astrology, in modern terms, very well and concisely written. One of the best modern works we have seen."

— CAO Times

"You have done a superb job on *Astrology, Karma & Transformation.* It is the kind of book that is going to raise the level of consciousness in the astrological field. I salute you for the depth of consciousness and the insight that is shown in your book."

— Isabel Hickey
Author of *Astrology: A Cosmic Science*

"I find it to be superior to any other astrology book I have ever read. It is a remarkable work of extremely meaningful material that is written in a very lucid and practical style, and that is why I tell my students that I consider it to be an absolute 'must'."

— Robert S. Kimball
Astrological Researcher & Teacher

Other Books by the Author

ASTROLOGY, PSYCHOLOGY & THE FOUR ELEMENTS:
An Energy Approach to Astrology
& Its Use in the Counseling Arts

ASTROLOGY, KARMA & TRANSFORMATION:
The Inner Dimensions of the Birth Chart

STEPHEN ARROYO'S CHART INTERPRETATION HANDBOOK: Guidelines for Understanding the Essentials of the Birth Chart

RELATIONSHIPS & LIFE CYCLES:
Astrological Patterns of Personal Experience

NEW INSIGHTS IN MODERN ASTROLOGY:
The Jupiter/Saturn Conference Lectures
(Co-authored with Liz Greene)

EXPLORING JUPITER:
The Astrological Key to Progress,
Prosperity & Potential

PRACTICING THE COSMIC SCIENCE

STEPHEN ARROYO

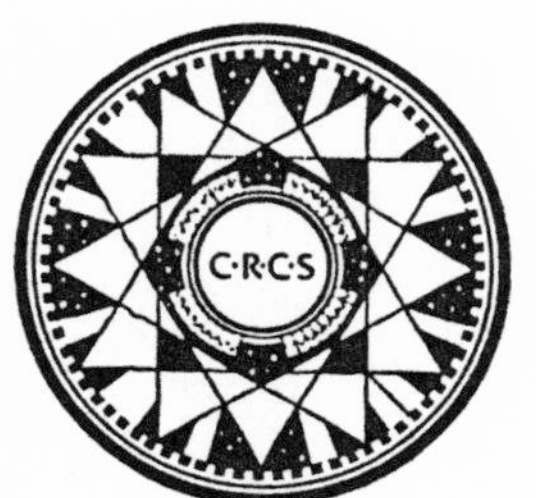

CRCS Publications
Post Office Box 1460
Sebastopol, California 95473

Library of Congress Cataloging-in-Publication Data

Arroyo, Stephen.
Practicing the cosmic science : key insights in modern astrology
Stephen Arroyo. -- 2nd ed., rev. & expanded.
p. cm.
Rev. ed. of: The practice and profession of astrology. 1st ed. c1984.
ISBN 0-916360-62-8 (pbk.)
1. Astrology and psychology. I. Arroyo, Stephen. Practice and profession of astrology. II. Title.
BF1729.P8A78 1999
133.5--dc21 99-28073
CIP

SECOND EDITION, REVISED & EXPANDED
INTERNATIONAL STANDARD BOOK NUMBER: 0-916360-62-8

Published simultaneously in the United States and Canada by CRCS Publications

Prologue

It is better to stir up a question without deciding it, than to decide it without stirring it up.
—Joseph Joubert

Many policies, procedures, and habits are taking hold in our society today, as well as in the field of astrology, without the essential factors or ultimate purposes being questioned. It is for this reason that a new, expanded edition of this book seems appropriate at this time. The original edition, entitled *The Practice & Profession of Astrology*, confronted many difficult issues and stirred up numerous questions that had not been widely publicized before. The new material in this book attempts to expand the scope of the subjects considered and to update observations on developments that seem increasingly important today, such as the extensive use of computers in astrology. I have also included a considerable amount of new material summarizing various astrological methods and interpretive factors that I have come to regard as extraordinarily important, from the perspective of over 30 years experience in the field.

I would like to thank the following people for their contributions to this book, either in its first incarnation or in its new edition: Kathe McDonald for transcribing, Aina Kemanis for transcribing and word-processing, Barbara McEnerney for proofreading, Jim Feil for developing the "brain-storming" idea that led to Chapter 6, Barbara Morgan and Rick Tarnas for inviting me to speak at the Cycles & Symbols Conference which led to much of Chapter 7, and Tony White for his cover design.

S.A.

Psychology textbooks of future generations will look back on modern psychologists working without the aid of astrology as being like medieval astronomers working without the aid of the telescope.

—Richard Tarnas, Ph.D.
Professor of Psychology

Contents

An unfailing experience of mundane events in harmony with the changes occurring in the heavens, has instructed and compelled my unwilling belief.

Johannes Kepler

Astrology is astronomy brought to earth and applied to the affairs of men.

Ralph Waldo Emerson

The natures and dispositions of men are, not without truth, distinguished from the predominances of the planets.

Sir Francis Bacon

Astrology is an acausal phenomenon . . . A horoscope is the equivalent of a mathematical formula. It is the mathematical pattern to which one human life functions.

Carl Payne Tobey

Astrology does not offer an explanation of the laws of the universe, nor why the universe exists. What it does, to put it in simplest terms, is to show us that there is a rhythm to the universe, and that man's own life partakes of this rhythm.

Henry Miller

I "believe in" astrology for the same reason that you "believe in" the multiplication table . . . It works.

Grant Lewi

Astrology would be a large scale example of synchronism, if it had at its disposal thoroughly tested findings. But at least there are some facts adequately tested and fortified by a wealth of statistics which make the astrological problem seem worthy of philosophical investigation. It is assured of recognition from psychology, without further restrictions, because astrology represents the summation of all the psychological knowledge of antiquity.

Carl Jung

Introduction

Health is the proper relationship between the microcosm, which is man, and the macrocosm, which is the universe. Disease is a disruption of this relationship.

– Dr. Yeshi Donden, physician to the Dalai Lama

The responsibility assumed by anyone practicing astrology with others is a weighty one, regardless of whether he or she consciously accepts that responsibility. Because astrology is one of the ways commonly used to re-establish the proper relationship between the microcosm and the macrocosm, those practicing it are undoubtedly engaged in practicing a healing art, whether or not they succeed in encouraging true healing. Because astrology is one of the few effective methods of rebuilding our lost connections with the cosmos, its practice is no less important, challenging, or sacred than the vocation of physician, psychologist, or priest–although admittedly the public often *pretends* to take the observations and advice of astrologers less seriously than that of these other practitioners.

The psychologist C. G. Jung felt that psychology's entire future as an effective healing art lay in this rebuilding of the lost connections between modern human beings and the cosmos. If this realignment between the individual and the greater whole of which each person is a part cannot be achieved, then no real healing can take place, as the quotation at the beginning of this Introduction states quite succinctly. I do not believe that astrology is the *only* way of encouraging this realignment, nor do I claim that astrology *by itself* (without other therapeutic or spiritual methods, practices, and attitudes) can achieve this cosmic harmony for the individual; but I do believe that astrology–properly used and properly understood–can be a tremendously effective harmonizing tool and a precisely accurate language of life that all people should learn for their own personal use.

This unity between the individual and the cosmos was taken for granted in many ancient cultures, but today we have lost the capacity to appreciate any simple thing in a simple way.

Nowadays, through study and effort and intricate analysis, we have to rebuild and rediscover the *reality* of that Oneness which our highly vaunted modern intellect has so violently shattered. I can only hope that many of us slowly learn to relax our taut intellects after all the study we pursue, enough to perceive once again the living reality of life's unity. If the study of astrology can even slightly open the door to this rediscovered state of openness and oneness, it will have made a profound contribution to modern life.

While speaking of astrology's place in the spectrum of the healing arts, I might also contrast it with modern medical and psychological orthodoxy (the "establishment") in the following way. One can easily make a case for astrology's being a major component of the feminine (or lunar) side of the healing arts; it deals with subtlety and with qualities rather than quantities, intuition rather than rigid logic. It is indeed the complement (although unacknowledged by most practitioners of orthodox methods) of the masculine (or solar) technological type of medicine and psychology of which the establishment today is so enamored. The technological-statistical-biochemical approach to the healing arts is a comparatively recent development and in many ways represents a destructive intrusion of the solar principle (or *logos*) into the domain that has traditionally been formed, developed, and sustained by those of a lunar/feminine/intuitive/caring orientation. In fact, any mention of the word "heal" or "nurture" summons the image of a lunar type of person and a caring, non-invasive sort of activity.

To carry this analogy further, the solar principle always tries to concentrate authority in itself and to shine as brightly as possible by polishing its ego through amassing social power and prestige, while the lunar principle by nature tries to sustain life (even at the cost of self-sacrifice), to help as needed while staying in the background, and to avoid conflict with those in authority. One need only look at the position of medical doctors in Western society (the "solar" exponents of the technological "healing arts") to see the aptness of this analogy and to what extent the healing arts have been made an arena of the struggle for social prestige and power, while the traditionally feminine domain of natural healing methods and traditions has been repeatedly violated. In fact, the unwarranted invasion by the solar types into the lunar domain of the healing arts is just one more example of the mentality which habitually insists upon *invasive* methods for the treatment of any problem.

Fortunately, after the attempt by the technologically-oriented to hoard all authority in the healing arts field almost succeeded, the pendulum has finally begun to swing the other way once again. However, those who have consolidated so much social power will not abdicate! And those who are devoted to one of the more lunar healing arts will have to assert their right to practice that art and to use those methods which are rightfully theirs and to which the public deserves to have access. In short, they will have to become somewhat more "solar." And, while engaged in this struggle, those who want a small place in the sun (i.e., who want to earn a decent living and have at least a modicum of respect for their profession) will not only have to confront the "authorities" in various ways and to educate the public more effectively, but also they will have to improve their public image and to some extent professionalize their field.

In spite of the thousands of people in the English-speaking world practicing astrology of one kind or another in a professional or semi-professional way, to my knowledge there has until now been no book that thoroughly treats the professional issues involved. (Dane Rudhyar's *The Practice of Astrology* and Dr. Bernard Rosenblum's *The Astrologer's Guide to Counseling* both discuss many important issues regarding the astrologer's responsibility, counseling impact, attitudes, etc., but the practical issues of astrological work as a profession and many of the other subjects discussed herein are also important and must be acknowledged.) Likewise, the whole question of astrology's place in modern society has to be addressed before any effective professionalization or organization of astrologers (or astrological counselors) can take place. Taking on subjects such as these has led me in many directions quite spontaneously, and the observations that resulted have not always been predictable nor comforting.

In fact, I seem to have the misfortune of being compelled from within to say those things that many (inside and outside the astrology field) do not want to hear. I fully realize that such statements do not make one popular. Also, since astrology is a religion to many thousands of people who therefore "believe in it" wholeheartedly and without discrimination, an indignant backlash can result when one seems to be attacking the high priests or the tenets of that religion. To say, for example, that there are limits to astrology's useful applicability is absolute heresy to those who believe "How can there be *any* limits to my own true religion?" As stated in this book, I have no intention of devaluing anyone's religion; those for whom astrology is a religion should probably not read this book. But for me, since astrology is not a religion but rather an art/science which is continually changing and being reformulated to suit the needs of a particular time period and culture, I have no qualms about stating precisely how I think this reformulation should take place.

In the last analysis, to rebuild our lost connections with the cosmos, we have to learn how to understand the cosmic language. We have to learn how to listen to the celestial music; *this* is a healing experience! Even to approach such an attunement is a great attainment, and a rare one. So, for ordinary mortals, this cosmic connection is only slowly perceived over time. While orthodox medicine, therapy, and psychology generally have no basis in philosophy or cosmic law, astrology is based on unchanging principles. The study of astrology *as a tool for self-development and self-knowledge* is based not on "new discoveries" but on a deeper penetration into those few ancient principles that are already known. Over time, we come closer to understanding and appreciating the ancient truths, perhaps through reformulating them or redefining them, but never replacing them with the constantly changing fads of every era.

1

Astrology Today & the Astrological Psychology of Tomorrow

The unprejudiced observer is the only true scientist.
—James T. Kent, M.D.

It is theory that decides what we can observe.
—Albert Einstein

As years go by, I'm more and more interested in the social implications of astrology, its place in society, and the philosophical foundations that it should be based on. So, although the first few books I wrote are filled with a lot of astrological details that can be used in chart interpretation, that's not what I'm going to talk about now, nor is that my main interest now.

Before anything else, I want to formally acknowledge my debt to British astrology. Other than the work of Rudhyar, who has lived in America most of his life, most of my first teachers in astrology (through books, not in person) were the great British authors. I feel especially indebted to Margaret Hone and Charles Carter. I'm not really trying to flatter you collectively by saying this, but generally there has been a tradition in British astrology of a sharpness of mind that is notably lacking in most of the American astrological literature. So, although books on astrology produced in the States tend to flood the market these days, it still seems to me that real progress toward a *psychologically-oriented,* modern astrology started here in Britain. One might say it started

---

This chapter is based on a talk given in Canterbury, England, at the Fall 1982 Conference of the British Astrological Association. It has been extensively edited from a transcript of the original lecture.

with Alan Leo, I suppose, although Isabelle Pagan and many others did excellent work as well. The British astrologers built up the theoretical and metaphysical foundations in a way that the Americans probably couldn't have, and the early influence of the Theosophists contributed an openness to the spiritual side of life that *must* be included in any comprehensive astrological psychology.

I have one more introductory comment. I don't associate with astrologers very much, and even with those that I know, I really don't know what they do in a consultation. I don't really know how they are with people in a one-to-one situation, except when I occasionally talk with a former client of theirs. So, when I make certain statements (and some are very broad and sometimes controversial statements), you have to assume that *I am referring primarily to the kind of astrology that exists in the literature on astrology.* I have a feeling that there are many, many astrologers (or astrological counselors–whatever term you prefer) who practice a type of astrology and astrological counseling that is much, much better than the kind of astrology that is presented in the literature. Many of those people are probably too busy doing their work ever to write anything, or they find their breadth of experience extremely difficult to condense into words. But, I wish they *would* write more things.

Unfortunately, I have to deal with the kind of astrology that is presented in the literature because *that* is what the general public often sees as "astrology." The only thing the average person knows about astrology (other than the prejudices and sensationalism that the mass media is always propounding) comes through books. They go to a bookstore and buy a book. If they are lucky, they happen onto one of the few intelligent books; but most likely they buy those cheap sun-sign books, and pretty soon they're convinced that all of astrology deals with superficial character analysis, predictions, or sex. The literature of astrology, I believe, is in shambles, and I think it is important for all of us to encourage those in the field who really *do* have something unique to say and who really are articulate, to put it on paper and get it in book form. I guess it's my Aquarius Moon coming out, but I think it's extremely important today that astrology be related to society more and more effectively. Not just propaganda, but *intelligence.* In fact, a lot of astrologers underestimate the intelligence of the general populace, as do many astrological authors.

Definitions of "Astrology'

I have to get into some definitions before talking about "astrology." You have to know what I mean by that term. But first, there's one quotation from Marc Edmund Jones that I want to read. No doubt there are many, many people in the field of astrology who have been active and who have studied and done thousands of charts for 30 and 40 years. Those are the kind of people that I keep trying to push into putting on paper what they have seen and learned. Marc Edmund Jones, after being in the field for 50 years, was at a conference a few years ago. A woman went up to him and said, "Oh, I envy the knowledge that you've accummulated on this subject." He replied, "Oh, my dear, I've been at it for 50 years and I've only just begun to scratch the surface." This is true today, even more than 10 years ago. The field of astrology is growing, developing, and expanding. But it's also fragmenting. No matter what you do, even if you spent all your waking hours studying different aspects of astrology, you can't help but just scratch the surface, because it's a profound, cosmic science–art. Thus, it can be applied, to some extent, to almost every aspect of life. Therefore, one definition of astrology in general, covering *all* its applications, is simply "a language of life" or, alternately, "a universal language of energy." So it's important when anyone talks about "astrology" to define what kind he's referring to. As Rudhyar once wrote, one should actually speak of "astrologies," because each type of astrology studies different things from a different perspective and applies the results of the study to different objects and for different aims and purposes.

More and more I prefer to use the term "astrological psychology." When I'm with just one other person who already knows where I'm at astrologically, I'll just say "astrology." But "astrological psychology," I think, is an important term and it's quite different from "psychological astrology," a term quite fashionable in the past 15 years or so. "Astrological psychology" implicitly states that *astrology is inherently a psychology,* in other words, a system with which to study the psyche! I also prefer to use Ralph Metzner's definition of astrology for the kind of astrology I'm most interested in. He's written a couple of books, one called *Maps of Consciousness.* He's not an astrologer per se. He's a research psychologist who is especially open-minded and intuitive, and he used to teach at Harvard University. He says that "astrology is astronomy applied for psychological purposes." That's a nice, short definition that satisfies me so long as the word "psychological" is taken in the broadest sense; "psyche" must be taken in its most inclusive sense.

This new "astrological psychology" is being born *now.* It is today *still* being born, so I can't purport to sound out all its dimensions, but it is getting increasingly clear *what it is not.** Very often, when some new idea or new direction or–in your personal life–some intimation of a new development in your life starts to become apparent, you don't yet know what it is or where it's ultimately going; but you *do* know what you don't like about the old ideas and directions. You know you *don't* want to keep doing this or keep doing that. You're not happy with various old patterns. So, what this new "astrological psychology" *is* will develop slowly but surely. But already, what it is *not* is becoming more clear.

As Dennis Elwell, one of the best modern writers in the astrology field, wrote over a decade ago:

> What exists today is not an astrological psychology, but an application of astrology to other psychologies. Instead of evolving a psychology congenial to itself out of its own unique vision of man and the world about him, astrology has always been constrained within ready-made, and to some extent alien, frameworks. It has been made to wear borrowed clothing, not always of the best fit.

I think I should say very clearly here at the beginning that, to me, astrology is inherently a psychology. Inherently, *it is a psychology!* C. J. Jung acknowledged that decades ago when he wrote that astrology incorporates all of the psychology of the ancient world.

---

*As Nobel Prize winning physicist Niels Bohr put it, great innovations inevitably first appear muddled, confusing, and incomplete, only half-understood even by their dis-

> Astrology is assured recognition from psychology, without further restriction, because astrology represents the summation of all psychological knowledge of antiquity.
>
> – C. G. Jung, Commentary on *The Secret of the Golden Flower*

Astrology, even in its current fragmented state, is inherently a psychology, and in my opinion, a better psychology, more accurate and, in fact, more scientific in the true sense of the word than any other psychological theory or system. It is a great descriptive language of all human functions, needs, energies, urges, archetypes, and dilemmas, rooted in real human experience and the cosmic order of life.

Recently a bit of Jungian psychology has been added to astrology, and some people talk about transactional analysis; every type of "psychology" now has been thrown into the pot. I'm not saying it's all bad or all good. I just think it's important to acknowledge what we're doing and to stick to the essence of our science as closely as we can, or else I think we lose it. Unfortunately, by default and by tradition, behaviorism has been the primary psychological emphasis of most astrological work and most of the literature. Again, to quote from the article Elwell wrote in 1970,

> Unfortunately, without the matter ever having been debated, astrology has aligned itself with behaviorism, which evaluates a person from the outside, in terms of observable characteristics.

Now this approach to astrology reflects, as Elwell writes, "a wish to describe people, rather than understand them." It's important in any astrological literature, certainly, to build up a body of accurate, incisive, descriptive characteristics of the various astrological types, and this could still be improved upon a great deal. However, if you just describe the obvious and don't have any understanding, it's pretty hollow. Unfortunately, that's what many people find when they go to astrologers, and especially when they get a computer print-out of astrological "interpretations" that give a lot of descriptions and *absolutely no understanding!* We need to evolve a *perceptive* descriptive language in astrology.

---

coverers and a total mystery to everyone else. There is no hope, Bohr said, for any speculation that does not at first appear (to most people) completely absurd.

I'm starting this talk off on the heaviest theoretical issues. For some reason, every thought I've had in the past few months opens up a giant chasm of ignorance. The more I explore it, the more endless it becomes. I see how little we know and how far we have to go in the field of astrology. So there are probably twenty-five or thirty issues that we might mention, and each one could be discussed for two or three hours in itself. In a way, I'm just skimming the surface, but there are a lot of questions that I never hear raised in the astrological journals or by astrologers at the astrological conferences. For some reason, I feel I have to talk about those questions.

What Astrological Psychology Is & Is Not

Now the following are *not* astrological psychology, which I feel *can* be a true science, especially when it's totally born. None of the following are really a science, nor even a consistent approach. And you have to question how valuable such contributions are to understanding human beings. These various approaches contribute little to a *perceptive* description and appreciation of human nature.

1) "Pseudo-original-theory astrology." This is the type that is based on the "let's develop what nobody else has" obsession. You really see this a lot. You see it at astrological conferences and in journals a great deal. But really, nothing in astrology is original. This is one thing that's embarrassing to me about people making a big deal out of me, because almost everything in my books is very ancient stuff. There's nothing new in it. I just know how to write English and how to think systematically. And that evidently seems new and unusual in the astrological literature!

2) Another type of astrology currently practiced is what I call "let's extrapolate a theory astrology." This winds up in lots of padded "cookbooks." A lot of astrological cookbooks flood the market. They purport to be comprehensive. There's all this speculation and endless analysis, and the worst part of them is that they come up with pat answers to every human problem or situation. We all know that it's not that easy. With every little conflict related to one of your hard aspects, you read these

books and you'll find all the pat answers and simplistic advice that you could ever imagine and a nice statement about how you can solve all your problems. That's not the kind of astrology that will encourage intelligent people to get involved in it.

3) Then there's the astrology with superimposed spiritual beliefs. I have no objection to anyone using astrology as part of his or her religion, but let's recognize it as such in those cases and differentiate it from an astrological psychology developing as a science of human nature.

4) Then there's the astrology with superimposed philosophical or social beliefs.

5) Then there's "advice astrology." This is very common, of course, and it's along the lines of the old fortune-teller school: "You should do this, you must not do that." I remember a friend of mine who once went to a very well known astrologer on the east coast of the United States. My friend was a Virgo and was seeing a Virgo Sun woman, and they were dabbling with the idea of getting married. Rather than any intelligent dialogue, and rather than any questioning by this astrologer of how they felt and what they were doing with their lives, she just reacted to their living together for so long unmarried, glanced at the charts, and started screaming at this guy hysterically, "Marry the girl! Marry the girl!" Of course, he didn't. He was living with someone else a year later. This advice astrology, I think, is very dangerous.

6) Another kind of astrology is "Guess what your karma is." I think more and more people are being cautious about rendering supposed karmic judgments about charts. I think there is more awareness now than there was ten to fifteen years ago.

7) Then there's "Aren't we clever astrology," which is based on the idea of "let's find a neat little correlation for everything." Even if it's not there, let's find it anyways!

8) Then there's "guessing game astrology," which is basically "let's predict events."

9) Then there's "pseudo-scientific astrology," which seems to imply that everything has to be statistically verifiable for it to be true. In fact, it's quite obvious that statistics *cull out* in-

dividual and rare truths in favor of a kind of mish-mash-mush of averages. And of course, those whose religion is *scientism* superimpose those religious beliefs and demand that reality fit those beliefs just as much as do those with metaphysical biases, as mentioned in # 3 above.

So, when I talk about astrological psychology, I can't mean any of these commonly-used approaches. Admittedly, it is hard to define exactly what I mean in a concise way, and it is impossible to define it without using a few abstract terms–terms which not all people will immediately feel comfortable with. Nevertheless, by "astrological psychology," I mean the study and the language of human experience that emphasizes and illuminates the archetypal levels of human nature. Specifically, I still feel comfortable with the terms I presented in my first book,* and these are the *substance* which any true astrological psychology that purports to be a science must include:

The *dimensions of experience* (the planets).
The *qualities of experience* (the signs).
The *fields of experience* (the houses).
The *energy substance of experience* (the elements).

One reason I'm emphasizing astrology's *own* inherent psychology and its *own* language (both of which must be allowed to develop in their *own* way!) is that astrology emanates from *universal mind.* You could use other words for it–cosmic mind, archetypal mind, collective unconscious, etc. Take your pick. Astrology, I believe, emanates from that level of mind in such a direct way that I think it's very troublesome and dangerous to impose a lot of overlays of man-made theory and intellectual gymnastics. Better to learn how to read the celestial language that's already there! Most of all, when I was doing a lot of consultations, I found that people could relate to and accept and understand the astrological language itself, *if spoken clearly* in a direct way. In spite of the fact that I had all sorts of psycho-

---

*See pages 79 and following of *Astrology, Psychology & the Four Elements: An Energy Approach to Astrology & Its Use in the Counseling Arts.*

logical training (by then I'd extensively studied Jungian and other schools of thought and I knew their terminology), I found that just by using the astrological terminology the average person could understand profound life patterns *if they were explained right.* I found just by experience that that was working best. Its simplicity worked! I didn't have to put on an overlay of other terminology or theory. The simplicity had a lot to recommend it. Also, man-made constructs are generally not well defined or well correlated to real experience. They tend to overlap a number of astrological archetypes. You can see this, for example, in Charles Carter's *Encyclopedia of Psychological Astrology.* He tried to define various man-made theories or types of behavior astrologically. He'd have to say, "Well, it could be Uranus in the 3rd house, or Mercury in Aquarius, or any number of other factors." Pretty soon it's very confusing.

A lot of what I'm saying today may at first seem terribly negative, and I'm hoping that all of you are at least slightly Plutonian and therefore see the need for a lot of garbage to be cleared out before astrology can, in fact, be reborn. In the astrological field, and especially—if I may use the term—in the astrological *profession,* it is necessary, I feel, to do this purging. I don't mean to imply that we throw away the basic traditions, but that we use them and build on them. Astrology per se, and astrological psychology specifically, is an already existing science, but it potentially could be a much greater and more useful science. First, we need to develop our interpretive language further. It needs more clarity and definition. More about the language issue in a few minutes.

But you might still be asking, what is this new "astrological psychology?" Again, I'd like to quote Elwell, because he has come closer than anyone I know of to putting it in words.

> For years a strongly *inward* psychology has been developing, a psychology of motivation and striving, in which behavior is reduced to the status of an almost incidental fallout, yet the mainstream of astrology has clung stubbornly to behaviorist thinking. Whatever their differences, the psychologists Freud, Jung, Adler and their followers all sought to identify an inner situation. Each drew a map of man's inner world. So far astrology has not seriously

> tried even to sketch the landmarks on its own map of the same territory, nor does there seem to be any real conviction that such an exercise might be worthwhile.

Now remember, this was written about 1970. Maybe I'm just optimistic, but I do believe that, since then, there has been a significant beginning to sketch those inner landmarks in astrology. The journals of the British Astrological Association and the Federation of Canadian Astrologers are good examples of the fact that this is happening. You can see it in some of the articles and in some of the letters to the editor. And there are a few books that have come out with that inward emphasis. I think it's especially significant that suddenly there are at least four books on astrological counseling that are all being published within a six-month period.* Previously, there hasn't been even one book solely devoted to the subject. All of a sudden, we have almost enough material for a curriculum on astrological counseling! Until now, the only book I know of that dealt with many of those issues has been Rudhyar's *The Practice of Astrology*. I guess one could call this an example of *zeitgeist*. It's really encouraging, I think, and I hope it marks a new level of sophistication for astrological practitioners to aim for.

For astrological psychology to develop further, my feeling is that there has to be a new attentiveness to basic counseling principles, and not just for the benefit of the client, but also because that's the best way the astrologer can learn—in a genuine dialogue with a person. You don't just do a "reading" while they sit there passively sorting and screening all this mental stuff through their belief systems and prejudices. You find out where they are, what they're experiencing, and then *you* learn just as much as they do! I don't know any other way it could happen. It seems to me that's how you really learn personal and inward astrology, and that way you learn it at a fairly deep level. It does take time and patience. It does preclude a lot of quick readings

---

*The four books referred to were *The Astrologer's Guide to Counseling*, *The Astrology of Choice*, *Astrological Counseling*, and *Healing & the Horoscope*. In subsequent years, a number of other books relating astrology to counseling and healing were also published. However, almost all of them went out of print after only one printing due to slow sales. Without a viable profession and its academic and financial support systems, such books cannot remain in print, although they should be required texts in any comprehensive training program for astrological counselors.

and so forth. But from such a first-hand application of astrology, a number of things can evolve:

First of all, a better astrological language can develop. You'll be able to see: What is your client responding to? What is the person actually understanding? If you say, "Well, Mars is in the 9th house and quincunx Pluto and so forth . . .", and you have a rapport with the client, then you'll *know* when you've failed to communicate. Whereas if you put that statement in a written chart interpretation, you will not know if you've failed to communicate or if your client has taken it all wrong. In other words, you'll be forced to develop a more effective language to communicate the astrology.

Also, from first-hand application of astrology a much greater understanding of people can develop, as they live and breathe and experience various transits and natal aspects and so forth. The importance of such experience should hardly be underestimated by anyone who purports to be an "astrologer." This is another thing that–from a writer's point of view–I find really abysmally boring about most astrological books. The human element is not there! How many times have you seen in an astrological book, "Well, one client said. . . . " Any reference to a human experience? Hardly ever! One gets the feeling that all astrologers simply sit in a back room theorizing in isolation. Astrology is a tremendous abstract study. But it does have to be brought down to earth if it's to be more accepted in society and thus used more widely. I'm not really hung up on acceptability per se. But if we believe that astrology has a lot of value, then we should also accept the fact that we need to do certain things to make it more accessible to people.

The Practice of Astrology & Its Effectiveness

Now, there are a number of questions about astrology's effectiveness, or lack of it, that I want to raise. I don't have any great, simple solutions for all of these questions. Some of them are admittedly challenges to astrologers, and the issues at stake must ultimately be acknowledged by astrological practitioners. These next few topics all have an impact on the effectiveness of all astrological counselors. Over 400 years ago, Paracelsus, who was a key figure in the development of medicine and a deep student of astrology, said that *the physician must cure the disease in the way that it wants to be cured, not in the way he wants to cure it.* Now if one is a counselor using astrology, I think it's important not to assume *anything.* Don't interpose theory between you and the client. Just keep your eyes open to see what is there! If you're really doing astrological *counseling,* you'll get "leads" from the person. *From the person* you'll find out what the problem is and you'll know where to go—you'll follow those leads. Astrology then becomes a fantastic thing, I think. It can then illuminate the whole inner situation of the person, whereas if you look at the chart first, and not at the person at all, you're not letting the problem or the astrology reveal themselves in a natural way. Wouldn't it be more effective if you'd let the person reveal himself or herself first? Then perhaps you could apply Paracelsus' advice and see how the client's state of "dis-ease" wants to be cured.

Admittedly, many clients don't want to reveal themselves, especially the Scorpio rising clients! They are the worst. One lady astrologer that I knew once finally took an oath never to do another consultation for a Scorpio rising! She found it exhausted her so thoroughly that she was just shot for the rest of the day. There was just so much resistance to break through, and so much reticence to reveal oneself. This is why I prefaced these remarks by saying that I don't have easy remedies for all these situations, and certainly I'm speaking in terms of ideals, to some extent. It is not with every client that you can have this perfect dialogue and clear communication where they give you all these great leads, and you then just take off on brilliant insights! Counseling, I think, is some of the hardest work I've ever done. It's really hard work, if you're going to do it right.

There is what I call the "know-it-all" syndrome among astrologers, and I'm not just basing this judgment on outside observation. I've also had some astrologers come to me for appointments. I never could figure out why, in those cases, because they inevitably did all the talking. It was obvious that no matter what I said, if I linked it to astrological factors, they were linking that same thing to other factors. Both people were seeing the same things in the same chart, but in totally different ways. However, their aim seemed to be to convince me that they already knew everything. This "know-it-all" syndrome is by no means found only in astrologers. The following quotation sheds some light on this peculiar characteristic. It was written by Samuel Hahnemann, the founder of homeopathic medicine, a true genius in the healing arts field.

Hahnemann's quote is about physicians, but it's equally applicable to astrologers, who at best often act as physicians of the inner person. He said, "preventing, relieving, and curing are the functions of the physician's office, not to pose before the world as expounders of the inexplicable and masters of all the unknowable in the universe." Preventing, relieving, and curing are much more important in all the healing arts and helping professions than posing as someone so brilliant as to know everything. This quote continues, "To be able to explain everything is the function of the sham—to cure is that of the true physician." A lot of astrologers could benefit by taking this observation to heart.

In spite of my seeming to put down certain kinds of astrology or astrologers, I really don't care what anybody does so long as the client is benefitting from it. I'm not setting myself up to judge that. That's purely from the client's point of view. The main thing from my viewpoint is: Is what you're doing working? Is it effecting a healing or curative type of reaction in the person? Those standards define my particular bias in evaluating the work of astrologers who do general counseling with the public.

For effective consultations, you've got to stress what you know and what you emphasize in your particular studies and practice and research. If the astrologer can clearly define his area of specialization, *his purpose*, then he'll also know when he should refer clients to people with other specialties. Astrology is fragmenting and increasingly specialized. I may be wrong, but I don't see any other direction it can go in than still more specialization. If one is going to be an economist—astrologer, or a medical-astrologer or a psychologist-astrologer, fine! So be it.

Let's just make it clear to the public what we do best. The field is just incredibly demanding. How can one be good at *all* those things? You'll never have time to research all those areas! Just like a good doctor will often admit uncertainty and therefore refer the client, I think astrologers should do this also. Unfortunately, right now there aren't even ways of knowing who you can refer to. An organization like the Astrological Association here in Britain could work on something like that, maybe a pamphlet of the members who are actively practicing, what their specializations are, and so forth.

The key issue when judging astrology's effectiveness or lack of it in a counseling situation is, I believe, *interpretation versus understanding.* Interpretation has nothing to do with understanding, necessarily. In fact, too much interpretation can inhibit your understanding. Now there are a number of things worth mentioning about this issue. One thing I've found is that there are many troubled clients who have dug themselves into a hole, a psychological hole. They come to you, and you see they have dug themselves into this hole, often through excessive self-analysis. If they're into astrology, it's often through excessive analysis of their charts that they've become so lost and confused. But instead of seeing what clarity and overview we can give them, they demand that we climb into the hole with them and play with their questions *at their level.* Now it's very hard to say anything about such a situation that will apply to everyone. In some cases, I think it is true that you kind of have to go down into the hole, onto their level of conflict and confusion, and sit and chat with them awhile. But in many cases, it's better to refuse to go down into that hole and instead to summon them out of it! Challenge them to take a different point of view!

Astrology's greatest strength, I think, is its perspective, not guessing at particulars. If you're at the top of the hole and they're in the hole, you've got an incredible perspective but they can't see anything. Especially during certain transits of Pluto (or other outer planets), even knowing some astrology people often aren't able to see anything clearly. Often if we can just summon them to adapt a different perspective, they can start thinking in a new way. Then it becomes a question of understanding. Excessive "interpretation" at a time like that will often just dig them deeper into an intellectual hole, a fairly deep hole that was perhaps caused initially by too much analysis. So, we're often not fulfilling our potential in this helping profession if we just deal with people by analyzing and interpreting a myriad of details.

As a matter of fact, I think the cosmos puts blinders on us at times, to force us to go through certain karma. I can look back now in my own life and see what transits were happening during certain crucial periods, but at the time I couldn't see those transits. I knew astrology then, but I couldn't "see" them. One time I had surgery, and transiting Pluto was conjunct my 7th house cusp *exactly* on the day of the surgery. But I didn't see it. For some reason I couldn't see it, and I went ahead and scheduled the surgery. If I had known about that transit I would never have scheduled it because of fear. There is a bit of superstition in all astrologers, and some desire in all people to try to avoid their fate, and Pluto, well . . . , has–shall we say– a rather bad reputation that would have caused me some anxiety. Anyway, it's happened with other people I know, too, who are deeply into astrology–when they get in a certain psychic state, they can't see it. They can't even use the astrology for themselves. Likewise, many psychics can't help themselves with their psychic abilities. This is a different subject, but I must say that astrologers would probably learn a lot by being clients. Go to some other astrologers, and don't tell them that you know any astrology. Then you'll be really shocked!

In emphasizing understanding rather than interpretation, I'm saying that encouraging the client to *face* himself or herself rather than running away from oneself, is in many cases the duty of the astrologer. It is also the most effective approach in counseling. Mere interpretation often encourages the client to run away from where they are and from their real feelings. In other words, it often seems that an overly analytical astrologer is trying to take out a little pain (by denying or dismissing it) and replace it with a whole lot of verbiage. That is not really curative, although maybe very transitory relief is provided in some cases.

This facing of self, even if painful (and it often is), can lead to the positive type of Pluto experience–namely, real transformation onto a new level of understanding. This is real growth of consciousness, and anything that leads to that is truly effective counseling. After all, "the truth shall make you free." If we align ourselves with that part of the client that wants to deny the truth, deny the pain and the vulnerability (a negative type of Plutonian behavior), we are helping to shield the client from reality and reinforcing his self-repressive tendencies that have already led to a state of misery. As Herbert Spencer said, the ultimate effect of shielding people from their folly is to fill the world with fools!

One example of understanding versus interpretation: at a Saturn Return, one often feels, "Oh, I'm so disappointed in so-and-so (some significant person–spouse, lover, friend, boss, etc.)." That client, that person, will feel depressed and crushed. But that feeling makes a statement about their *expectations*! It doesn't necessarily make a statement about the other person's true nature. If Mary says, "Oh, I'm so disappointed in John. Here I thought for years that John was such a great guy, and now this relationship is a disaster and John is just a big pain. He's been using me for years!" Well, maybe John isn't so hot, but Mary is also revealing her expectations, and she needs to acknowledge her own expectations during that Saturn Return. This is what I mean by emphasizing *understanding* in an inward kind of astrology, rather than an astrologer just saying "Well, let's see, you have your Saturn Return now, Mary. Are things rotten with John? Well, don't worry, it will pass." With a Saturn Return you deal so much with your past expectations that are now being shattered in the light of reality and experience. So, what is the person revealing in their statements, or in their problems, about their expectations, priorities, and ideals? Can you help the client clarify those attitudes and values? All of that is just as significant as any listing of events.

Another factor that relates to the effectiveness of an astrologer, or the lack of it, is the need to keep focused on the *purpose* of the consultation. Otherwise, it is very easy to get lost in infinite information. There is something sort of seductive about astrology, for some reason, that just pulls you in. Many people here have experienced that when they first got into astrology. They were just so utterly fascinated by it that they almost got lost in it. It's important to keep focused on the purpose of the consultation when you're with a client, to guide you through the innumerable combinations of symbols in every chart. Otherwise the chart might start doing a little dance in front of your eyes, and if you start following every little moving symbol on the chart, in no time the appointment is over. Then what was the purpose of all that?

To quote from Rudhyar:

> Knowledge which does not take into consideration the knower can cause incalculable harm, especially if forced prematurely on the other person. Many astrologers think of astrology as a definite system of "knowledge" which is based on a multitude of observations recorded by generations of theoretically careful, scientist-astrologers. They feel that this system is "true" and that it can definitely predict events. Furthermore, many astrologers unquestionably believe that "forewarned is forearmed," regardless of who the person is and what his feelings and way of thinking are when the future event is announced to him, and regardless of the way in which the prediction is made.

Astrology has an inherent power. I don't believe we have to try to *make things happen* as much as we're tempted to, in counseling clients particularly. It has an inherent power. The chart is a "grid," if you want to put it that way, that connects the individual to the whole of creation. People can get a sense of cosmic order in their apparently chaotic experience. And that is what many people get out of astrology. It's that sense of order, that inherent power to tell people that it's O.K., to restore their self-confidence and their peace of mind, and if the counselor is good and effective—to encourage self-acceptance. The purpose of astrology is not to encourage confusion, fragmentation, mental tension, and anxiety about the future.

I should probably tell you, since this is perhaps seeming very "preachy," that when I was doing a lot of counseling, I would say maybe 30 to 40% of my clients came to me *after going to another astrologer.* It infuriated me to see and hear what was being done in the name of astrology. In a sense, I had to spend a lot of time trying to undo damage, trying to reassure them that, "No, this is not necessarily fated," etc. That gets tiresome, too, but you have to do it, I guess. Anxiety about the future had become an almost crippling disease in many of these clients. And very often the seed of that anxiety had been planted by the astrologers! That's a very heavy thing to do, I would say. So, please forgive me if I seem unduly critical of many astrologers. But to me there is no doubt whatsoever that large numbers of practitioners are irresponsibly putting their egos and need to pose as "know-it-alls" before the welfare of their clients. Such pretentious behavior also damages the reputation of all practitioners and of astrology itself.

Now the following is a real challenge to astrological counselors, I think, and there's no easy answer. A major and frustrating problem in astrological counseling stems from the fact that you're dealing with the client's level of self-knowledge. The "knower" matters at least as much as the "knowledge," as Rudhyar pointed out in the quote we read a couple of minutes ago. You have to go *through* their level of self-knowledge. The chart may show the truth of that person's energy attunement, but it does not show that person's level of consciousness and self-awareness. In addition, self-deception is a major tendency of human beings. So there you are, the astrologer, having to go through layers and layers of self-deception, and layers and layers of ignorance or wrong self-knowledge, that is, inaccurate beliefs about oneself that the person is holding. If you cannot establish real communication with the person by *beginning* at their level of self-knowledge (something that often requires much effort and patience), your "counseling" will probably be ineffective. To make this a little more realistic, I'll give an example.

If one has a lot of Scorpio, he or she is likely to be afflicted with some degree of jealousy. But if that person's Moon is in Aries or Sagittarius or Aquarius, the "Oh, I'm never jealous" signs, he may think of himself as not jealous, as personally above that petty sort of stuff. Now if, in fact, you're counseling somebody who has a lot of Scorpio, and he or she has the Moon in such a positive sign (and the Moon has a lot to do with your self-image, how you feel about yourself), you immediately have a problem if that person doesn't know himself too well. I'm not saying there's only one way of dealing with this, or one grand solution to this problem, but it's a very common problem.

Sometimes, the client's self-knowledge is so pitiful that it is just like talking to concrete. In situations like this, you are asking a client to trust you, if he is going to reveal himself. In fact, *you're asking the client to trust you and to trust astrology more than his own emotions and self-image.* You're dealing with all the psychological patterns that that person is into, which that person does not want to give up. You're asking him really to trust you and astrology rather than all those feelings. If what you say contradicts that person's beliefs or life-long images of self, that is a tremendous thing to ask of somebody. You're really asking them to open up and look at themselves. So they've got to trust you and you've got to be trustworthy. You've got to seem trustworthy.

Also, this need to establish trust might be another good reason to set up more than one appointment with a new client. I don't know how people do practices here, but in the States most astrologers have one-shot appointments. Many of those people they will never see again. I would think that the fact that you are asking a client to trust you so much is an excellent reason for (if possible) setting up two appointments right at the start, maybe even three—something to get them used to you and you used to them. There may be a lot of advantages to that kind of approach. Of course, you're demanding more of a commitment from the client, then. But that may be good. I mean you'll have to charge more, so you'll be screening out some people. That might have disadvantages in some cases.*

Also, once that person leaves your office after the appointment, as many of you know, you often suddenly start seeing a whole lot that you didn't see when they were there. I don't know exactly why this is, but as long as I'm in the presence of somebody, I can only think within certain parameters. I can only react to certain things, and other things I can't even see clearly. When I did one-shot appointments, I learned to make a ritual of leaving the room after the first hour and walking outside for a few minutes. I would often get all these revelations then. Suddenly my mind would be free again. I have a very strong Neptune

---

*See Chapter 4 for further discussion on structuring a practice.

and a packed seventh house, so I just soak in the other person if they're present. The person's expectations could actually restrict what I could see, and what they didn't want me to see. Very often, as I was walking around during the break, I'd go, "Aaaaahhh!" and suddenly would realize something crucial. It was usually the right thing. I mean, you've got to work with your own psyche too, your limitations, and the way your psyche functions. I can't purport to know how anybody else functions. The practice of astrology is a totally individual art.

Astrology gives incredible keys to understanding. We know that. These keys to understanding are astounding. It is the only system I know of that lets you get inside the other person so deeply, in an almost frightening way sometimes. This level of understanding and this profound scope of understanding is part of the cosmic connection. The chart is a grid, showing how one fits into the whole cosmic order. If you can successfully communicate this understanding, your counseling will no doubt be effective. You don't have to have nice simplistic answers and easy solutions to all personal problems to do this. Even if you have no answers, *just outlining clearly and graphically what the current situation is often gives so much clarity that that in itself is curative or healing.* If you can do this, then you've gone a long way towards effective counseling–if you can successfully communicate this power and this incisiveness of astrology. It's got to be through understanding; it can't be just through interpretation. As it says in the Bible,

> "Wisdom is the principal thing; therefore get wisdom: and with all thy getting get understanding."
>
> – *Proverbs* iv, 7.

The Magic of Astrology & Its Relation to Healing

In spite of the tyranny of materialism posing as true science these days and the related attempts to disprove or deny astrology's validity, the magic of astrology is real and I don't think we should even try to remove it. The very fact that every aspect of astrology is surrounded by so much controversy suggests that some deep and genuine issues are at stake. I don't know the whole situation in this society, but I gather that the B.B.C. has not been too cooperative in broadcasting any accurate portrayal of astrology, in spite of a show being developed some years ago. In the United States, this media blackout* is also present for the most part. The reason for all the often-bitter controversy about astrology is that there are *incompatible world views* clashing whenever that subject is discussed. The dominant world view, the one that the establishment supports, is the so-called "scientific" world view (otherwise known as the pseudo-scientific, materialistic world view). Now astrology cannot be proven materialistically—at least not yet. Probably, it never will be.

However, astrology may well be provable, or even *already* proven, within the domain of *true* science—"Science" meaning "I know," from the Latin word *scio.* If we understand science in its true meaning, then astrology should indeed strive to improve itself scientifically, to refine itself so as to make it closer to truth, to real knowledge. A broader definition of science needs to be acknowledged, and that of the philosopher Herbert Spencer is, I feel, quite satisfactory: "Science is organized knowledge." On the other hand, a misguided attempt to substitute materialistic measurements for real science in some vague hope of the establishment's approval is quite a mistake in my view and diverts astrology into the wrong channels.† We might also better understand this question of science by listening to this quotation from Bacon:

> Books must follow sciences and not sciences books.

To me this means that the search for truth and knowledge must come first, and that then the books will come later to report on the findings, to present systematically the organized knowledge that has been discovered. And yet, what is happening today in most of the "scientific" establishment is that the books already written are considered some sort of gospel, and the new discoveries and the open-mindedness that leads to new discoveries are inhibited by this worship of the old mental framework. In other

---

*See Appendix for more on this subject.

†The ramifications of relying only upon what is easily measured are explained in the footnote on page 26.

words, the sciences and their development are following books for the most part, rather than a totally open path of research. This quote explains the situation:

> Orthodoxy cushions the impact of new ideas by surrounding them with a wall of paper so thick that the average inquirer can barely make a dent in it.
>
> – Harrison Coulter, from *Divided Legacy, A History of Homeopathy*

Although I feel that astrologers should not *cultivate* mysteriousness unnecessarily, as they often do, I suggest that we should not persist in the attempt to remove all the mystery from astrology either, because the mystery is inseparable from the magic. And it's the magic that has such a healing effect on people–both through individual study of astrology and in consultations. Most of us got into astrology, I assume, because we sensed a certain magic in it. It performed magic in our lives and helped us to feel better, to understand things more, to see people more accurately and objectively and tolerantly. So, I think mis-applying the so-called scientific methodology cannot do any good, and often one of the motives of those doing so with astrology is to try to remove all this annoying mystery! "The black mud of occultism," as a skeptical Taurus friend of mine used to call it. "Let's make it nice and clean, squeaky clean," they seem to feel. Anything that can't be easily pinned down and categorized seems to create frustration in such people.*

But astrology is far more profound than just the two-dimensional, limited, analytical mind. It goes beyond that. You see, an inheritance from 18th and 19th century rationalism–the religion of rationalism–is the belief that the primary task of science, including the healing sciences, is to "explain" phenomena. To do this, they had to devise *theories,* based on various assumptions, which are usually not acknowledged. Those theories then slowly become accepted as dogma, and people stop seeing them as mere theories, and as mere provisional views. Ultimately, these dogmas have come to dominate our sense of reality, our beliefs, and they now tyrannize our minds. We want to break free of their restrictions, but it's a difficult struggle.

---

*This common approach is explained by Daniel Yankelovich like so (quoted from A. Smith's *Supermoney*): "The first step is to measure whatever can be easily measured. This is okay as far as it goes. The second step is to disregard that which can't be mea-

Astrology, I don't think, should do this at all, *i.e.,* attempt to "explain" phenomena by concocting endless theories; but rather we should stick to empiricism and just look at what is there and at what works. It seems to me that only by trying and experiencing astrology can the magic be seen, not by *á priori* reasoning. You have to enter into astrology to a certain level of depth before it reveals itself. You have to come into a relationship with astrology, almost like you do with another person, before that person really reveals himself or herself. You've got to *give* something first! Or, as the philosopher Pascal says,

> Earthly things must be known to be loved;
> Divine things must be loved to be known.

In this sense, astrology must be considered a divine thing. There's another old saying: "Wise men sit around a table and prove conclusively that something cannot be done. Then a fool goes out and does it immediately!" So it seems to me that those astrologers who are doing the healing and counseling work should busy themselves doing the magic and encouraging the healing and forget all the pointless argument about science this and science that and proving this and that in terms that are really inappropriate to astrology.

The cosmos, as Elwell wrote in the same article that I quoted earlier, has its *own* priorities and speaks its *own* language. We have to accept that fact and listen to that cosmic language receptively, rather than imposing our limited concepts and demands. The vast cosmic power that is reflected through astrology is a mystery and will remain so. How can such a power, such a cosmic language, be anything but a mystery? After all, it *is* beyond our rational understanding. It therefore seems quite a bit better to call astrological psychology "a healing way," rather than a science in narrow modern terms. With the public at least, it's more useful simply to call it a *healing way* or something like that, to let them know that it can in fact be therapeutic.

Astrology in Modern Society

As I mentioned at the beginning of this talk, I'm getting more and more interested in the question of astrology's place in

---

sured. . . . This is artificial and misleading. The third step is to presume that what can't be measured easily really isn't very important. This is blindness. The fourth step is to say that what can't be easily measured really doesn't exist. This is suicide."

modern society. This subject could otherwise be called "what we are up against!" There are a couple of facts that immediately clarify the situation. One is that the main religion of the Western world now is *scientism.* It's not science, but scientism. These "scientists" hold forth as the high priests of humanity, often funded by the state, and offering to "unravel the mysteries of life," which is of course historically a religious function. That's quite a claim, I would say. I think it's important to realize that when many scientists speak publically, they're not speaking as true scientists. They're speaking as high priests of the dominant modern religion. Now *scientism* arises from the methodology of science being mis-applied, by taking that fruitful *method* (which *has* produced a lot of useful discoveries) and applying it as an all-embracing world view!* Then there arise philosophical and religious overtones to what really is only a methodology. The reason people get so emotional when they're discussing "astrology versus science" is because they are actually confronting conflicting world views, each having various unacknowledged assumptions and a lot of emotional investment.

However, it's important that astrologers don't do the same thing that we often see adherents to scientism doing. That is, astrologers are also often tempted to take our fruitful method and apply it as an all-embracing world view. Astrology simply *is.* Astrology can be an all-embracing world view for many people, in the sense that it becomes their religion. But in general, I think it's more fruitful for astrologers to acknowledge the limits of their particular type of astrological practice. This is repeating again, in another way, what I said before. But if you acknowledge what your specialization is and don't take on more than you can effectively handle, or don't bite off more than you can chew, as the saying goes, you can keep it simple, and you can keep it much more precisely accurate. Then also, your clients will have a lot more respect for you because you know what you're doing and you know what you *can't* do.

That astrology is getting more technical and "scientific" today is just a fact. No doubt, given modern society, that trend is going to continue. And the computerization of astrology will continue broadly both in good ways and in very negative ways,

*As Ken Wilbur writes in *Up From Eden,* "There is no scientific proof that scientific proof alone is real. . . ." Hence, those who believe that scientific proof alone is real are adhering to a *belief* that is a fundamental religious tenet of their overall life attitude.

because whenever there's money to be made, a lot of people will go after it. There's going to be much broader sales of pseudo-astrology computer programs, for example. To some extent this is inevitable. But while this is happening, it seems to me that those people who are really the guardians of astrology during this era and who are the teachers, whether just with individual clients or in classes, must repeatedly emphasize the important philosophical anchor of astrology that is so neglected these days. There must be that respect for and acknowledgement of certain philosophical and ethical moorings to ensure that astrology promotes understanding and appreciation of people and their differences, rather than fostering manipulation, which is one of the dangers that could happen to astrology in the next few decades–it being used as a tool for manipulation. Without these moorings, astrology and its varied applications will no doubt drift from its use as a "healing way" into whatever unthinking functions people find convenient or amusing.

That philosophical anchor has to be maintained, no matter what kind of astrologer you are, it seems to me. What are some of these philosophical foundations? First, that astrology is somehow an emanation of archetypes or is somehow connected to a universal mind pattern of some sort. Some kind of incredibly broad cosmic pattern is thus revealed in astrology, a pattern that is then reflected throughout life on many levels. Our personalities, activities, and thoughts are all part of this grand pattern. Astrology can also reveal the cyclic nature of life and human development; particularly transits and certain progressions are the best examples of that cyclic predictability. I think people today are finally ready to see things in terms of cycles. There are a number of non-astrological best-selling books that are emphasizing life cycles now. The general public seems to be more and more able to accept the idea of cyclic patterns in life. This is a perfect "in" for astrology. It's an "in" because astrology is a study of cycles, certainly.

Astrology also has another of its philosophical moorings, from my point of view, in the religious awe of the cosmic order that it inspires. It has been called a "divine science" throughout the ages. I would not be one to contradict that. The more you see it work and the more you see that there is such a cosmic order, if you are open to it, you can't help but have a religious awe of that order. Likewise, astrology gives you the tools to get into conscious alignment with that order, or at least to begin to so align yourself. One person called it "a conscious alignment with the timing of God." By using astrology properly, you can begin to get into attunement with that larger order. It is no easy task. But it is a beginning. I cannot deny that, in astrology, there are implicit spiritual and religious essences. That is why the conflicting world views, the scientific-materialistic view and the astrological world view, are probably permanently antagonistic—a case of irreconcilable differences.

The Language of Astrology

A key to astrology's development and wider acceptance is how successful we are at developing a good, clear, practical astrological language. This is no doubt a key to its wider acceptance by the general public. When you're doing a consultation, for example, the person usually hears a great deal of astrological jargon that he or she perhaps can't understand. If that's the case, you may have failed to communicate. You are, after all, talking about a *person,* not a chart! Now the care with which one should choose one's words, while always important, is even more important in written astrological work than in in-person consultations. When you're with a client, you could say, "Oh, well, Saturn's going into your second house," etc., and you can immediately see and sense the client's reaction and whether or not the client has understood you. If not, then you can reiterate it, or you can shift your words around and use additional explanation until you make real contact.

But when you do written interpretations of a chart,* then the potential hazards of using imprecise or careless language become all the more dangerous, because the written word tends

---

*Note that I said "written interpretations *of a chart.*" Whereas an in-person consultation provides the opportunity for a real dialogue *with the person,* using the chart as a guide, the vast majority of by-mail work deals not at all with the person, but only with the chart in the abstract—a chart which many people may in fact have.

to be cast in concrete. People tend to think, "Oh, there it is, that haunting fact again. I wonder if it's really true!" And often, with these by-mail chart interpretations, many people will read them over and over for years! You're not even going to have the option of changing it, or gently altering the person's attitude. So this is one element of the question of *language* that is really difficult.

It's very exhausting to use the right language in a consultation, because of the intensity of concentration it requires, but I think you have to do it. Astrology includes some kind of cosmic hierarchy, and these symbols are *already* a language. We're interpreting something *up there,* but we're *down here* with the English language; and we're trying first to interpret cosmic symbols and then to interpret them once again into English! So it is exhausting. You're doing double interpretation. This is the reason I've always felt that children should be taught the astrological language starting very early. But how do you get the schools to do it? Parents will have to do it themselves! Then you wouldn't need to interpret for all these clients. They would know the language and would just speak it. They'd feel it. It would be natural to them. But until that time comes, obviously the astrologer has the role and the duty to interpret this astrological language into the English language. And that is really difficult without having a great command of both languages and using a lot of nuances, as well as making sure that you really are establishing a rapport with the client.

To paraphrase Dennis Elwell one more time: "So much of astrology is a matter of definition, and yet hardly anything is ever defined." The next paragraphs are from Elwell too. In his research into this language issue, it turns out that, quite independently, he found the same thing I did; and he expressed it so well that I'm quoting him directly.

> When I started to study the subject, I became obsessed with the idea of achieving precision of statement. But I increasingly found that to reach a greater degree of accuracy, both in dealing with human nature and future events, it was necessary to limit oneself to the inner situation.

To limit oneself to the *inner* situation! You can be much more certain of the inner situation than of the outer. The inner situation, in a sense, is simpler and thus more precisely symbolized by the astrological glyphs and configurations. Once that essence manifests out in the world, it immediately fragments and can become almost anything. The one becomes the many.

> To attempt to describe behavior, or the outward circumstances of life, brought in an element of guesswork; and the more trivial the behavior traits one went for, the more ephemeral the events, the more guesswork played a part.

I think that is really accurate. In the astrology field, if one is going to be truly scientific, one must emphasize the inner dimensions! When you start dealing with trivial behavior traits or outer events, more and more you have to guess, "Will these symbols manifest like this or like this or like that?" The astrologer thus merely involves himself in an endless guessing game. Elwell continues:

> It was purely on the score of the greater degree of accuracy achieved that I was forced to conclude that astrology's true subject matter must be concerned with consciousness and mind–concepts which behaviorism rejects. If one had to go inward to discover the characteristics which were *invariably* present with this or that aspect or planetary position, surely astrology itself must be essentially a science of inwardness.

When I read this article many years ago (I've read it about ten times now), it especially struck me that he was looking for those characteristics or qualities which were *invariably* present if a certain astrological factor was there. That is what I had always been looking for, too. I was also obsessed with achieving precision of language–a truly scientific, reliable type of astrology. That's really why I *had to* write some books, because I had to put down on paper *for my own use* what approaches, definitions, and language I was coming up with. Most of the existing literature failed me completely; when I looked to it hoping to find some *reliable* statement of what was invariably there if a certain astrological factor was present, it was hardly ever accurate. I mean, it was 95% wrong. I don't think I'm that abnormal! I just think that many of us have outgrown the old astrological literature's level of consciousness. So, basically I went on that same sort of quest that Elwell talks about. You can use very precise language and achieve a very high degree of accuracy *if you stay to the inner situation.* And to me this means that you reject both the old, fatalistic astrological language of black and white categories and ethical judgments *and* the pseudo-scientific language of statistics or pop-psychology jargon; you reject all irrelevant overlays in favor of a language of *experience*—a real language of *energy* that people can feel and identify with.

It's late, but there is time for a few questions.

Question: Where can one find examples of this "language of experience" that you talk about?

Stephen: People understand when you talk about needs, urges, energies, dilemmas. All I can really do is point you toward the first two books that I wrote, because they were both attempts to speak clearly about things that seemed to need more definition. In addition to the strong emphasis on the four elements as types of life energy that people can *feel,* I think it's at the end of Chapter 9 in *Astrology, Psychology and the Four Elements* that you'll find about eight or nine pages of keywords. Those keywords and key phrases were synthesized out of every other keyword system I could find, refined through long use and teaching many classes, and then a few more were added. They're very condensed and concise, and the keywords can be put into very accurate interpretive phrases too. I'm not saying that that's the only way to do astrology, but it can be very useful—for beginners especially, and for teachers, I think. Obviously, Margaret Hone, Ronald Davison, and other people set up keyword systems a long time ago. Mine was just an attempt to do it a little differently, with a degree of precision with which I could feel comfortable. I think a lot of the writing in *Astrology, Karma and Transformation* is also along the line of what I'm pointing toward about language. Especially when it gets into the interpretation chapters, there's a certain carefulness in the language that I was trying to use.

Question: Regarding "esoteric astrology" . . . [inaudible] . . . how do you see that?

Stephen: The magic of astrology, I was assuming, would be pretty obvious to most people here. Those of you who might be beginners will see it soon enough. But regarding esoteric astrology, not only are there many kinds of so-called esoteric astrology, but also that is such a personal preference that there's not too much I can say about it. I think astrology had to go through that phase, especially with Alan Leo and the theosophists. That's one way that astrology became reinstated in the Western world. And I'm not one to discard all of the subtler and esoteric and spiritual implications of it. Astrology often becomes mostly a religion, and if you want to do that, it's OK if it is your religion. But what I'm talking about is more of an astrological psychology, one that you would use with clients. In that case, I don't think there would be much point in bringing in those "esoteric" kinds of considerations *unless* the client was already into that. If the client was already a spiritual seeker of some kind, or a theosophist, or whatever, then it would be a way of relating to them. Otherwise, it seems like esoteric astrology in many ways is a personal religious preference, which is OK. And there are many times in counseling when you do have to discuss religious questions and even share your own values. Astrology, by its nature, *is* esoteric to some extent. So this is a rather big question, actually, and it becomes a question of what is comfortable for each counselor to do and what feels within his or her proper domain. I do think astrologers should be extremely cautious about playing the role of spiritual teacher.

Question: I wonder if you would care to comment on the time of . . . [inaudible] . . . when they consult a horoscope and take that into consideration.

Stephen: You're talking about the "age factor" of the person. Well, have you read Ruperti's book, *Cycles of Becoming*?* That book deals very thoroughly with that factor, and as I've become older I see the value of what's in that book more and more. There is generally very little mention of the individual's age in

---

* Available from the publisher of this book.

astrological books. In fact, about three weeks ago I got a letter from an Australian who said that very thing, that in astrological literature there's almost no mention of the age factor. Everything is interpreted in this broad way, as if it applies to everyone. I've often found it more interesting to deal with people who were past 40. They seemed to have manifested a lot more of their chart. Their life was half or more over; and they were more interesting in the sense that it wasn't just potential anymore. Everyone has infinite potential, but how many use it? Some quite young people—even in their teens—are very interesting. The really creative ones that are already starting to manifest their potential are especially interesting. But some are rather boring too, because there's so much potential, and yet at that age everything is so unformed, you know. It's something that should definitely be acknowledged, I think, in astrology and in astrological literature. And there are a lot of studies being done now in the psychological field about aging and about life cycles and all that which could easily be grafted onto astrology.

Question: (Here a question was asked about the houses and the Ascendant.)

Stephen: I've used both equal house and the Koch system simultaneously for the last eight years. More and more I'm Ascendant-oriented. I've been pulled more and more toward equal houses, actually. But that's not saying anything, since I know that the Koch cusps are quite reliable with transits. As I get older, anything that's simpler and more geometric I tend to gravitate toward. But still, the fact that I continue to use both shows that I find value in both.

Question: (Another inaudible question—about the Ascendant, aspects, etc.)

Stephen: In relation to her question, *any* major aspect to the Ascendant, I'm finding incredibly powerful, including the semi-sextile and quincunx. Any trine to the Ascendant, with a fairly wide orb (5–6 degrees), I'd say is really significant. In chart comparisons, even a sextile from somebody's planet, especially if a "personal planet," to your Ascendant is a very significant factor. It's just that that planet will be felt strongly in that relationship. For example, say somebody's Moon trined, or sextiled even–which some people would dismiss as less important–your Ascendant. Somebody's Moon sextiles your Ascendant. If it's real close, particularly, you may feel encouraged by that person, cared for, nurtured. Their lunar energy flows well with your Ascendant–the whole way you are in the world, the way you express yourself in the world. I guess my language is very much that of flowing energy. It's hard for me to define it, but I always think in terms of energy. I see astrology visually as energy flow.

Question: (Inaudible question about the expectations of the public and the frustrations of dealing with the public.)

Stephen: Can't please everyone. It's terrible. In fact, all the people I know who are the best in astrology have quit doing consultations! That's one thing that's getting me more interested in activism, in terms of professionalizing astrology; because as long as the public sees it as fortune-telling, it will be hell to be an "astrologer" in many ways. Not that there aren't rewards. But all the people that I know, and all my best students, have quit doing it for the public, often because they just couldn't stand it–they were just so sensitive. They were gifted, actually. But they were so sensitive that they got sick of people's games and expectations. It's a real big problem. And that's why I think education of the public is as important as any issue in astrology right now. We should aim not just at the survival and acceptance of astrology, but I think astrologers should be able to make a decent living with some dignity in the Western world. But now it's very difficult, unless you're a fortune-teller or purport to do predictions or stock-market forecasts that people will pay big money for.

Question: (Inaudible comment about explaining to clients what astrology really is.)

Stephen: True. It just gets tiresome to do a mini-seminar on astrology with every client since their expectations are so bad! I used to have to spend literally four to nine hours per week doing that kind of explanation, and my clients were generally a fairly educated and intelligent group.

2

The Purpose & Profession of Astrology

Man's unbelief and opinion do not affect truth.
— James T. Kent, M.D.

The human phenomenon must be measured on a cosmic scale.
— Teilhard de Chardin

The main purpose of this talk is to outline some of the major themes of this conference. This talk is mainly about the *profession* and the *purpose* of astrology. The *practice* of astrology will be dealt with later in many different ways during this conference. How much everybody here puts into the conference and the small group sessions will really determine if you define something for yourselves and clarify significant issues for yourselves during the coming week.

Although we will be talking about the Saturn/Pluto conjunction on many levels during this conference, and about various psychological dimensions of astrology, some of the underlying themes that I'll emphasize are, in my experience, neglected at most gatherings (and I've been to many astrological conferences). Various fads or supposedly "new" techniques, which in many cases are many centuries old, or an over-emphasis on the basics, often dominate astrology conferences. This is another thing

---

*This chapter is based on the keynote talk of the 6-day Saturn-Pluto International Astrology Conference, held in Berkeley, California in late November of 1982. This conference, and hence this talk, was devoted to the theme of clarifying all important issues related to the "Purpose, Practice & Profession of Astrology," and this talk attempted to survey many of the key topics which would be talked about during the 6-day event. The conference was a tightly-scheduled, "working conference" that challenged astrologers to evaluate all aspects of their work. Among the methods used to facilitate this were small discussion groups and "brainstorming sessions." Much of the material in this volume is an outgrowth of that innovative conference.

we're going to try to get away from. This is a *very* advanced group—there are actually thousands of years of astrological experience in this room.

As Saturn and Pluto conjoin, shall we entertain the thought that the *profession* of astrology might be *transformed*? I think a lot of us feel like it can and should be transformed, or you probably wouldn't be here. Shall we posit that during this Saturn/Pluto period (Saturn, of course, traditionally relating to vocation, structure, career, profession; Pluto being transformation)—shall we posit that the practice of astrology might be and can be cleansed of some of the useless and even harmful debris that still clutters it up from centuries of all different sorts of applications? Might we think that those practicing astrology, in whatever capacity—informally or formally—might go through a period of self-analysis and self-transformation so that a higher consciousness might shine through their work?

We have all seen astrologers gather together, talk to themselves in their own language, and announce many dozens of "new" discoveries. They often get real happy for a short time. Then they go back home, all without bothering to ask some of the larger questions about the profession, the practice, and the purpose of astrology: what its place is in society, what can be done to improve astrological practice, and what can be done to make it more available to the public. And we should also ask, "What can be done to further the acceptance by the public of the value and wisdom that astrology can provide?" So, we can go into questions like this during this conference. Facing yourself and facing tough questions about yourself and about your life and profession is often difficult. It's often painful, too. But how better to use a Saturn/Pluto conjunction? You might as well be a little bit masochistic!

I feel that astrological counseling is an incredible force for good, but only when used in the right way, when in the right hands. I feel astrological counseling must become further established as a legitimate helping profession. It has *begun* to be so established, especially since the 1960's. But it has a long way to go. Admittedly, there are a great many established power structures in this society, and also there are rigid patterns in most people's educational and religious background, that resist any diffusion of astrological wisdom. In other words, there are a lot of vested interests, and there is a lot of prejudice and resistance that one has to contend with if one is destined to or wants to work in the field of astrology. But there's relatively little that we can do, in a quick way, to change all of those things.

What we can do, however, is to take a hard look at ourselves and see what we, as astrologers or astrological counselors, are doing ourselves that might need some improving! What are we doing that inhibits the development and the broadened acceptance of this great science–art? So . . . some self-criticism, a bit of cleaning up our own act now seems necessary. You know, one of the meanings of Pluto traditionally is cleaning out all the waste and useless remnants. It's sort of the cathartic of the solar system. Saturn and Pluto are both soon going into Scorpio, too, the Pluto sign. Naturally, these forces will manifest all over the world on many levels, not just in astrology. But, in the astrology field, "The time has come, the Walrus said, to speak of many things. . . . "

This self-examination and self-improvement, I feel, must be a prelude to astrology's further acceptance as a valuable helping profession. My feeling is that we do not need to run around trying to please "authorities" or to adapt the language of other fields of study. We have our own language that's better than any other. What *can* we do to further the acceptance and the wide acknowledgement of astrological counseling as a valuable helping profession? My feeling is that what we can do is simply to do our work *so well* that no one and no vested interest group can do anything to stop the growing awareness of astrology's value. It just happens that people look for value. They are also looking for meaning–not all people, of course, but many. Those of you who are in practice know that your practice spreads by word of mouth twenty-five times more than through any form of advertising.

In addition, helping each other to clarify our role and purpose in astrology is a goal of this conference. We are all different and we have different approaches, different values. And, although each can be helpful to a certain group of clients, it's rather unrealistic to speak of only *one* purpose of astrology. I'm not a Sagittarian! There's not just one purpose of it, one meaning of it. The point is to *define* your purpose. It's an individualized meaning—an art. So, some self-questioning, coupled with an honest and, I hope, tolerant dialogue with others in this conference, might in fact produce something really special. And from this delving into the deeper questions of astrology and our use of it might come an increased self-confidence based on a truer and firmer sense of our capabilities and our purpose.

Self-confidence is an issue I'll bring up a number of times during the conference. I'm personally convinced that a lot of astrologers' problems come from a lack of self-confidence. Particularly, the Neptunian and Plutonian types of astrologers often have very little confidence. Now this questioning of ourselves is especially appropriate now that Uranus has entered Sagittarius. If you look back to the last time Uranus went through Sagittarius, at the turn of the century, there was a small explosion of increased interest in astrology on many levels. There was a proliferation of astrological magazines, journals, groups, organizations, and a noticeable increase in the number of people interested in the metaphysical and spiritual dimensions of astrology. Of course, the Theosophical Society had a great deal to do with the spread of that kind of astrology.

Some of the questions that we are going to be asking, and I assume some of you already ask yourselves these questions, are extraordinarily complex. There are not at this time any easy answers. So it is a *questioning* that I want to do, more than providing a lot of pat answers. I think asking the right questions is important, and *asking them bluntly!* So, in that sense, in a sort of Sagittarian, wide-ranging exploration of many key issues, I intend to quote today from a number of sources both within the astrology world and from outside it, and I'll mention quite a few different challenges that we need to face. I'll start out with a quote from a 1975 letter that Dane Rudhyar wrote. Most of you know who Dane Rudhyar is. Perhaps more than anyone else, he began the development of a more intellectually and psychologically sophisticated astrology, beginning in the 1930's. He sent copies of this letter to nine people in 1975, all of whom were particularly interested in his approach to astrology—what he then called "humanistic" or "person-centered astrology," as differentiated from event-centered astrology. He wrote:

> Humanistic astrology certainly does not need to become more "popular." Its public will increase automatically as the ideas presented will be formulated more convincingly by teachers who can be exemplars of the values that such an astrology is presenting. We need *quality and clarity, not quantity and glamour.* We need *practicality and intellectual honesty* in dealing with whatever issues present themselves.

This next statement is particularly powerful to me. So often, we hear "Let's serve astrology. Let's give ourselves away to some abstract that is called *astrology*."

> Yours is the moral and cultural responsibility to practice astrology for man's sake, not for astrology's sake—or for self-aggrandizement.

That's a very important differentiation. Unless astrology is our religion, we're not really serving *it,* we're serving *people.* We're serving clients and, hopefully, ourselves, using it as a tool for self-knowledge.

> Humanistic astrology is only a means . . . to assist individuals in a time of world wide challenges to personal integrity as well as integration. Do not ask too much of it, and do not intensify the general confusion by mixing it with other techniques from other cultures, and other psychic approaches. Keep your mind focused and free from emotionality.

That's the end of the quote. That's a pretty powerful quote. You may not agree with everything in it, but to me, there is a lot of truth in it. *Focus* is, of course, a Saturn and Pluto thing—concentration. You can't do good work in anything without concentration. I just read an article saying that if you have insomnia, concentration is one of the best ways to get to sleep. If your mind is too scattered, you can't even sleep, let alone do something very effectively while awake. Concentration and focus are desperately needed in astrology, especially today, when it's such a fragmented field of study. Astrology is fragmenting today like crazy! That's one reason there's a need, I think, for such conferences as this. Divisive issues can be discussed so that a unifying philosophy can develop.

My feeling now is that astrology simply *is.* Today it need not really be *talked about* too much anymore, but rather the question is: how can it be *used,* how can it be applied and understood in life? How can it be used *in life*?—not just abstract speculation and theory about astrology. Although my first couple of books might indicate that I'm very theoretical, I'm not so much anymore. I'm interested now in how we can *use* astrology. The theory is all there for anybody that wants it; but, for those devoted to astrology or whose vocation is wrapped up with astrology, it seems to me that a major focus now should be these practical questions: how can it be used and applied? How can astrology and its value be presented to a broader variety of people in an *intelligent* way?

That's the challenge now and that is where astrologers, as a group, have seriously failed. I think many, though probably not all of you, will agree. It is not legal recognition or licensure that will enable the great values of astrology to be infused into society. You can't correct all of *our* own thoughts and incompetence by calling on the government to do something for us that we can't do ourselves! So it seems to me that a common-sense, practical, intelligent, and rather dignified presentation of astrological wisdom to people, in a way that commands respect and an intelligent reaction, is the way to go now, at this point in astrology's history. This is needed for what I consider to be a modern, useful type of astrology to develop and to expand.

Any sort of Aquarian call for action like this inevitably elicits a lot of political questions and organizational questions, most of which I'm not going to deal with now, although there are a few things I'll mention at the end of this talk. These questions will be discussed in the small group sessions. But I've got to point out that if all the best people in astrology constantly quibble, you can be sure that those whom I like to call the "enemies of truth" will prevail. They have a vested interest; they're busily organizing and consolidating power; they're projecting phony images of astrology to the public. And these false images of astrology are not being projected to the public *only* by the anti-astrology pseudo-scientists, such as the 186 "scientists" who signed that anti-astrology statement a few years ago, pretending that they knew something about the subject. Fortunately, some real scientists criticized those who signed it, calling it an incredibly authoritarian misuse of their reputations and of their role as supposedly "objective" scientists. So, there are some people in the scientific community that are fair-minded. In addition, there are the media sensationalists misrepresenting astrology. There are also certain types of astrologers who project what I consider to be a totally inaccurate image of astrology to the public through their practice, by the way they do things and the way they use it or misuse it.

So, in regard to "the images of astrology"–what are they? What needs to be done? In my view, a great deal of work needs to be done. As I said earlier, it's only since the 1960's (in my opinion) that astrology has begun to develop some roots as a legitimate helping profession that can begin to be widely accepted. There are a lot of people now, especially in this country, who do recognize it as a legitimate helping profession. We all know that there are various people in other professions who now recommend their clients to astrologers. They see that it does have a role. It can do something and contribute something to people's lives that nothing else can do.

What needs to be done, then? First of all, traditional astrology needs to continue its reformulation. It has already started. It is sort of arbitrary to set a time for the beginning of this reformulation process, but I can't help but think of Rudhyar's publication of *The Astrology of Personality* in 1936, which was a profound book on the psychological and philosophical dimensions of astrology. All of a sudden a lot of highly educated, formerly skeptical people started to think, "Amazingly, this kind of makes sense!" Whereas, when it had been presented before merely as a fortune-telling game, few paid attention to it except those who wanted their fortunes told. So, this reformulation and modernization that has been going on for about 50 years, I believe, needs to continue. It is still happening now, fortunately. It's slowly taking place, as evidenced by the writings of all of the speakers* at this conference, for example.

---

*The speakers at this Saturn–Pluto Conference were Liz Greene, Tracy Marks, Donna Cunningham, and Stephen Arroyo, all of whom are known for particularly clear, modern presentations of astrological psychology.

As Rudhyar wrote in 1970,

> We should not repudiate the old symbols and entirely discard the old interpretations. What we must do is to thoroughly *re-think* them and reformulate them in terms of our own collective and individual mentality. Above all, we should reformulate them in terms of our NEED. As I see it, the most crucial questions to answer now are:
>
> 1. How can astrology today answer the deepest need of individual persons in our confused and disordered society?
> 2. What kind of astrology can help distraught individuals to find a deeper peace, . . . a more complete actualization of their innate potential?

Another thing that's needed today is education of the public. And I'm afraid that we can't rely on the mass media to do that. The media still ignores the facts, still ignores the value and the modernization of astrology that *has* occurred—undeniably has occurred—and is still happening. The media totally ignores significant scholarly work in astrology. I don't have time to explain all of the facts that substantiate that assertion, but definitely it's true.* Many, many editors of the major magazines and newspapers in this country, as well as the head of the Federal Reserve, the head of the Treasury, and many other media people, have been notified of the astrological research of Barry Lynes and his impressive findings. His work is very good astrological research on world affairs and economics, predicting exactly to the day, in some cases, specific turning points of the economy and various crises that would affect interest rates and international stability. Not one of the media people ever printed it or put it out. It was buried by all of them. By pure journalistic tradition and practice, it should have *at least* been reported, because he had substantial evidence to back up his conclusions. The *Christian Science Monitor* editor wrote him a letter saying, "We don't put stuff like this in, because *we don't believe in astrology.*" Well, does a true journalist have to *believe* in everything they put in their paper? No. They put murder in their paper! Do they believe in murder? It's just an incredible prejudice.

Even *Newsweek,* which is sometimes regarded as a fairly good magazine and somewhat objective in some areas, printed the following in their issue of August 30, 1982. *Newsweek*'s

*See Appendix for the details.

staff is so completely ignorant of astrology and so irresponsible that they can write the following even in today's time—1982. This is a direct quote:

> Except for the millions who follow the horoscopes in the local paper with unfailing hope and longing, nobody has a good word to say for astrology. Its premises are dismissed by sensible folk, its pretensions mocked, its impositions upon the gullible lamented.

Who have they been talking to? They're just talking to themselves in their heads and not paying attention to what's really happening at all! The *facts* have been completely ignored! And that is where the astrologers have failed. They have not communicated astrology's definition, value, premises, and myriad practical uses. There is not one astrological organization in this country that has a public relations department or anything like that to give the media constant information on something truer and more positive about astrology, and also to contradict inaccurate reports in the media. Even the biggest astrological organization in the Western world, the American Federation of Astrologers, has—as far as I've seen in the past fifteen years—made no effort to contradict the media's attempts to make all astrologers a laughing stock. And that organization could easily afford to do so because it has plenty of money. But nothing is ever done, in spite of its ostensible purpose being research and *education*! How about *educating* the *public*?

An author named Malcolm Dean wrote a book entitled *The Astrology Game,* from a purely journalistic point of view. He did many, many interviews, and he did years of research. It's a bit of a pompous book, but I liked reading it. There's a lot of very interesting information in it. I get a little tired of his snideness, since he is one of those who seems to have swallowed—hook, line, and sinker—the pseudo-scientific approach to astrology, the kind that assumes "the only way to make astrology modern is statistical studies like Gauquelin's," which I don't agree with at all. In *The Astrology Game*, he makes some very hard, harsh—but, I'm afraid, true in many cases—statements. The first concerns the ignorance with which most people approach astrology. He is a "believer" in astrology, by the way, in the sense that he knows it can be valuable. He doesn't believe in everything about it. But he has seen it work in his life. So, he isn't a skeptic in the usual sense. And the book does have a considerable degree of objectivity.

> The ignorance in which most people approach astrology is an important issue, because astrology, as the proto-science of cosmic influences in human behavior, will only break out of the closet when this vicious circle is broken. (page 206)

There *is* a vicious circle of ignorance regarding astrology, and no one is going to break it except the astrologers themselves. And if the astrologers don't, it's never going to be broken—at least not in our lifetime. For this vicious circle to be broken, Dean writes,

> . . . there must be a greater awareness that astrology has a history and a logical direction of development. . . . Astrology must be seen as a central theme in man's continual struggle to come to terms with his cosmic environment. If astrology and astrologers have accomplished anything, they have kept alive the tradition that there is an intimate relationship between man and the cosmos. That alone is enough to justify all the apparent absurdities which have been perpetrated in astrology's name. Since many have devoted their lives, sat in jail, and even died in concentration camps for their love of astrology, their efforts deserve more compassion than the ridicule which is heaped on astrology at every possible turn. (page 206)

Another quote from Malcolm Dean deals with the sad fact that the astrologers themselves are perpetuating this vicious circle of ignorance just as much as are the mass media and the biased pseudo-scientists and academicians.

> . . . if the planets move in circles, so do astrologers. Without the benefits of the establishment—funding, scholastic institutions, archives, and libraries—astrologers have left the history and development of their techniques as virtually unexplored territory, a territory which is rapidly crumbling into oblivion. Even today, the best astrological organizations have poorly maintained libraries, and there is no single definitive collection of astrological publications anywhere in the world. Public and scholastic libraries often look upon their astrological collections more as nuisances than fascinating repositories of a proto-science. . . . Astrologers therefore live in a kind of never-never land in which the past is continually forgotten and only the present exists. He who does not remember the past is condemned to repeat it. And so, cut off from

> their roots, astrologers even today are "discovering" concepts and theories which date back centuries, and in some cases, millennia.

So ignorant are we of our own history! There is today a desperate need, I feel, for a general, collective recognition in the astrology world of the excellence of certain presentations, concepts, books, and underlying philosophical principles, all of which should form the basis for any formal curriculum or course of self-study. However, in order to accomplish this, we have to be able to *discriminate,* and we have to be willing to put an end to astrologers' current habit of readily considering every conceivable notion to be an idea worthy of serious study and research! Although the traditional openness of astrologers to the new and the unorthodox is commendable, there must be some standards used to evaluate "new" ideas. There is, after all, a big difference between a healthy *broad-mindedness,* and a totally undiscriminating, naive open-mindedness.

Astrologers Today as a Professional Group

This may be an overly rough attempt at self-evaluation of astrologers, but I'd rather it be honest and blunt than self-congratulatory. Saturn-Pluto, after all! Admittedly, the role and vocation of astrologer are not easy ones in today's society, that is, if you are a responsible person who sincerely desires the well-being of your clients. Also, admittedly, it is difficult to make statements about "astrologers" when they are such a diverse lot. Therefore, a lot of these statements won't apply to all of us here today. In fact, I'm sure that *we* are just the most intelligent of the lot, and that all the criticisms apply only to the dumb astrologers! However, the following observations from numerous sources will, I think, ring true about the field in general.

Over fifty years ago, Charles Carter, one of the greatest astrologers, I believe, and quite a scientific one in the true sense of the word, wrote in a pamphlet called "The Seven Great Problems of Astrology":

> It is perhaps open to question whether astrologers have not, in their enthusiasm for their neglected science, claimed too much on its behalf, thereby leading ultimately to its losing credit, rather than winning credit.

It's easy to see how astrologers can become defensive in our society and thus want to compensate for their lack of recognition, lack of credibility—and the accompanying lack of *confidence* that we all experience—by exaggerating or sensationalizing astrology's claims and capabilities. It is a temptation, I know, one that many astrologers give in to regularly—exaggeration, sensationalizing, overly-specific predictions, and so forth. Such behavior, however, does not help astrology's public image and reputation, that's for sure. It is generally an attempt to *impress* others rather than *help* others, and such exaggeration loses credit for astrology. It's that simple, I believe. No matter what you may say about extravagant predictions, or even whether or not they can be accurate at times, if it's done wrongly, in the wrong way, it will be a negative thing in more ways than one. If astrology is really a science, we should be able to use it reliably within a realistic framework. But that's another subject, and I'm not going to debate predictions today.

Practitioners of any essentially lonely and arduous type of work, whether in astrology or in other fields, who don't get much reward in terms of money or recognition from the work to which they are devoted, often will be an eccentric group of people. And often they will be susceptible to institutionalized efforts that promise to lift their burden, such as licensing ("Let's establish licensing laws and it will solve all our problems!"). So we're susceptible to those kinds of vain promises or misguided schemes. Also, anyone in such a field is also susceptible to flattery or to attention of any kind because they're so neglected and often derided, such as going on the local news for 30-second spots so everyone can laugh at them. I'm sure some of you have been on the local news and television. Television is much worse than the radio, in what they usually do to astrologers.

While I was in England recently, I had been talking about some of these very issues with a very intelligent astrologer there—the nature of astrologers and why astrologers act like they do and why they often exaggerate. He ambled up to me and whispered (so no other astrologers would hear!), "You've really got to wonder, don't you, if they really believe in it." So much of their behavior seems to indicate that they don't, really! Well, his comment really hit me, because just a couple of days before that I had scribbled this little note: "Why are astrologers," I wrote, "always exaggerating astrology's authentic scope of application?" It has a tremendously broad scope of application, but why do we tend to exaggerate it? Let it just do what it can do best, and let's be realistic about how specific it can be. It can do infinite numbers of things, yes, but how many can it do really well? Then I wrote, "Do they secretly doubt its veracity and its accuracy and thus try to compensate, like 'true believers' in a religion, who secretly doubt they are going to Heaven?" They secretly don't think they are really saved, so they tend to compensate with fanaticism or with preaching to everyone else.

"Do astrologers secretly doubt themselves and the value of their work?" That's a real question, and it's hard to think it's not true in many cases. For example, this self-doubt explains, to some extent at least, why astrologers so often undercharge for their services, or don't charge at all, and why they often sensationalize their knowledge so that people like them or pay attention to them, so they really seem to be giving something to clients for their money. I know astrologers have terrible hang-ups about money. A lot of them feel horribly guilty about taking money for their work. Part of that is the rampant Neptunianism that pervades the psyches of astrologers. You know, you want to give everything away, and what you often do is that you give everything away, everything, until you're exhausted *and* broke. At least, if you're going to be broke, be energetically broke!

So, this self-doubt and exaggeration points to either a massive self-deception on the part of some astrologers . . . [Are we really fooling ourselves? Do some of us doubt A, B, and C traditions of astrology? And if we do, let's ignore those traditions and use just what we know works!] . . . or it points to, again, this lack of confidence we mentioned before. Charitably, we would have to say that for most sincere astrologers, it probably points more to a lack of confidence.

Now, for some years, I've noticed a characteristic common to many astrologers, as I'm sure many of you have. Perhaps it's partly the Uranian lack of cooperation—the inability to cooperate and the insistence on doing one's own thing. But, no matter how much lip service is given to cooperation and to the "good of astrology" and things like that, there's often a self-destructive tendency, often related directly to the inability to see the greater good of the astrology field and the profession as a whole. After considering this trait for a long time, and after looking at a lot of astrologers' charts, too, I came to the conclusion that astrologers are not just Uranian and Neptunian, but they're also often *Plutonian*—you know, the planet of self-destruction. We like *depth,* you know, and hidden secrets and all Plutonian things. But Pluto can also be incredibly self-destructive, and Plutonian people can undermine themselves. The self-destructive tendencies (to use a Scorpio sort of analogy, these tendencies to "sting themselves to death") to undermine themselves by behavior or by simple lack of responsible action are self-evident. This tendency is also evident in the lack of support for positive new forces in the astrology field.

Malcolm Dean, after researching the matter for his book *The Astrology Game,* concluded that, unlike the popular opinion that the mass media tries to promote—that astrology is like a "spreading infection with hundreds of thousands of adherents, rapidly falling into the abyss of superstition"—in fact worldwide membership in astrological organizations totals only about 10,000. There are a lot more people practicing it in one way or another, and many taking money for it. But how many support *any* organization?

Another example of the lack of support for positive developments in astrology is the failure of quite an intelligent magazine, *Astrology Now,* which was published for a few years some time ago, sold quite cheaply, and always included quite a few intelligent articles. It had its problems, admittedly, not the least of which was its publisher and its habitually late publication schedule, but it was not expensive. It folded, mainly due to lack of support, lack of subscriptions. I don't think it ever got even 5,000 subscribers in the whole world. It was an international effort, too. People from all over the world published in it. Its overall high quality should have earned it far more subscribers, especially at its low price, in spite of its often being behind schedule. It was worth the wait!

One friend of mine referred to this last year when we were discussing how astrologers create problems for themselves. He said, "I've noticed that the astrologers often have a type of self-subversion. They subvert themselves, somehow." And lest you think that this is just my private fantasy, and that I'm totally paranoid or overly-critical, many people have noticed this tendency. Once again, Malcolm Dean writes,

> Among most astrology groups, there seems to be an almost suicidal urge to discredit themselves through ill-conceived actions, immature behavior, and a lack of any concerted research efforts. And the picture does not get any better out in the "boonies." Outnumbering those in organizations by at least ten-to-one, there are thousands of amateurs who really know almost nothing about their field, or that there even exist astrological organizations and serious journals to which they might profitably subscribe. Yet they hang out their shingle, place an ad in the *Yellow Pages*, and even willingly appear on the local radio station to discuss astrology. (page 40)

Now I'm sure that none of us are like that! However, we have to admit that there is a kernel of truth in some of these descriptions. Of course, it would be uncharitable to infer that astrologers have more than their share of personality defects. Other than the lack of sufficiently broad intellectual background, I have to assume that once again the issue of *lack of confidence* and *lack of self-esteem* lies at the bottom of astrologers' behavior. It's hard to develop any real, rooted, unswayable confidence in oneself and in one's work if the educational, religious, social, and legal systems all tell you repeatedly, from the moment you begin astrological study, that you are a fool, a charlatan, a swindler, a gullible twit, a starry-eyed wimp, or a complete moron! It is not easy to develop any kind of confidence in that kind of atmosphere! And, especially since astrologers are a gullible lot, you can't help but start to believe it. Even subconsciously you start to think, "There's got to be something wrong with me. Maybe this stuff doesn't really work, maybe it's totally untrue and I'm just an idiot!"

This lurking suspicion, then, gets even worse when your supposed colleagues, upon whom you'd like to rely for support, start acting like juvenile delinquents chasing after any idiotic fad in their adolescent excitedness and regularly displaying what I call "schizophrenic inconsistency." So you look at the astrology field and you want some support, and you ask yourself, "Why am I like this? Convince me that I'm really all right and that being in this field is OK!" But your lurking suspicions sometimes are even magnified by what your "colleagues" do. They aren't always models of stability! So, it seems to me, the situation is that we have no choice but to look within. The real confidence can only come from within.

The word *confidence* means "with faith." And you can't create faith. Faith comes of itself. Real faith, if it's faith in a *truth,* is the same as inner knowledge of that truth. That knowledge can only come from experience. So you just know it in your bones. This confidence has to be born spontaneously when we face our doubts and our questions, our lack of confidence, our confusion; we have to face the truth about ourselves and about astrology, and achieve some kind of spiritual, mental, physical and emotional integration. Then you can start to be a bit centered, and you can start to know something in your bones, not just in your emotions or your intellect. Then you can't be swayed so easily. You don't have to be so defensive anymore.

I think that's one thing astrologers individually should aim for now—*a state of personal integration.* This is a trend already that I especially like, that finally many people in this field are now pursuing different types of activities that aid their own self-integration, whether it's meditation or some sort of healing art or psychological study, or whatever. That's where the real self-confidence will come from—when you know at an incredibly deep level, through a wide variety of experience, what you are and what you're doing. You may not know *why* you've been chosen to do it, but at least you can know what you can do well.

I remember a quote from an interview with Isabel Hickey that was recently reprinted in the Canadian Journal. She was saying something like this (I can't remember the exact quote): she had a Catholic mother, Presbyterian father and, a Fundamentalist grandfather, or something similar. When God "told" her in some way, "Guess what? You have to be an astrologer," she replied, "Oh, God, No! Please, no!" And also, she was raised in conservative Boston. You can imagine what kind of abuse she had to deal with. Some of us, I think, feel like that at times. "Why me? My mother told me to be a civil engineer; you can make lots of money."

So much stress is felt by many intelligent people, and especially by particularly sensitive people, who get into the field of astrology! So much stress is felt that the best people often leave the astrology field or just start doing it secretly only for a few friends. Or they get tired of the criticism, or the raised eyebrows and the sneers and so forth. Many of the best astrological counselors that I know have quit doing it professionally in the last ten years, which is one thing that motivates me to say some of these things, harsh criticisms though they may seem to some of you. I think it's a pity that many of the best people—and often the most sensitive, who are the most effective with others in counseling and in healing—quit because they can't stand it. The psychological pressures are too much, and also they can't make ends meet. If they have children, how would they feed them? It's a rare astrologer that makes a good living. And the psychological pressures are astounding.

Fifty years ago, Charles Carter wrote about a related issue, and what he said is equally true today; the issue is "*Who* should study astrology?" Those of you who teach know that, generally, you'll take anyone who shows up for your class. I don't blame you. But we might ask who, ideally, should seriously study astrology?

> Because the study of Astrology may tend, when it is improperly understood, to promote a fatalistic attitude of mind [Notice he said "may tend." S.A.] and so work dire consequences, it is a matter of some interest to consider whether it should be studied by all and sundry. . . . It is quite certain that there are some, nay many, people to whom it would be almost criminal to introduce Astrology. Only people possessed of considerable moral courage should study their own maps, and only those endowed with more than the average common sense and sense of responsibility should study others'. Every atom of sensationalism should be banished from the attitude of the professional astrologer, but this ideal, I fear, [He said this 50 years ago! S.A.] is by no means always realized at present. The nervous and the fearful should leave Astrology strictly alone. . . . (*Symbolic Directions in Astrology*)

Of course it's impossible, nowadays, to control who studies astrology. I'm not saying that's bad; I am sort of an Aquarian type, after all. Astrology today is easily accessible to the masses, and I think it should be seen by them as a *language.* Astrologers have to educate the masses in that view of astrology. It is no longer an initiatory science. You don't have to be a high priest, or an initiate of a religion, to learn it anymore. We cannot control who studies it, but we *can* make an effort to have intelligent educational opportunities and materials available, so when people do study it, they can find a decent class, or they can read a decent book that presents astrology in a modern way—as a language and as a practical tool for living.

There are many people publishing astrology books today. And many of these publishers, in fact, have no editorial expertise in the field. They publish almost anything, regardless of quality or originality, as we all know from trying to read many of these books! Some of them don't have even one part-time editor who knows astrology! That's the pathetic truth. Now a good analogy would be with physics or chemistry, also very intricate sciences. Would a publisher publish a book on physics without having an editor who knew physics? No. That's because the physicists wouldn't buy it. But to some extent, the astrologers buy anything. The general public, also, buys incredible amounts of pseudo-astrology and superficial "entertainment astrology."

Before you all get terribly depressed, I should emphasize that we have come a long way in only 50 years. Modern, psychologically-sophisticated astrology is still extremely young. It's only about 50 years old or so, if you date its beginning to the publication of Rudhyar's *The Astrology of Personality* in 1936. There were glimmerings of it earlier, in the work of Alan Leo, Isabelle Pagan,* and others. Some of Alan Leo's work is quite perceptive, and Isabelle Pagan's writings were way ahead of their time. That was long ago, about 1900. But even if you consider that period to be the beginning, I think it has come a long way,

*So far as I know, the only work by Isabelle Pagan currently in print is *Signs of the Zodiac Analysed* (formerly entitled *From Pioneer to Poet*), published by the Theosophical Publishing House and very much worth reading by all students of astrology.

thanks largely to Dane Rudhyar's work. One more quote from Malcolm Dean before moving on to the next topic:

> If Rudhyar accomplished one thing as an astrologer, it was to bring home the realization that astrologers had to accept responsibility for their actions. In his 1968 work, *The Practice of Astrology,* Rudhyar commenced with chapters on understanding the nature and purpose of what one is about to study and assuming personal responsibility for the use of one's knowledge. This sensitivity to the effects of astrology's application was virtually unheard of at that time. Everyone was so busy trying to outdo other astrologers in predicting events or proposing new techniques like the latest Paris fashion, that hardly any thought was given to what astrology might be doing to those who came into contact with it.

So I would say that we have come a long way from that state of affairs, or—to put it more accurately—some of us have come a long way. Many astrologers now do pay close attention to the effect it has on clients, unlike the typical practice of 50 years ago.

Science, Scientism & Astrology

The status of astrology in modern society today cannot be explained thoroughly without looking at the current power structure, "what we're up against," you might say. What sort of trends dominate this society? Not only America, but also the industrialized countries in Europe; and these dominant trends are spreading rapidly to all the developing countries.

First of all, the main religion of the Western world now is *scientism*—an "Ism" based on science. No matter what people say, no matter how many people go to church and so forth, the dominant religion is scientism, since it unconsciously shapes our attitudes, thought processes, and beliefs so thoroughly. And of course the high priests of this religion are the "scientists," some of whom are true scientists; others are merely pseudo-scientists. Many of these pseudo-scientists hold forth as the high priests of humanity, offering to "unravel the mysteries of life." We're all supposed to bow down and worship them and their latest "discoveries" and the latest gadgetry. This scientism is the dominant religion of the culture we live and work in, and the dominant (though unconscious) paradigm of the modern view of "reality." Now I don't think it's too strong to say that a lot of phony "experts" make statements on astrology. And the media, of course, helps them to get lots of publicity. By "phony experts" or pseudo-experts, I mean those who have not studied astrology at all, or if they've touched upon it, it has only been superficial. They've never entered into it deeply and spent enough time on it to understand it.

Therefore, first of all, I have to say that these kind of people's opinions should always and immediately be considered worthless until proven otherwise by the strongest possible evidence! Those who follow any number of academic fields know that the opinions of so-called experts change almost daily, according to the latest fads and peer pressure. They're not dealing with truth; they're dealing with fads, ideas, concepts, what's "the latest." It's funny that they keep rejecting the things that were "true" just yesterday, huh? And they reject yesterday's "truth" in favor of a new "truth" which they now defend just as strongly. On the other hand, astrology has lasted, in one form or another, probably longer than history records and is found universally in advanced civilizations!

For example, what I mean by this phony "expert" business is this: I cannot calculate the velocity of a falling brick. Even when I took physics in college, I didn't do it too well. But I'm not making any claims about physics. I'm not saying anything about physics. I don't know anything about it. That's all I can say, and that's all I would say if a media person asked me about it. And yet those who cannot even calculate a birth-chart feel no hesitation in saying anything they want about astrological subjects. Those are not scientific opinions. They are opinions based on beliefs, on their belief system. Many media-created "experts" (Carl Sagan is one of my favorite phonies) use their authority to put people at odds with their real experience and inner knowledge.* They also put people at odds with their traditions, dis-

---

*See page 83 of *New Insights in Modern Astrology* for more information on the media's propagation of the "scientist" as high priest and its inherent hypocrisy. This book, by Stephen Arroyo and Liz Greene, is available from the publisher of this volume.

couraging people from trusting their own intuition and values. Often then, not only the general public, but in our case the practitioners of astrology also, lose confidence in themselves, even subconsciously. And we often subtly start to submit to the "certified wisdom" and the "education" of various "specialists," all of whom are thoroughly ignorant in the field of astrology. They seem familiar only with their own biases and absolutely predictable opinions.

These comments critical of the Church of Scientism are not meant to demean real scientists–those who are motivated by wanting to find truth or by wanting to produce methods or products that indeed make life better for human beings. They are directed to the power-hungry, rigid-minded authoritarians who misuse their authority, who have lost the true spirit of science, and who completely lack any intellectual honesty. So, the target of these remarks is the negative establishment that basically seeks to perpetuate its hold on people's minds. There's a lot of vested interest involved. Think of the funding and the well-paid jobs available.

When we see how entrenched in the society's power structure anti-astrology views are (which are fundamentally materialistic views), one cannot help but conclude that astrology arouses such hostility and such feelings of insecurity and even panic in many people because their materialistic belief system and astrology represent *totally incompatible world views.* There won't be a meeting of minds, ever, between materialists and those astrologers who see a higher level of life through astrology. (No doubt, however, there are materialistic astrologers.) So, incompatible world views, I feel, lie at the bottom of the hostility and the diversity we all observe. But that's all the more reason not to go chasing after some illusory marriage of astrology and materialistic science. Astrologers would do better to clean up their own act than to waste their energy trying to change the establishment. Neither should we naively jump into the mental quagmire produced by such limited minds in the futile hope that we can "prove" astrology to them.

The incompatible world views I just mentioned also find expression in two radically different paradigms of reality. The paradigm of materialistic science is quite familiar to us: causality, linear thinking, measurement of forces, and so on. By contrast, implicit in the reality that astrology reveals is a holistic paradigm, which shows the interrelatedness of man, the planets, and all the rest of creation within a dance of energy that exhibits *all-at-onceness* that transcends the space/time limitations that traditional scientists tend to believe in. Although paradigms are admittedly only models that are set up in order to try to understand certain things, it is possible that some paradigms are better models of ultimate reality than others; and this suspicion tends to create a certain amount of insecurity in some quarters. I believe that we should acknowledge the radically different paradigm that is implicit in astrology, as well as the philosophical and religious/spiritual implications of the vistas that astrology reveals. And to me, perhaps the most pointless venture of all is for astrologers to limit themselves by remaining stuck in the old materialistic paradigm while purporting to "test" astrology. There are, after all, many ways to do research; and such attempts are like mixing apples and oranges—to no avail. I am not saying that astrology cannot benefit from more critical thinking and a sharing of observations, even those that may refute some traditional notions. But the kind of research we use should be appropriate for astrology and should develop out of astrology's nature and uses, not be a foreign overlay.

There are many reasons for our acknowledging these different paradigms, and we do not have the time to explore the entire philosophy of science. And yet, at the risk of belaboring a point that few people seem willing or interested enough to understand, I feel that I must at least outline a few facts, just for the record. I feel this must be done because so many people in the astrology world seem amazingly unsophisticated about the intellectual distinctions and the philosophical implications of enthusiastically adopting the limited methodology of a materialistic science that in fact is already being outmoded even within the domain of science. Roy Alexander, an astrological counselor in London, has written some very good material on this entire issue, from which I want to quote a couple of things:

> It always seemed to me that the scientific investigation of astrology rested more firmly on misconception of what science was

> about than it did on logic, since the techniques of quantitative objectivity that were supposed to reveal all were already in serious trouble in their own discipline, in the realms of relativity and particle physics. What was to be gained by the attempt to make astrology conform to an outdated nineteenth century science was never clear to me. (*Journal* of the British Astrological Association, Spring, 1984, in an article entitled *Context: A New Dimension in Astrology*)*

Mr. Alexander also wrote a long and excellent letter on the subject of the different paradigms we confront in the science vs. astrology controversy, which was published in 1983 in a British magazine. I refer anyone to the entire letter if interested in exploring this subject further. However, I do want to excerpt a couple of quotations.

> This paradigm, that the universe is essentially a machine, whose laws and workings can be understood by detached observation and analysis, was invented sometime around the last half of the 17th century by people like Newton and Galileo and other lesser lights whose names are hardly or not remembered at all.
>
> Again, taken as a set of rules, this paradigm has been outstandingly successful in enabling us to understand and manipulate the material world. It has been so successful, in fact, that we take it as being axiomatic and have come to believe that it represents the truth about the way the world actually is. It is completely ingrained into our habits of thought and feeling. Even those who dislike and oppose its implications are held within it. This is why researchers have such an easy time of dismissing the arguments of those who oppose or are unsatisfied with research. The researchers are aligned with the prevailing paradigm in a way that their opponents are not and their arguments therefore carry very great weight. A case in point is Eysenck and Nias in their book, *Astrology: Science or Superstition?* They admit that they could not interpret a birth chart with any confidence yet state that it does not matter, since statistical analysis is competent to investigate the validity of astrology. If a tone deaf music critic who had never listened to any music were to claim that this was no bar to practising his profession, we would all instantly see how absurd his claim was. But Eysenck and Nias are speaking in full alignment with the Newtonian paradigm and their claim sounds convincing. (*Correlation,* 1983, Vol. 3, No. 1, pp. 54ff.)
>
> Applying the quantitative, Newtonian techniques to astrological phenomena is mixing two opposing paradigms. It just does not make sense to think of astrology in terms of man separate from a mechanical universe. Quantitative research in this context is merely chasing its own tail since it is pursuing phenomena that it

*"Materialism starts from the assumption that only matter is real," says Cambridge-educated biologist Rupert Sheldrake, Ph.D., and using mechanistic theories to try to explain living processes or the "realm of spirit" he characterizes as "the last survival of the nineteenth-century worldview of science, a kind of living fossil." The author of

> is specifically designed to exclude. It is no more logical to expect statistical research to say anything useful about the validity of astrology than it is to expect astrology to give us such hard and specific information as the atomic weight of copper. (ibid.)

I think it is particularly interesting and disturbingly true, as Mr. Alexander's quote states, that the dominant paradigm of any time period becomes "ingrained into our habits of thought and feeling." You see, this paradigm is a trap; it is not a truth but a purely mental construct that should be used only for specific purposes. But yet, it somehow creeps into our attitude toward reality itself. It is the old story of man being eventually controlled by the tools he creates. The dominant characteristic of the materialistic methodology and model is that of *limitation*—it systematically *excludes* much of reality. And its main tool is "logical deduction." In an excellent article, Stanley Schmidt explains how the old paradigm can never give birth to a more inclusive new paradigm through conventional procedures:

> But *formulating* a new theory (as distinguished from a special case or extension of an old one) *cannot* be done entirely by deductive reasoning. By definition, a really new principle cannot be logically deducted from old ones. A proposition which can be so deduced is not something fundamentally new, but merely something which was already implicit in previous knowledge (or beliefs). Relativity, for example, could in no way be deduced from classical mechanics, because it requires fundamentally new concepts of space and time, or (as it historically happened) the postulate that the speed of light in vacuum is a constant for all observers. Quantum mechanics could not be deducted from classical mechanics because it required the new postulate that matter exhibits aspects of both particle and wave behavior.
>
> In each of these cases, the new ingredient that made the breakthrough possible was something which not only could not be deducted from the premises of previous theory, but actually *contradicted* those premises—was logically inconsistent with them. In each such case, the breakthrough required a largely intuitive leap to a radically *new* premise. (From *Non-logical Processes in Science & Elsewhere,* CAO Times)

The above observations explain clearly why astrological hypotheses and principles are never arrived at by orthodox scientists who are still limited by the old paradigm. One must make a leap to a new level of understanding and to *a new scope*

A New Science of Life, Dr. Sheldrake has hypothesized "morphogenetic fields" (M-fields), "invisible organizing structures that mold or shape things like crystals, plants or animals, and also have an organizing effect on behavior," fields that exist quite apart from material structures and closely resemble Jung's concepts of archetypes and the collective unconscious.

of openness to reality on all levels if one is going to be able to see the reality of astrology and its great value. One must be able to accept a new paradigm, one that has far fewer limitations than the materialistic one. Without such an intuitive leap, all types of human endeavor stagnate, including all branches of science. And the science of psychology and all attempts to understand human nature will inevitably stagnate whenever they persist in trying to evaluate human complexity through the narrow paradigms of material science.

And yet, what is the state of things today? What is the state of modern consciousness in relation to these questions? Are we beginning to seize control of the monster of materialistic science and its methods and implications and force it once again to serve us rather than to enslave us? It seems to me that fewer and fewer people all the time bother to ask *any* philosophical questions, particularly those people involved in "science." So, what are people who are deeply involved with astrology to see as their role and purpose and place in modern society? In fact, what are we up against? The unconscious assumptions and conventions of our entire society mitigate against our astrological claims and knowledge. But it is obvious that "science" will never supply the human being with the real substance of life: meaning. It has never done so, and it never will. As Laurence L. Cassidy, Ph.D. has written:

> Science neither asks nor answers any questions of meaning, but only provides definitions of operational function so that, at the end, as at the beginning, the important questions such as "Why?" are left outside the scientific universe of discourse. . . . Science is meaningless in terms of asking or answering any question concerning the reason why. Is it any wonder that our scientific age is characterized by all but universal scepticism?
>
> . . . science overemphasizes the role of objectivity and thus leaves no room for the personal, subjective side of human knowing. The result is, of course, the alienation of man from his environment, from his fellows, from himself and from his God. This has become a major theme, with variations, of contemporary art and literature. It is also one of the prime factors in the rejection of astrology by the scientific community, because our discipline is principally concerned not with the planets themselves, whatever that means, but with their influence on mankind. (*Science and Astrology: The Anatomy of a Philosophical Conflict,* © 1981, Astrologer's Guild of America, reprinted in *CAO Times.*)

In fact, science rejects all other ways of knowing. In *Astrology, Psychology & the Four Elements,* I went to great lengths to explain the different ways of knowing and to contrast them. The negative impact of the denial by science of so much of reality and human experience is powerful and profound. This negative impact is outlined in the following observations. They are taken from a lecture by Da Free John, a spiritual teacher who, I understand, is also writing a book on this subject. The talk was called "The Asana of Science" and bluntly states the facts of science's position in our society today. I will simply list the key observations that he pointed out. [Quotation marks indicate a direct quote from the lecture.]

1. Science is a *pose* that we assume to do a particular kind of work. And, years ago, when people had a more holistic view of life as their habit on both conscious and unconscious levels, the scientific pose was considered to be a certain type of madness, of which people were naturally suspicious.
2. In spite of the fact that science assumes that only the material universe is real, we do not exist merely in a physical universe. In reality, "we exist in a multi-dimensional condition, every aspect of which is totally real." All the levels of reality in which we exist comprise a far larger domain than the limited universe that science is investigating.
3. Science acknowledges a "reality" that "is only a fraction of the condition that we are directly aware of in every moment." The physical universe that science investigates is only a narrow portion of a wider scale of dimensions in which we participate. "As human beings we simultaneously exist in many dimensions and fluidly move attention through many dimensions."
4. "Science is a dehumanizing adventure when made into an absolute philosophical point of view," because it excludes man and makes the physical universe superior to and more real than the being of man and his full dimensions–his energy and his psychic dimensions.
5. When you use science, "if you don't understand that you're just applying a discipline in order to get to know something but rather make this discipline the model of existence, the model of your entire presumption about existence, then you'll find yourself doing more than science." You'll find yourself making the assumptions of that discipline and making that model the way you see the relationship between all things.

It was also pointed out in this same talk that scientific materialism is in fact another kind of cult that wants to dominate society and the modern mentality worldwide, in association with the state. I have felt for some time that the official spokesmen of academia and "science" (the high priests of the religion of scientism) generally enforce the standards that suit the state; and the state in turn enforces the exclusive view of reality (through laws and funding) that allows the religion of scientism to flourish. An excellent example of this is the great number of TV shows that bow low in respectful obeisance to any sort of new technique or gadget of technological medicine, whereas unorthodox natural healing methods and radical changes in lifestyle that often improve the health are either criticized, ignored, or made the butt of jokes and curiosity features in "Isn't this a silly world?" shows. All this is done in the name of health and education and "progress," whereas health and education are really not even minor considerations. They are really self-congratulatory incantations.

Before we take a much-needed break, I just want to read one more quotation. This also points out the negative impact of our contemporary use of and worship of science. I believe we should take these observations as warnings. If we cannot change these trends in the society at large, at least let us be aware of them in our private lives and in relation to our professional practices. Those practicing astrological psychology or astrological counseling can serve as a counterpoint to the dominant trends of society, and seeing clearly "what we're up against" should ultimately make us stronger, more confident, and more appreciative of the great value that astrology can contribute to modern people. This quotation is from Maharaj Charan Singh, a spiritual master who has hundreds of thousands of followers throughout the world:

> It has been the aim of mankind to make a kingdom of man on this earth with the help of science and technology. But where is that kingdom? The entire world is strife torn; the entire humanity is in a state of high tension. The modern man has lost faith in everything. Fear born of hatred dominates him and his kingdom. The pursuit of science is directed towards destruction of both. . . .

The way we are using science today is leading to the destruction of both the individual and this mythical kingdom that science is supposed to give us. And of course the environment is also being destroyed. Astrology, on the other hand, is a tool that can increase harmony, tolerance, and understanding in the world, so I don't think we should betray its value by forcing it into the mold of a world view that has produced worldwide mass psychosis and destruction. Now that's a good note to end on, right?

After the 15-minute break and before continuing with the prepared lecture, Mr. Arroyo made the following remarks to acknowledge the mood of the audience and the fact that many of his observations were indeed rather "heavy" and perhaps even a bit depressing to some conference attendees.

[This is of course the "Saturn-Pluto Conference" and we should not expect that everything done or said during such a working conference will be light and happy and pleasant. Saturn of course traditionally rules Capricorn, and many people think Capricorn is a great negative and depressing sign. Pluto of course rules Scorpio, which must be acknowledged as a very negative sign in many respects. So Saturn and Pluto are both negative. However, negative and positive go together—like yin and yang. One cannot expand continually in a Jupiterian fashion; sometimes, you know, you have to contract and consolidate. So, in the lectures I'm giving during this conference, my aim is to consolidate and define; my aim is not negative, but in any growth cycle there is a period of contraction. One has to, at some time, turn within to assimilate a great deal of outward experience and development. And so these periods of consolidation may seem quite negative in comparison to the excited periods of extraverted growth. At various phases of any growth cycle, there is a period to get things together, to evaluate one's recent experience and discoveries in the light of history and various standards. Without such a phase of inwardness (and seeming negative experience), you continually expand until you suddenly explode, and then everything is diffuse. Everything goes out into the cosmos, and you've wound up with nothing. So, in this light, astrology has expanded so incredibly fast in the last couple decades, on many, many levels, that I think some consolidation is in order. I know that most astrologers hate any type of discipline, but some self-imposed discipline is absolutely necessary for astrology to continue to develop in a healthy way and for it to take a great role in modern society. There has, in my view, been a great deal of absolutely useless and pointless "progress" in the astrology field in recent years, but—unless these new ideas are harnessed and channeled more intelligently—it will amount to just so much wasted energy. As Jean Cocteau said, "The speed of a runaway horse counts for nothing."]

Astrology is a True Science

Before we go on to the question of the purpose of astrology and to some of the professional issues, for the sake of completeness and at the risk of boring some of you, I simply have to make a few observations that point to the conclusion that astrology is in fact a true science. It is futile to belabor the question of whether astrology is or is not a science unless one immediately acknowledges the assumptions one is using about science and the definitions being used. What I've come to now is just a simple matter of definition. So, I'll briefly give you those definitions, and then if anyone ever wants to argue this issue with you, just refer to these definitions, and—with God's help—perhaps they'll go away!

As Stanley Schmidt wrote,

> Science attempts to formulate, in words and equations, the laws which the universe obeys. It does not legislate; it describes. Its fundamental presupposition is that the rules are already there, independent of man; the scientist's job is to come up with statements which describe those rules as accurately as possible. In general, his statements are only approximations, and each generation of scientists tries to improve them, bringing the approximate statements into closer correspondence with actual behavior. A crucial part of this process is checking the predictions of theories against actual behavior, especially in previously unexplored regions of experience. (From *Non-logical Processes in Science & Elsewhere.*)

By this definition, astrology is definitely a science, for it formulates and describes laws which the universe obeys or exemplifies. And, just as no science is perfect and complete and unimprovable, astrology likewise is in a constant state of development, or at least it should be! We should be constantly trying to make our astrological statements, our astrological language, more precise and a closer approximation of observed experience, behavior, and phenomena. And to do this, instead of mathematical equations, we must achieve greater mastery over the English or French or whatever language we speak. A language of *quantity* won't help us at all in making our statements about human experience more precise, because we are dealing with *qualities* and *dimensions* of experience that are far subtler than measurable reality.

The word "science" is supposed to mean something other than what most people today understand it to be. The word "science" comes from the Latin word "Scio," which means "I know." So science is supposed to represent *what we can know.*

It doesn't say how we get that knowledge at all; it's just what we can know. All knowledge is included in what is called "science." Now today the field of science (that is, what is popularly known as science), including many so-called scientific approaches to astrology, embodies a great deal of what in olden days used to be called "speculative philosophy." What is now popularly known as science is often not science at all, but speculative philosophy. By contrast, much of astrological knowledge (I didn't say ALL, but *much*) is based on repeated observation and so, in fact, can accurately be said to comprise a segment of true science. It does not fit the categories, as some detractors claim, of mysticism, or even philosophy, or speculation or superstition. The real core of astrological fact is a science. Why else can you do what you can do with it? Why else on certain days do you guess five people's Sun signs in a row? The odds against that are astounding.

For example, take an experienced, observant astrological counselor who has worked in person with hundreds of clients. (I emphasize "in person" because then they get feed-back, they can see something, they don't just stick something in the mail and never see the person's reaction.) Such an astrological counselor can know much more about any person's true nature than a practitioner from any other field of science. A psychologist, for example, with his hands full of psychological tests, cannot possibly discover as much precise information as can an experienced astrologer from a birth chart. And if this isn't knowledge, what is? If it's true knowledge, then it comprises a science.

Now the problem comes in here. One *does* need a broad, wholistic view of life in order to reach the deepest understanding and knowledge that astrology can provide. It's not available to just any lazy or cynical intellectual with a closed mind, who is completely blind. It's only accessible to those with a large vision. The fact that such a breadth of vision is necessary to utilize astrological science effectively does not deny astrology's scientific precision and value.

In other words, just because not everybody has that breadth of vision, that doesn't deny the value of astrology. If somebody's blind, they just can't see—that's all. So they don't know what's there and they have no business talking about it, either. Now this broad vision is the astrologer's chief tool, even beyond the chart itself. It's this broad vision, this wholistic vision, the wholistic view of life. Just as a chemist must learn to use his laboratory tools and instruments before he can effectively use chemical science, so we have to learn to use this broad vision. If somebody does not know how to use a chemical laboratory, he has no access to chemical knowledge. So what we have is a situation where this necessary breadth of vision *does limit the number of those who can verify the truth of astrology.* Others are simply not qualified to validate or to invalidate astrological statements. Similarly, it's only those who can operate all the instruments and who know how to do the experiments in a chemical laboratory who can validate the truths of chemistry. So I guess that's enough to say about that.

So, the guide in any truly scientific search should be "I know." That should be your end, your aim, to arrive at someplace where you can say "I know this." The point of true science should be attaining knowledge and understanding, not absorption in limited methodologies, such as statistics. A modern trend in all of Western culture, of course, is to see statistics as the only means of validating or arriving at "knowledge." People can get funding to study almost anything statistically, although you can't get a dime for studying anything astrological. The statistical trend is also increasingly visible in astrology.

Now again, just briefly, we have to touch on the Church of Scientism. Every church has prayers. Well, numbers and statistics are modern scientism's accepted language of prayer. Quantitative information is considered sacred. (Qualitative descriptions are considered to be nothing at all—unreal, biased, subjective.) Quantitative information is considered to be "the word of God," the *last* word in any judgment of a theory or the truth of any method. Now, of course, this approach crowds out people's own experience, people's own common sense, and in astrology it crowds out the qualitative judgment of people whose years of experience has made them true artists in working with people on subtle levels, and in dealing with people and their inner workings in times of crisis. The quantitative approach makes no allowance, it gives no space, it puts no value on a qualitative type of expertise.

I'm not saying you shouldn't use statistics for anything, but that method has its limits, and one has to acknowledge it. Those limits have been discussed a great deal by Jung and others.* Those who want to believe in that as prayer don't want to see it as limited. In fact, percentages and statistics can be a convenient cover when you really don't have the vaguest idea of what the truth of a given matter is. But when you have a method of penetrating to the truth on a very essential level, especially with people, through an immediate access to a universal level of knowledge (astrology gives you an access door to the universal order), you don't need confusing numbers. You don't need silly tests that somebody made up out of the blue with purely artificial concepts and categories, which have nothing to do with archetypal or cosmic categories. If you know astrology deeply based on considerable experience with people, you can very often know that you are right on about somebody, and very quickly understand many of their facets. Then who needs the rest? If the goal of using astrology in a practice is clarifying the client's needs, helping to meet that person's needs and giving him some perspective, then *everything else* becomes extraneous.

So when astrologers try to reach out to the outside world to communicate what astrology is, I keep coming back to the conclusion that it has to be represented to the public, not as a materialistically scientific system ("Oh, look! We have found evidence for cosmic rays affecting this, and the lunar tides affecting such and such. . . . "), not as a pile of categorized traits that have been statistically compiled, not as a magic cure or a form of prophecy, but merely as a language. How do you relate it to people? How do you say what astrology is? I just keep coming back to the fact that it's a language of life. You can apply it on

*Mathematician Jules Henri Poincare, for example, said that you can't get numerical values for many phenomena, and even if you could, they wouldn't tell you what you wanted to know. See also Arroyo's *Astrology, Psychology & the Four Elements* for a discussion of this subject. (Arroyo started college as a mathematics major.)

any level. With people, it's a language of experience. On all levels, it's a language of energy.

The Purpose of Astrology

This is a vast subject. Of course trying to define the "purpose of astrology" implicates one's philosophical views. In fact, it implicates one's entire philosophy of life. Each person's philosophy of life and each person's specific purpose in practicing astrology is colored by all kinds of different influences: your values, where you grew up, what background you have, your age, what kind of clientele you have, your beliefs, and so forth.

There are actually many kinds of astrologers, and there are many kinds of astrology, as defined by the astrologer's *purpose.* This is one reason why it's so difficult to get any group of astrologers together in any way, let alone to organize them for anything. It's also why speaking of "the astrological community," which we hear a lot, may be a bit of a self-deception, because actually there are many diverse little astrological communities. If, however, some agreement about the philosophical priorities of astrological practice could be generally agreed upon, even by a small minority of astrologers, it could then be possible to bring about a little unity among those astrologers.

Now of course nobody else can tell you what your purpose or philosophy should be. The important thing is to define for yourself what it is, because without a philosophy and a clearly defined purpose (especially in a professional practice of astrology), it's impossible to evaluate the factors in a chart and their relative importance. Without a definite purpose, you have no goal, no standard, by which to measure. And it's almost a certainty that you'll go off on many different tangents, if you're without that guiding philosophy always bringing you back to the purpose of a consultation or the purpose of your personal use of astrology. The purpose gives you a direction. It's like the Sagittarian arrow, OK? Sagittarius is the sign of philosophy, traditionally. Its energy is going someplace; its got a target, an aim. So whatever that aim or purpose may be, you've got to define it, in order to focus. And if you do, you'll be much less tempted to go off on incredible numbers of tangents, as so many astrologers do.

"A little knowledge is a dangerous thing." We've all heard that. The philosophical dimension has to be recognized as fundamental in astrology. In any field of knowledge, whenever sufficient depth is reached, one encounters philosophical questions. That's why in other fields you hear of "the philosophy of science," "the philosophy of history," "the philosophy of religion," etc. We all know that unless the astrologers respect and acknowledge their philosophical moorings and their ethics (another Sagittarian thing), this science can be used as a means of manipulation, rather than as a means of understanding and appreciation. And I know we've all probably used it as a means of manipulation, and certainly we've seen it be used that way. And that is not only wrong in many cases, but dangerous.

This danger becomes stronger the more astrology is "accepted" by those who have purely technological minds. If astrology starts to be "accepted" by such people, the philosophical and spiritual dimensions may be ignored totally, and the science used for questionable purposes. Again, what can we do? Primarily we can get our own act together. Ultimately, maybe there could be some kind of organization with certain ethical codes and clearly defined philosophical principles that really mean something instead of the double-talk in the codes of ethics used by most astrology groups.

The purpose of astrology . . . this is a bit of a redundant definition, but I like it anyway, so I'll venture this idealistic definition: *A major purpose of astrology is to clarify to individuals the purpose of the heavens.* That assumes, of course, that there *is* a purpose to the heavens. That assumes that all of these cosmic laws that you can observe through using astrological principles are all purposeful *and thus meaningful* to some extent. If so, then there is a purpose—a higher purpose you might say—somewhere, not only to astrology but to life.

So then what is the astrologer's purpose? *To clarify to individuals the purpose of the heavens.* Actually, we can never achieve this ideal fully, but *working at it in a close dialogue with the client* is what matters. This effort can help them to define *their own* life purpose; you can't impose it, and you should never try to. Now that can get dangerously close to a priesthood type of role, which I'm never comfortable with. Ideally, we read the language of the stars and we interpret according to our ability. And ideally, we do not impose our concepts and language and priorities on the stars. In other words, we have got to be open to the revelation of that higher purpose. Who are we to tell the heavens what to do?

Another definition of astrology's purpose is a little bit more down-to-earth: simply to re-establish order, confidence, peace of mind, and to encourage self-acceptance, in oneself or in others. It's purpose is not to encourage confusion, fragmentation, mental tension, and anxiety about the future. The cosmic grid of the horoscope has the inherent power to connect the person with the whole universe. That's a tremendous power. And one can use it purposefully.

Finally, I want to quote from Dane Rudhyar a brief section from one of his booklets that not only touches on the astrologer's purpose but also serves as a good lead-in to the final part of this talk, regarding professional issues. As the professionalization of astrologers proceeds, it might be well to consider Rudhyar's definition of astrology as "a form of personal guidance." This quotation in fact comes from his booklet *An Attempt at Formulating Minimal Requirements for the Practice of Astrology,* something he felt compelled to write a few years ago when the legalization of astrology and its licensing by the state was at least temporarily a pressing issue.

> For the "person-centered" type of astrologer, astrology is a form of personal guidance aiming at assisting an individual in the process of actualizing as fully as possible his or her birth-potential. He is therefore concerned with events only in so far as they can be given a deeper, more encompassing meaning in terms of the whole life-pattern and the individuality of the person whose birth-chart is being studied.

In concluding these brief comments on "the purpose of astrology," it only remains to emphasize that it is the aim of this conference to provide a structure within which each one of us can further refine and clarify his or her purpose in using astrology, whether in one's private life only or whether also in a professional practice.

Professional Issues

Astrology has increasingly been recognized as a legitimate helping profession, I believe, especially since the 1960's. But it still has a long way to go. A lot of these questions will be brought up in the evening meetings, and then everybody can throw in their two cents, but I want to introduce the subject with a few comments and observations. In an ideal world, of course, we would not have to worry about professional questions. We wouldn't have to worry about professional images and labels and fee schedules and sliding scales and all of this. We'd just be fed manna from heaven! However, most of us do have to earn a living; some of us have to support children; most of us would like to have a decent old age. It's hard for me to understand, therefore, the short-sightedness of many people in astrology. And there are many who are paranoically against any professionalization efforts. By professionalization, I do *not* mean legal licensing. That's a totally separate question.

The *key question* to me is really: "Do we think that astrology is valuable and thus should reach people?" If we do, then we simply have to build channels and structures through which it can do so! And this includes a more professional image, as well as more sophisticated professional organizations and standards. If you don't believe that astrology is valuable, or if you're just too cheap to want to share it with anybody else and you just want to use it for yourself, then all these professional questions are irrelevant for you.

We live in an age of increasing specialization and economic pressures, and we have less and less time due to life's hectic pace. It seems that life's pace gets more and more hectic all the time. In this age of specialization, especially given the fact that astrology is fragmenting and expanding in so many directions, you've got to specialize in astrology, too. Nobody any more can honestly purport to be an expert in all the different branches of astrology; there is no way! One has to do astrology many hours a week to become really good at it, and you've got to keep doing it quite often to stay good at it, to stay attuned to that way of perceiving. It's like, if you want to be a good athlete—you have to "stay in shape" and keep your astrological muscles toned. If we don't professionalize astrology to allow intelligent, active, goal-oriented people to make a decent living from it, then we're ensuring that a mediocre calibre of practice may continue to dominate the field.

This brings up the practical question (which I won't go into in detail, because it's so different for everybody) of what you want to do with astrology, whether you want to make a living out of it, and so forth. But in 1920, Charles Carter wrote:

> It is irrational to declare that astrological work should not be charged for. The effect of such a rule would be to deprive us of all astrological help, except such as would be provided by amateurs.

So I feel that the "fee" question has to be addressed by anybody practicing astrology. Also, the anxiety and ambivalence about fees among astrologers comes from many sources, and I don't purport to understand it completely. It might come somewhat from the high priest role that a lot of astrologers like to play, either overtly or unconsciously. It's like dirtying their hands to ask for money. They want a "donation," but they don't want to charge a set fee. That goes against the Neptunian feeling of universal obligation. Of course spiritual guidance *does* become a dimension of some people's astrological practice, and so feeling like a priest at times is understandable. That may well be fine. But the fact is: if you don't charge, then you have to beg! If you're trying to make a living at it, you have to charge or else you'll have to beg. *Or* you have to go get a job somewhere else that ensures that you're always in a state of exhaustion, and you have no time for astrology then, either. Nor do you then have the psychic energy left to do good work with people when you have clients. So it's a tough question.

If one is doing good work with great thoroughness, it's usually difficult to charge what your time is worth. If you're really doing good work, you're still not going to get paid what union members get for steel work or carpentry, if you consider the hourly wage you're getting for all the time involved. This is one good thing about computers; they can really cut down on time spent. They can save you incredible numbers of hours of tedious calculations, because you can instantly get all the calculations done. That really helps make astrology a more financially viable profession, I would say.

We've got to look, though, at the question: What does the public *value*? The public pays outrageous money to lawyers, for example, even though often they don't know anything. They pretend to know something, but they often don't know anything. And you go to another lawyer and get a totally different opinion. And yet the public pays for that. Now I'm *not* saying astrologers should become like lawyers; don't jump to conclusions. But obviously the public does pay a lot of money for many personal and professional services, most of which have far less to offer than astrology. One has to conclude that the services of the astrologer are often seen as not worth very much.

I think that for some practitioners it might be better to charge $100 or more for a long, in-depth consultation, or maybe for a series of two appointments, than charging $25 or so for quickie "readings." At least you'll learn a lot more astrology doing the former! Ultimately, you'll probably get as much or more money. You may temporarily get four times as many clients if your fee is low, but there is a sacrifice in the quality of service you can give if you do quickie stuff and try to "process" people. It's like what's happened in medicine, and some chiropractors are doing it now too—processing 60, 70, 80 patients per day. How can you have any semblance of understanding of that human being? It's just totally impossible.

When speaking of professionalizing astrology, one cannot ignore the question of professional organizations. There is some historical background here that I want to explore. The purpose of reading the next couple of quotations is to point out the really complex issues that arise in any consideration of an astrological professional organization. Now pay close attention to this quotation:

> An influential profession will be the only possible successful bulwark against the multiform manifestations of quackery.
>
> [Our] profession has a power for good in the community which is not equalled by that of the clergy or the legal fraternity. Its power is, however, not exerted. It is dissipated by lack of concerted effort, and wasted by internal differences of opinion. . . . Why is it that after 100 years . . . our influence is so transient, so feeble, that the most absurd fad, the most hare-brained delusion, the most fantastic fraud that comes along spreads its pernicious poison among the people? How much weight has [our] opinion . . . in a public matter, and with what smiling indifference do not those who make the laws listen to [our] protests? There is something wrong here. . . . One cause . . . stands out as first in importance. It is lack of organization.

That was the status of allopathic medicine in 1901. That's a quote from the American Medical Association *Journal,* in 1901. Allopathic medicine is the dominant medicine now. Then it was only one of many types of medicine, many branches of legally-practiced healing arts. I am not saying that astrologers should emulate the allopaths and set up an A.M.A. sort of organization. But at the turn of the century allopathic medicine was only one of many types of healing that had a widespread following and many thousands of practitioners. One of the most popular types of healing then was homeopathy, so popular that in Boston alone there were many hundreds of practitioners at the turn of the century. They were fully trained medical doctors; they could do surgery, give drugs, and all that. But in homeopathy they only give infinitesimal drug doses, so that it stimulates the person's own being to recuperate through its own vitality—it doesn't drug you into another state of being.

Now homeopathy contributed to its own downfall partially through errors in judgment in how it managed its professional organizations. They had a great opportunity to become established nationwide as a powerful and effective healing art. But they sowed the seeds of their own decline as a profession to the point that homeopathy almost entirely disappeared in the U.S.A. It has been only in the past fifteen years that renewed interest in it has been noticeable and fairly widespread. This is just a parallel, and I'm drawing it because it might caution us what can happen to astrology if you organize it wrong, if you have some serious misconceptions, or if you are too idealistic.

The next quotation, to me, shows why, if there is to be any astrological organization that's going to be worth very much, it's got to be *focused* on a definite purpose; it's got to have very clear principles and philosophy. And thus it has to be rather *exclusive.* It cannot purport to include all people who say that they're astrologers. And the reason I'm saying this is well illustrated by what happened to the homeopaths.

At one time the homeopaths had a tremendous following among the masses, especially in the small towns and the countryside. They always had little political power compared to the allopaths, but they weren't interested in political power very much. They were healing arts purists. They adhered to a strict science and philosophy in homeopathic practice, one principle of which was "Do no harm." That was a primary law, which of course most allopaths do not follow. Some of the homeopaths got the idea that if they would simply "extend the liberal hand of fellowship to the allopaths," in other words let them into the homeopathic organizations, it would be greatly to their benefit financially. You see, the homeopaths then had the same problem that the astrologers have now–if you do good, thorough work, you can hardly get paid for your time. Homeopathy takes a long time to deal with each person. As you get more experienced, it gets shorter and shorter, but still it's very time-consuming. And nobody will get outrageously rich doing homeopathy, which is one reason why it got less popular among graduates of medical schools. So this quotation is from the president of the American Institute of Homeopathy over 100 years ago, in 1882, and it shows clearly their misguided attempt to consolidate their professional and financial power through diluting their standards and naively believing that overlooking their distinctiveness would strengthen their profession.

> We should extend the liberal hand of fellowship to the allopaths. . . . Toleration begets friendship. . . . It may be urged by some that this measure will eventually bring the two schools together and extinguish homeopathy as a special school; that practi-

> tioners of all shades will simply adopt parts of homeopathy and will forget what is distinctive in it. But we do not fear the result.

But that's what happened. And homeopathy almost became extinct. In fact, if it hadn't survived in India and Mexico and a few other places, it would probably have died. It's now having a rebirth in this country. You may draw from that example the conclusion that if you're going to organize, make it a bit exclusive, and have your principles drawn out clearly. Some may disagree with that. It's a far cry from what most astrological organizations do now, where you virtually have to believe in nothing. You don't have to do anything or commit yourself to anything. I think we could all agree that the field of astrology could use an organization that calls press conferences to refute misrepresentations about astrology, that has a Public Relations Department that can educate the public, that has a Legal Aid Department to assist practitioners who are being harrassed or deprived of the freedom to practice by unconstitutional laws . . . in other words, an organization that would be truly effective and supportive of astrological work as a profession. And, since I feel that there will be further attempts to develop such organizations in the coming years, I wanted to state for the record the experience of the homeopaths as a cautionary note. Astrology does not need further misguided, poorly-thought-out organizational schemes. And we can learn from past failures within and without the astrology field.

Licensing

The whole question of licensing–I don't really want to belabor that point. I don't really believe in any sort of government licensing for astrology. Who is to judge? How can they figure out anything? We need to clean up our own act and to agree on some basic principles. The government can't keep its own books balanced, and we're asking *them* to clean up *our* act, because we can't do it? A quote from Rudhyar, which he wrote about 1970, clearly states the crux of the matter.

> As an astrologer comes face to face with an eager, perhaps confused or even distraught client, intellectual knowledge (including statistical knowledge) is not what really matters. The human

> quality of the relationship brought about by the astrologer's personality and his feeling-responses often is what is most important—and that quality cannot be standardized and even less subject to legislation. (From *An Attempt at Formulating Minimal Requirements for the Practice of Astrology*)

So rather than licensing, my main thought along these lines, in terms of how astrology can be related to the public, is the importance of educating the public in whatever way we can. In addition to improving ourselves and our own work, in whatever way is possible, we have to educate the public about what astrology really is and what it can do for them, *without overstating the case.* To me, that kind of education is much more important and more effective than any form of licensing.

And yet, given the fact that the professionalization of astrology will ultimately force us to confront this issue in some way, certain standards have to be set and certain steps taken before they are taken for us. (Also, the other various counseling and therapeutic fields are jealous of their territories and will not take kindly to what they will see as an intrusion into their domain and into their pocketbook!) As Simon Best wrote in an article called *Astrological Counselling and Psychotherapy* (*Journal* of the British Astrological Association, Summer, 1983 issue),

> We really have no alternative. Either we put our house in order or someone from the establishment will sooner or later take great delight in doing it for us, or, alternatively, taking it apart brick by brick.
>
> Such is a client's heightened suggestibility in counseling and the potential for disaster at the hands of the incompetent or ill-informed, that such a monitoring of astrologers by astrologers—as all similar psychological and medical bodies operate—should no longer be delayed.

In that same article, Mr. Best outlines some very specific steps that might be taken in setting up qualifications, training, and so forth. Going into such detail is beyond the scope of this talk, but I would suggest that anyone interested in pursuing such developments consult his entire article. I would only urge, in conclusion, that great care be taken in the kinds of definitions used when a new professional organization is developed. If astrological *counseling* is to be the primary focus of such an organization, it should be clearly stated, and that will inevitably mean the exclusion of many types of astrological practitioners. There is a long road yet to be traveled before astrological counseling or astrological psychology will be firmly established in its own right, but a journey of a thousand miles begins with one step.

3

Counseling & Astrology as a Healing Process

To cure sometimes, to help often, to comfort always.

– 16th Century French Proverb

There is no therapeutic technique or doctrine that is of general application, since every case that one receives for treatment is an individual in a specific condition.

– Dr. C. G. Jung

Considering my own background, I don't think it's necessary for me to emphasize that I do see considerable value in practitioners of astrology studying many things outside the astrology field, including various types of therapy and healing. However, more and more I see astrology as a direct emanation from a very high level of universal mind. And that's one reason I believe that it constitutes an inherent and complete psychology (psychology being defined as a study of the mind). If in fact you have a system that is a perfect reflection of the higher mind of which we're just little microcosms, certainly that is a profound and complete psychology that includes all potential mental patterns.

So I don't think we should overdo the current propensity to overlay onto astrology lots of labels, concepts, and techniques from other fields or from other therapies. Not that one shouldn't study these things, but do whatever you're going to do and then use the *astrological* language. More and more I believe that.

A friend of mine thought of the analogy of an ice skater training for the Olympics. What do ice skaters do? They skate many hours every day, yes. But they also run, they study ballet, they do yoga, they swim, who knows what else? They may meditate. But when they get on the ice, do they meditate? No! When they get on the ice, do they do yoga? No. When they get on the ice, do they run? No. They just skate! See, all the rest is preparation and self-improvement. But when you do your primary thing, you focus on *your* art. I think that's a very good analogy that astrologers can learn from. By all means improve yourself, but too many extraneous concepts, I think, becomes a problem. It relates to one of the issues that someone brought up last night: how to demystify astrology and make it more accessible. You have to keep it a bit simple if you're going to make it accessible.

I mentioned Dennis Elwell before, and I want to read a quotation from one of his articles that supports the notion of astrology's relation to universal mind. I might mention that when I first met him in England, we talked about our backgrounds and how we arrived at our astrological concepts. I told him that I had pretty much just studied astrology on my own, mostly from observation and trial and error, and had just "done charts" for many, many people in person for free for the first few years. Likewise, he had to learn astrology almost solely from observation. He said that when he was growing up there were no books on astrology in the library, and he was so poor he couldn't afford to buy any. So he had to develop it himself just from scratch, through observation. You see, he had the great advantage of not relying on "astrological literature," much of which is relatively idiotic. This is the quote I mentioned:

> The realization that bursts upon anyone who . . . [researches astrology deeply] is that he is dealing not so much with processes and laws as with mighty thoughts. Not only the ultimate nature of each sign, but the way the entire zodiac locks together in a complex system of relationships, suggests that its reality consists of mind-stuff, and that in turn suggests the existence of a Universal Mind.
>
> [This is] an audacious concept, but one which I believe will force itself on any astrologer who abandons the onlooker standpoint and tries to get to the heart of the principles known by the names of the planets and [the signs of the] zodiac. . . . Whatever

> else he is—as a result of his heredity, environment, training, and opportunity—man is larger than he guesses: cosmic thoughts think in him. (From *Towards a New Science of Man*)

In a sense, we're all channels for something much bigger than ourselves—the ancient microcosm/macrocosm idea. If astrology is in fact an emanation of universal mind or "collective unconscious" or anything like that, then instead of imposing a foreign dogma on astrology, I would say, "Let us open our eyes to what astrology *already is!* Let's acknowledge its inherent, extremely sophisticated, psychological dimensions." It's all there. It's a tremendous tool, a language of consciousness and inner experience, and it has an inherent healing power for this reason: because it is an emanation of that incredible universal mind. If in the right hands, if used in the right way by the right kind of person, its inherent healing power can then contact others—a client, a patient, a friend, a relative. And how does it "heal"? It does so by attuning the client to the cosmic order, or at least encouraging the client to tune in to it consciously. But that is a large order for any astrologer, we must admit, for us to be "fine tuners" to the cosmic order.

Anyone researching and using astrology for very long with people, *in person,* should have no hesitation in declaring that astrological psychology is the best psychological system, purely from the point of view of accuracy and practicality, even without any reference to "universal mind." It's certainly the best theory of human personality, if you compare it to all the others that are taught in universities, and it certainly is the truest *psyche-ology* ("psychology"), i.e., study of the human psyche.

The healing power inherent in astrology is at the center of any consideration of astrological counseling and astrological psychology. This healing power can be distorted, however, or it can be inhibited, by the astrologer. The astrologer is a channel, and doing astrological counseling raises the question of how good a channel, how pure a channel are we for that power, for that cosmic order and that knowledge? This healing power comes from a higher level of reality. It's one reason why we as astrologers cannot talk to most people in other fields, because we're really dealing with something way beyond the usual run-of-the-mill mental studies, the very limited intellectual studies, and materialistic studies. It's a different order of the universe. You can't use the same standards. Again, to quote Elwell, from a private letter he wrote in 1979:

> The idea is to demonstrate that the zodiac is an archetype, not only within the collective unconscious, but within the fabric of reality itself, [*It pervades everything!* S.A.] as a ground plan of creation. This archetype has not been invented. It exists, and knowledge of it has developed in step with evolving human consciousness. . . .

Now that's a really profound statement, that our consciousness determines our level of astrological knowledge. This is one reason why *traditional* astrology has become quite meaningless for many of us; the astrology has not for the most part evolved to keep pace with our growth of consciousness. At least we may hope (and I think there is some evidence) that there *is* some evolving human consciousness. And it's why every culture has its own astrology—the consciousness of that culture determines what level of understanding they can have of astrology. This is also why importing extremely fatalistic German or extremely fatalistic Indian types of astrology is often rather hopeless and often rather useless with intelligent Westerners who don't have that type of consciousness. I'm not saying that it's worthless to study those things. But to import it intact and try to pretend that it can apply to all modern Americans will get you into a bit of trouble.

So, as Elwell said, knowledge of this higher reality has developed in step with evolving human consciousness. It's only as we develop the capacity to understand more of life that we can understand a bit more of astrology.* It's always going to be ultimately beyond our intellectual grasp, because the universal mind is beyond intellect, and much vaster. It's also beyond "reason." So much of traditional astrology for many of us has

*Along these same lines, in an article in the summer, 1983 issue of *Aspects* magazine, the astrologer Noel Tyl wrote that if we relate a client's life only to what we know about various astrological rules or traditions, we "run the risk of confining the life to what we know about astrology. . . . Our craft takes us well beyond textbooks and lessons, indeed. What we know about life quickly becomes a lot more important than what we know about the tools of astrology."

become totally meaningless and quite outmoded, partly because our consciousness has grown past that level.

Another explanation of why astrology has such a profound healing power comes from this particular letter, written by a man in England and published in the Winter, 1981–82 issue of the British Astrological Journal. His name is P. R. Lewis-Bizley. It's a very good letter. He says:

> . . . a rather disturbing trend . . . seems to have been gathering momentum over the past few years, to suppress or discard the spiritual, philosophical, holistic foundations of astrology in favour of subjecting isolated parts of it to the restrictive, detached and rather presumptuous analysis of today's scientific statistical methodology. It even appears by implication to accept that satisfying, or failing to satisfy, these statistical tests is in some way proof or disproof of the validity of astrology as a whole.
>
> This I believe is in danger of doing astrology a profound disservice, whether it is the materialistic-scientific community we are thus trying to convince, or, via the media, the world at large. It is perhaps even more damaging potentially to the astrological fraternity themselves, especially to those younger members who have not as yet the experience on which to base a deeper insight.
>
> I am in no way criticising statistical methodology itself; in its right context—the material sciences—it is an indispensable tool. However, attempting to apply it, as a criterion for validity, to a Science and Art that far transcends the material raises the whole question of what we are really trying to do.
>
> Is it really our ultimate aim to see isolated parts of astrology (removed from the context of the Whole) accepted and taught in schools and colleges so that all and sundry can dabble in and amuse themselves with it? Are we really raising the status of astrology by making it 'acceptable' enough to take a (completely irrelevant) place alongside physics and chemistry in our seats of higher learning?
>
> If so, I have no hesitation in saying that we are prostituting a divine heritage that has been vouchsafed to us, presumably for the sake of gaining worthless recognition and acceptability on a superficial level of experience. The Higher and Spiritual cannot be subjected to the Lower and Material; the Truth inherent in the Whole cannot be subjected to a statistical examination of artificially dissected and isolated parts.
>
> Do we judge the greatness of a noble symphony by measuring the extent to which a chord or a passage follows an artificial predecided criterion? Or an artistic masterpiece by analysing the chemical content of the paint or the canvas? Would we accept, as proof or disproof of the validity of a great religious Faith, a statistical analysis of the instances in which prayers for material benefits

> (others could not be judged anyway) are answered, not only to the satisfaction of the supplicant but of a detached scientist with his rigid set of criteria?
>
> "Thy Faith hath made thee whole". We must first have that faith in the Whole–in the Divine–of which I believe astrology is an expression; then–and only then–shall we and, through us, the world in general, be made whole in all its manifold parts.

This wholeness and this spark of the Divine in astrology is the real source of astrology's great healing power. We must be careful not to fragment or discard it.

We all know that today we live in a fragmented and rather schizophrenic society. This is one reason why the healing power and the unifying magic of astrology is so needed today. But if we ourselves practice a fragmented form of astrology, then we can hardly claim that astrology's power to unify and heal will remain in our practice. If we're all fragmented, or if we're always confused about what techniques and methodologies to use, that will distort the potential for wholeness that astrology can contribute to people. In fact, if our mind is so scattered by reason of our not having defined our purpose, goals, and philosophy, there is little doubt that the great integrating power of the cosmos as a whole will be only dimly and distortedly reflected through our turbulent minds.

So once again we get back to the question of the astrologer as a *channel*. In that sense, the *astrologer* matters more than the kind of *astrology* being used. Someone just mentioned to me yesterday that he recently talked to a siderealist, and the person said a lot of things that were right on. Well, of course! It's a lens. And if you use just one lens and you keep using it and keep using it, you can see more and more clearly. It's like you're polishing that lens, and you can get a sharper and sharper focus. Astrology is a psychic art as well as a profound science. I'll touch a bit on that today, too–the psychic-energy dimension of astrology.

So, in many, many ways the *astrologer* matters more than the kind of *astrology*. Obviously, certain techniques seem to work better for certain purposes than others. But even with moderately inferior techniques, you can still do some very good work with people if you yourself have what it takes. As Jung said, it's the personality of the doctor that has the curative effect. I feel that both the astrology and the astrologer have an impact on the curative or healing effectiveness, or the lack of it. The astrologer can be a channel for that great magical healing power of the cosmos, but only if he himself (or herself) is living quite effectively—that provides the focus.

There are a number of quotes I'll read today from a book by Dr. Marvin Layman, who by training is a sociologist and a minister. But he has also studied astrology quite deeply. He wrote a little book called *Interviewing and Counseling Techniques for Astrologers* that is hardly ever found in bookstores. I'll be refering to it now and then during this talk. One thing he mentions is that

> Religion, Psychology, and Medicine all have a healing role, i.e., the making whole of the individual. . . . Never before has there been a greater need for such "physicians of the soul." For in our corrupt and spiritually bereft society, those who have psychic wholeness are desperately needed bastions of strength for many others. Therefore, a truly qualified consultant astrologer must be more than merely technically proficient. Such a one must have a genuine feeling for people, a considerable maturity, and some degree of wisdom and inner "soul quality."

This is a tall order and a difficult challenge for astrologers to meet. However, astrologers have no choice but to improve themselves, to make themselves better channels if they are to do justice to the profound truths and to the wholeness of the heavens that they claim to interpret. Otherwise, we had better be careful what we say to the public about what we can really provide. The more we improve ourselves, the more we can really give. As philosopher Leopoldo Luchs once said in a talk I heard him give, "If a man offers to give something that he doesn't have, he's a fraud." So, let the wisdom of the heavens come of its own accord. Perhaps we can help to elicit it from the client through good counseling and honest dialogue. But for *heaven's* sake, don't promise that you can deliver it anytime you want!

Charles Carter once wrote that the one above becomes the many below; the unitary above manifests as multiplicity in everyday life. So, if astrologers work at *raising* their consciousness to a higher level, they can perhaps begin to see the one in the many.

They will begin to perceive simplicity in the apparent chaos of life. So it is my view that astrologers should focus on increasing their *awareness,* not the number of factors and techniques used on the chaotic level of multiplicity. As our awareness increases, we can be more effective at enhancing the awareness of our clients. In other words, the consciousness that pervades all your astrological work is ultimately what has an effect–not mere "facts" or mere words. I recently read a study of "communication skills" that concluded that only 7% of in-person communication consisted of the actual words exchanged. The other 93% was tone of voice, body language, attitudes, vibrations, and other energies. And remember that all 93% is missing in computer horoscope or mail-order horoscope interpretations!

Now there are two extremely important points that can help the practicing astrologer to keep focused and to keep in the right frame of mind with a little bit of humility. These two observations cannot be dismissed lightly.

1. *Either consciously or unconsciously, in the mind of anyone who goes to an astrologer, is the belief that behind the astrologer's statements lies the power of the cosmos.* Even if on the surface they're skeptical (say the client's a Capricorn with 7 planets in Virgo!), they still wouldn't be there if they didn't have somewhere down deep the feeling that "what this astrologer says may be the truth of my life. Maybe it's the cosmos' truth."

So then the question arises: how many of us have what it takes to interpret the cosmos? That's really what we're doing; we're interpreting the cosmos. We're interpreting the state of the solar system as it's reflected in an individual's life. That is a profound task. Again, it brings one, I would think, a little bit of humility, and the realization that we have to acknowledge our limits. The second point is closely related to the first.

2. *You are dealing with something sacred when you are counseling another person about his or her deepest needs, feelings, and aspirations.* You're not just dealing with an object to bounce your ego off of. You're not dealing with something to treat like clay and push around. It's a very sacred interaction. And you should be aware that you can only interpret the cosmos, and thus that person's life, up to your highest level of awareness. That person may have much higher consciousness or higher aspirations than you do. You have to allow room for your ignorance! For all you know, 90% of your clients may be more aware than you are. You've got to leave space for that. Acknowledge your own ignorance.

For example, a particular Neptune factor in a certain chart can indeed be self-deception, but it can also be a tremendous spiritual dedication or idealism or devotion. It could also be both! So you've got to leave space for that person. You can't just preach, "Oh, that's self-deception." You don't necessarily know what that person's aspirations are at the deepest level. So, as they say in homeopathy, "first do no harm." Let people be what they are. It's hard to let them be what they are, especially when so many of them play games with you, when they won't give you anything, they won't open up. So if you let them be what they are and nothing happens, you're both silent and awkward. But that's where you get into the art of counseling, how to evoke and listen to things.

Significant Issues of Astrological Counseling

In the remainder of this talk I want to touch on some important issues of counseling. Each could easily be explored in an entire workshop or discussion, but at least we can raise the issues. First of all, I think it's good that there are now more and more astrological practitioners getting counseling training, learning counseling techniques, and so forth . . . especially for those to whom it does not come naturally. My experience is that most people who get into astrology deeply are not natural counselors. The natural counselors often don't need much training, but the others could benefit from it.

But I also have to say that, although it's probably a good trend for astrologers to get training and education in psychology and counseling, *truth transcends counseling techniques.* Once in a while you just have to lay it on them! Techniques go by the board. In other words, you can't do good counseling just through techniques. Sometimes you have to confront the person with your view of the truth of their nature–not in most consultations, but once in a while. Most people can't take it. They're not ready for it. But once in a while you've got to do it, even risking a rather angry response. And in some cases this can be the best "technique" in counseling, but only with some people and only in some cases.

Clients with mutable signs rising, you have to be especially careful with them. They're so suggestible. Those with the cardinal signs rising, they keep going wherever they're going anyway, no matter what! And don't be fooled by the seeming sensitivity of Cancer rising—they're not really so easily influenced as they appear. The fixed signs rising . . . well, who knows? Nothing you say will probably affect them anyway, except that the Scorpio risings will no doubt resent it! But with the mutable signs rising, any statement can affect them very deeply; so you have to be really careful about laying on what you think is a "truth."

It is, in my experience, a rare client who really is ready for and open to the truth. Once you've found those clients though, they're a joy to work with, because it's so rewarding. You just start striking home about the truth of their lives. It's an *art* to *apply* the truth. Even if you can see something that is absolutely valid and precisely accurate about that person, it is still an art to discover how best to approach and express it.

It must also be said that no counseling or psychological theory or procedure can replace immediate observation and experience and the intuition and insight that accompanies direct interaction with people. It's fair to say, I believe, that the astrologer often falls into the temptation to place a theoretical overlay onto every problem, just as is done by orthodox psychology and technological medicine. Along these lines, there's a great parallel here between physicians and astrologers. This next quote is from an excellent book by Harris Coulter, who is a medical historian very sympathetic to non-traditional methods. These comments are equally true for astrologers as physicians.

> The *observation of the patient is no simple thing. It is by far the most difficult task of the physician. For this reason he has often wanted to skip this stage and to interpose a tissue of theory or speculation between the patient and himself.* The natural desire to simplify the task, to bring some order into the variety of phenomena, to consider some symptoms "legitimate" and others "illegitimate," has always induced a part of the profession to advance the claim that the physician *could* see through the skin and *could* attain reliable knowledge of the underlying pathological processes.

Likewise, astrologers, I think, sometimes overdo their claims. Admittedly, astrologers do have a decided advantage over practitioners of the other healing or counseling arts, in that the astrological system itself does give profound insight (and is potentially very accurate) into the deeper and inner levels of the person's being. It gives a picture of it. But still, do we really know the *causes* of a problem ultimately? Do we really know what the person *should* do or should not do? I don't know if we really have that kind of wisdom, and yet astrologers and astrology books seem to be full of pat advice and wide-ranging explanations of the "causes" of all kinds of problems.

Our mind likes to *impose* an order on things. In fact, one of astrology's greatest values is that it can reveal a *higher* order in the apparent chaos of daily life. But I said it can *reveal,* and you can't *push* a revelation. You can't make a revelation happen. The cosmic order *will* often reveal itself after one discusses things with a client really honestly, after listening to the person, after evoking the person's feelings and deeper thoughts. After doing all that, the cosmic order may sometimes start to surface and reveal itself. But trying to impose an order artificially is usually futile. In any case, it will break down within hours of the person leaving your office, since it's treating symptoms on a very superficial level.

I suppose it's true for many other people, but when I first started doing astrological consultations, in those days it was more one-sided, more of a "reading" than a dialogue of discovery. Very often I would feel a panicky need to "help" them: "Let's put this all together in a nice little package before they walk out of here." I found out later, by subsequent appointments with the same people, or just by running into them on the street, that in most cases those artificially imposed structures and neat little theories collapsed within days or weeks of when they left my office. Why? Because it didn't come out of them! It was *my* mental order put upon them, just so *I* could feel better, as if I had done something real for them.

We should not minimize the chaos of life. Sometimes you can't say anything very comforting to the person in response to a given question. Very often things are totally out of control, or the client is totally out of control. You can't stop that chaos from happening. Sometimes you can help them to sense an order in what looked like chaos, or to get some perspective. But there are chaotic transits, you know, that don't bring about order; they bring about chaos.

For example, if the person has very powerful Uranus transits, or if Neptune is hitting something and dissolving it, the person can feel incredibly chaotic and uncertain for years. Or if Pluto is powerful by transit—the outer planets are going to rip up the structure that Saturn symbolizes. So during such transits, people may feel that everything is falling apart. They may get very frightened. They may feel like they're going crazy. At such times, people are disoriented at a very deep level. By denying it, you're just trying to dismiss it and it won't do any good; it won't comfort them. Trying to minimize that state of mind with all kinds of clever reasoning and analysis or trying to dismiss it as insignificant won't touch them. It won't reach them. At that time the client may need, *more than anything,* a great deal of support and reassurance that *it is all right* to be so crazy at this stage. This is the way it is. This is part of a larger cycle and series of phases. This insanity and chaos is a prelude to a new order developing of its own accord. Such an approach is much more effective than any kind of "advice" when a client is in the midst of huge changes and has lost all perspective and all sense of stability.

The counselor's goal should be to help the client develop enough awareness of his or her situation and feelings and fears that he or she can begin to make their own decisions and to take some steps to put those decisions into action. The astrologer should aim to clarify the situation and perhaps to reinforce any positive statements of new awareness or new plans or intentions that the person comes up with. Then the astrologer might support that and might even suggest some alternatives. But only rarely should one assume the burden of giving advice unrelated to all the details of the person's entire life context.

As an example of such a chaotic period, I'd like to ask those people born in 1945, '46, '47, '48 who have had transiting Neptune opposing natal Uranus in the past few years about their experience. I'd just like to see a show of hands as to how many experienced some form of real chaos, where you were almost going crazy and your mind was going out of control. [Some hands are raised.] About six.* That's enough crazy people for one room! How many who had transiting Neptune opposing natal Uranus in the past few years did *not* experience anything like chaos, going crazy, and so forth? About nine. Obviously it would depend on the individual charts. I would not expect any specific transit to manifest the same in everyone. I was just curious to see how widespread that feeling was when that transit occurred, because it's only in the past few years that I've come to see that an outer planet transit *to a natal outer planet* can be much more powerful than I ever thought before. I used to think that the transiting outer planets aspecting the natal *personal* planets were the key things, and they *are* for most people. They are powerful experiences for everyone. But if you're *especially attuned to the outer planets,* then those natal outer planets being activated by transiting outer planets can also be incredibly profound experiences in themselves, and very long-lasting periods of change. And of course, to interpret them you have to look at the individual's chart, how the natal outer planets aspect the personal planets, and what houses are involved as well. Entire life-attitudes can be totally transformed during such transits.

Perhaps the most important guideline for anyone trying to do in-depth counseling is—as I mention so often—encouraging the client to face himself rather than to run away from himself. Doing this will require the counselor to have considerable strength and perseverance, since most people habitually resist looking at themselves honestly. Pushing too hard in that direction may be especially frustrating when the client is having Uranus or Neptune transits, both of which especially pressure people to seek out new and exciting activities or escapist experiences. However, encouraging the client to *face self* is especially important and often the only appropriate course of action during powerful transits of Saturn and Pluto. The transits of Saturn and Pluto (as well as certain progressions involving those two planets) often force people to go inward, and in many ways these are the best times to go deep within yourself.

---

*This was actually quite a high percentage, since probably less than 30 people in the room of the 150 present were born during those years, and many did not respond to the question at all.

Related to the question of healing is the need to bring to consciousness that which is unconscious or compulsive. Often, transits of Pluto and Saturn do this, and it is often a prerequisite to wholeness, and therefore healing. Astrology is one of those very rare tools that can encourage such heightened awareness and can provide accurate insight into those forces that are unconsciously but powerfully motivating us and which are often interfering with our own wholeness and so preventing healing. In this way also are astrological counseling and healing directly related. With Saturn and Pluto, we can go within and concentrate on self-knowledge instead of going outwardly with frustration and destruction. This is something that Jung emphasized about the long road of gaining self-knowledge. One is often tempted to run out and away from the pain. But, as Jung wrote, there is no coming to consciousness without pain.

The Issue of Language

So much of astrology is a matter of definition. I think the ideal would be that everyone learn the astrological language starting in kindergarten. Then you could talk to them without having to translate. We are really translators. There's the universal mind at its level, and there's the astrologer with the astrological language, and then there's the people speaking English or whatever ordinary language. So no wonder it's so psychically exhausting; we're translating this cosmic, universal-mind language into Western astrological language, and then this language into English. So simultaneously we're doing double translation. No doubt many of you have seen how much easier it is to have consultations with people who know the astrological language. It is a real challenge to put into clear English what the astrology means. I do think it's often quite effective to say, "Well, Saturn's this and that, and traditionally Saturn has to do with . . . " but if you start throwing out too much jargon then you really lose them.

Because so much of astrology is definition, choice of words is incredibly important. It's even more important when you do any astrological work by mail, because then you cannot correct a wrong impression or a bad reaction. You don't see the person's face when they read it. That's why doing by-mail consultations raises the question of how you can do that well, especially if you aren't a good writer! How then can you explain such profound things?

Precision of language is also a key to astrology's development and wider acceptance. If astrologers can begin to use a bit of English clearly, without much psychological jargon and without excessive astrological jargon, I think that will make it much more accessible to many people. We have to ask ourselves seriously: What are the effects of my statements to clients? What are they feeling? Are they interpreting it all wrong? We have to be aware of the power of our words. Read the Gospel of St. John: "In the beginning was the word" . . . the *logos.* The power of words should not be underestimated. Even if somebody thinks of dismissing them, words are seeds. They are airborne thoughts, airborne power. Some people, many people, are going to want to see you as an oracle, whether consciously or unconsciously, and you must be aware of that responsibility and must use care in choice of language. It seems to me a good focus is that ultimately you aren't talking about a *chart.* You're talking about a *person,* to a person. The chart is secondary. It's the person who should always remain the focus. It's always easy to get lost in details if you focus on the chart, while the person sits idly by and listens or watches. One needs to engage the client in real communication, real dialogue, and that is best facilitated by a simple language of experience and energy.

Three experienced astrologers from England have made some interesting comments on the language issue. Margaret Hone, one of the most experienced astrological teachers and a great force in modernizing the teaching of astrology through the keyword system that she developed, was an air sign Sun (Libra) with an air sign Moon (Aquarius). She advised her astrology teachers, "Before you teach them astrology, you have to teach them English." You know, teach them how to think and speak in English! You get the point. Clarity of expression is really important.

An English astrologer named Doreen Tyson wrote, "The written word is ineradicable." She's talking about written chart interpretations now. "And that analysis will be read and re-read over the years, and even one word out of place is a disaster."

This is also true for taped charts; people may listen to them over and over and over.

Sue Cook, another astrologer in England, writes:

> The Golden Rule to bear in mind is that the astrologer's primary aim and objective is to help his/her client, not to demonstrate how clever astrology is. It is essential not to be unkind. A brilliant astrologer could prepare an astoundingly accurate analysis and then demolish the client's confidence by wording that is not chosen with the client's character and needs in mind—usually too direct and brutally blunt. It is not necessary to withhold unpleasant or unpalatable facts—wording and phrasing are all-important. . . . It is not what one conveys, but how one conveys it. As astrologers we are privileged to be given the opportunity to study our fellows in depth and we therefore need to be doubly careful about how we tackle sensitive areas. And some folks are more sensitive, touchy, or downright prickly, than others. Mutable Angles, for example, need kid-glove handling.

The symbolism and terminology of astrology does constitute a rather specialized and esoteric language, admittedly. But it is in that respect no different from many other specialized fields of study. There is in America a long tradition of the public making fun of arcane academic studies, based evidently on the assumption that knowledge ought to be common and available to everyone. But yet, most disciplines have succeeded in at least establishing for themselves some sort of niche in academic or scientific circles, even in spite of the public's general disregard for them. In some cases, extremely specialized subjects have even earned general respect from the public. The specialized languages used in various fields of study are, as Director of the University of Chicago Press Morris Philipson says, developed by specialized groups for good reason.

> Not because they're secret societies but because in order to understand what is going on you have to have a body of learning that initiates you into the discipline of thought. (From July 6, 1984 *Publishers Weekly*)

The field of astrology constitutes a specific body of learning with its own discipline of thought, as well, but it is a field that has no niche in modern society. The fact that the astrological language is incomprehensible to many people is not a unique situation.

> . . . how do you talk with a layman about particle physics or field and ring theory in mathematics, or debates over the nature of evolution in biology, or even over differences of points of view in literary theory? There are different languages being spoken, and unless you learn the language you cannot really understand what a thing says. (*ibid.*)

However, in all of the fields mentioned in the above quotation, even if many of the activities within those fields are utterly worthless to society, or even harmful, those active within those fields at least have a professional home base wherein they can do their work and communicate with others.

People active in the astrology field, however, have no home base, no academic niche, no government funding, few job opportunities, and in addition they are constantly subjected to all sorts of derisive comments by ignorant people who cannot even know what astrology "says" because they have not learned the language! Does it not seem time for professionalization and organization of astrologers in such a way that the great benefits of astrology can be made more widely available? After all, many specialized academic fields (if not most) do not *even* have to justify their value to the public! And their highly specialized languages do not prevent them from maintaining a place in society that allows for some professional development and research.

I mentioned earlier that greater precision of language in astrology is a key to astrology's wider acceptance. I have no doubt that astrology will have to justify and prove its value to the public, to the masses, before it is accepted (even if grudgingly) as a distinct field of study and research, with its own specialized language and domain of understanding, on a par with other professional and academic fields. I cannot help but feel that a major step toward that distant goal is for the astrologers to learn to communicate more effectively with the public, *in a non-specialized language.* In true Aquarian fashion, I feel we must go over the heads of all the "authorities" direct to the masses, similar to how Aquarian politicians go over the heads of Congress direct to the people. Astrologers have no niche in the establishment. To survive and thrive, their work must be of obvious value to the public in large numbers, and better communication skills must therefore be developed. The highly specialized language of astrology will of course remain and continue to be used *within the profession itself,* but a simpler language of common sense and practical experience must be used with the general public. And that is where we need to use greater precision of statement.

Understanding, Expectations & Ethics

It is difficult for many people to accept and harmonize with others in both personal relationships and with clients, unless they can somehow see inside the other person. Astrology lets you see inside somebody else, and that can lead to a fuller understanding of the other person. In that sense, it's almost embarrassing sometimes–what you can do with that chart. This understanding, of course, is much more important than speculative theory, especially in counseling. And in the area of one's personal relationships, as one spiritual teacher said, much more important than so-called "love" in close relationships is *understanding.* Especially with Uranus and Pluto having recently gone through Libra and then Scorpio, relationships have been a big focus for many people. I mainly emphasize this because real understanding is so much more important than the transitory, emotional "love" that just happens to you and which everyone seems to yearn for. Once the bloom is off the rose, there are the thorns. And at that point, understanding is necessary, or nothing in the relationship will work. Astrology can help you develop that understanding. It can let you have what Carl Rogers calls "unconditional regard" for another person, whether it's for a client or a lover or a spouse or a friend. You can then say, "That's the way they are." Let them be it. Acknowledge it. Accept it. You can have real objectivity toward others.

The issue of client expectations is something to be aware of. Ultimately, I got to the point that I would just have to force the client to define his or her expectations *on the phone* before I would even make an appointment with him. I wouldn't make an appointment until he would say what he expected, what he really wanted. Very often I would turn him down then, when it became obvious that the person wanted something that I did not or could not do. But some people would then call back, thinking, "Well, maybe if I said it this way, he'd accept it." I even found that people would lie to me at times to get in. And then at the appointment they would say what they really wanted, which wasn't too pleasant a situation.

I think it is important to make the client *define* his or her expectations *before* the appointment, if possible, whether you do it on the phone in advance, or mail them some kind of instruction sheet that demands that they think about such questions. At least let them know you are serious and that you demand something from them. Let them know that you need them to focus. This will save you a lot of time in the long run.

Rudhyar's quote on clients' expectations is to the point:

> One of the real possibilities of psychological harm, or at least confusion, faced by anyone consulting an astrologer results from the enquirer's false expectations of what the astrologer can reveal to him.

Again, the oracle expectation–people project this oracle or high priest image. Unfortunately, some astrologers encourage that. Rudhyar continues,

> Many people expect that the professional astrologer they consult will be able to tell them exactly what will happen to them and how whatever type of activity they are engaged in will work out. Others expect neatly formulated solutions for their psychological problems, and possibly definite reassurance as to the validity of their ambitions, their marriage or their new love . . . freeing them from anxiety, insecurity and doubts, and above all telling them precisely what to do and when to do it. (From *An Attempt at Formulating Minimal Requirements for the Practice of Astrology*)

Then we come to ethical questions. One thing that I think is really important with astrology–you've got that tool to get inside the other person, you can see their strengths, their weaknesses. This brings up profound ethical questions. So, if somebody comes to you, you have to pay attention to how they are going to use this information. If you're just going to pour out information, how are they going to use it? For understanding and appreciation of someone else or some situation, or for manipulation or some destructive purpose?

Very often a person will come to you alone and ask about someone else's chart, or somebody else . . . usually their lover or husband or wife or sometimes their boss. Is that legitimate? I'm not giving you rigid answers here. I think it depends on the case and on your judgment. But if the person is going to use that information as a club to smash home their will on somebody, then it's totally unethical to provide it. Quite often one is tempted to say, "Let's just grab the ephemeris and look up your spouse's chart." Sometimes that's fine, but you have to be really careful with it. There can be an ethical problem in giving out too much intimate information about others. It's important to be sensitive to that. How you want to handle it, I really can't say in any general way. It is simply part of the art of counseling.

The Psychic Energy Dimension

The psychic energy dimension of astrological consultations is rarely discussed. A lot of astrologers pride themselves in being "psychic." Well, in fact, we do have to acknowledge that we use *psychic energy*; "psychic" in the broadest sense does not necessarily mean that you're a clairvoyant. It's psyche-ological energy. But it's a little more than just psychological. Psychic energy is a profound-concentration type of conscious energy. A great concentration is required to channel one's psychic energy effectively. And to do good astrological work, in my experience, can be profoundly exhausting. It takes a great deal of concentration to do good astrological work. You have to tap your psychic energy, which is all the more reason to know your ideals and your motivation, like "Why am I doing this and what am I really trying to do for myself and for this client?" A strong focus can help to conserve your energy. You definitely pay a price if you regularly use your psychic energy. I'm not saying we all should stop doing astrology. But if you're going to use that kind of energy, you do pay a price, so learning to use it purposefully and conservatively is required for a professional astrological counselor.

It's not just in this field; it's many other fields too. Many psychologists, teachers, and counselors are familiar with it and with the depletion they often feel. Many people in the healing arts have to deal with this kind of question: How much of themselves should they give? If they start totally collapsing, are they suited for that kind of work, or should they maybe restructure the way they do their work? People in many fields experience psychic "burnout."

Also, in relation to this psychic energy issue, the astrologer can be influenced by the *desires* of the individual seeking guidance, even if they are not expressed overtly. The more sensitive and psychic you are, the more you'll notice, "Aha! That's what they're after." But you can be influenced by their desires *even if you're not aware of it.* So at times you have to ask yourself, "Does this person want the truth, or do they simply want to try to manipulate their fate? Do they simply want to try to fulfill short-sighted desires?" Again, that gets back to *your own purpose.* What kind of an astrologer are you going to be? Are you going to talk to one client about real estate and the next one about the soul? You do have to adapt to your clients, after all. But don't you want to do your best with each one? Many astrologers do have a broad range of work that they can do effectively.

The motivations, attitudes, skepticism, level of understanding, and the desires and intentions for using the information received on the part of *not only the client but of anyone present* at the appointment all affect the quality of the energy you can channel, the quality of the information that you can get access to, and the results of your dialogue. Anyone in the room, in other words, affects your psychic energy. I know a lot of astrologers have the experience of a Scorpio rising, for example, coming in and refusing to say anything or give out anything. You start getting exhausted. You start getting drained and don't know why. (I'm not just picking on Scorpio risings. We could pick on a lot of things!) You've got to sense what's in the air. What's this person after? Aha! They're actually much more skeptical than they pretended. All those things affect you. It makes it really tough. But if you acknowledge it: "You don't believe a word I'm saying, do you?" Bring it out. Often they won't even realize what they were doing or what they were really after, or the double messages they were giving you.

In a similar vein, *unity of thought and purpose* is incredibly important for astrologers who are very sensitive. By this I mean that you may find that you can only work well with one person in the room. That is the main person who called you. If there's an onlooker or a spouse or somebody else, it can negatively affect the psychic atmosphere and thus your psychic clarity. This is where I really disagree with a lot of the pat rules of traditional marriage counseling. They so often tell you, "You've got to have both people there to sort out all the problems." But if you're dealing at a level of truth, rather than of problems, you have a whole other situation. What I wound up doing ultimately was questioning whoever called for the appointment. First of all, I demanded that people call for their own appointments. Very often the wife or the secretary would call for somebody else, especially for men. I refused to make those appointments. I wanted to hear the person and his intentions and see what the "vibes" were, and I wanted to be able to ask any questions that seemed pertinent.

Another thing is if somebody said, "So and so would like to come too." Immediately the red flag went up in my brain, and I quizzed them on the phone so I could eliminate curiosity-seekers. "Who is this person? What is their attitude toward astrology?" and so forth. If there was any doubt, I said, "Sorry, no way." I couldn't handle it in the kind of in-depth dialogues I preferred. The other person's thoughts would filter in to me constantly, and it really was difficult to concentrate. It also distracts the client who is supposedly there for a purpose, who is then thinking, "Well, what is my friend going to think of this?" Pretty soon you have this huge social game rather than anything real happening. Frankly, I don't have the patience for such a superficial waste of time.

General Observations on Astrological Counseling

The vast majority of people who come to you will bring in problems that involve their emotional life: love, marriage, children, religious beliefs, and there's also a big emotional charge around career and vocational decisions. Obviously, if you cannot deal with emotional problems adequately, you probably shouldn't be in any kind of counseling work. And most astrologers, in my experience, are very mental and excitable people. It's quite a step for them to get into their emotions, and thus to deal effectively with their clients' emotions. As Dr. Layman points out in his book,* what is *possible* in terms of delineation and interpretation for you to do is not always *wise* in terms of effective counseling. Persons with problems enough to ask for advice usually need more than just simply information, especially if there is an emotionally charged issue there. Too much information can just scatter their minds and make a real mess. Also, too much information delivered too quickly, or without the right kind of emotional sensitivity, is inadvisable.

We often hear that every factor in the chart has to be considered in relation to the total chart. That's true. Maybe it's just my Libra prejudice, but the interaction with the person, for me, was always necessary. There was no such thing as a "whole chart" without seeing the whole person. My experience was that you could only really and readily look at the whole chart if you had the whole person sitting there. Then the whole chart does come alive, and you can begin to perceive its wholeness and main themes.

One of the first things anybody learns in counseling training is to encourage clients to "ventilate." Ventilate is not the same as babble. It's quite different. Especially if you have an exceptionally mutable person . . . often they're just hiding in a mesh of words. As Dr. Layman wrote, to ventilate is to express their feelings, their doubts and fears *freely*. By "freely" I mean that obviously there shouldn't be any moralizing about it, unless they bring up a moral question. That's something else. Then you can help them clarify the whole thing. All problems have a certain amount of emotional disturbance connected with them. Clients should be encouraged to release that. Until they release their emotions, especially the negative ones (Saturn, Mars, Pluto), they cannot think positively or rationally about their problems. They're at the mercy of them. They're at the mercy of those emotions. It's compulsive then.

---

*Dr. Layman and his book were introduced on page 87, in case you've forgotten by now.

The following is a quote from Dr. Marvin Layman's book, *Interviewing and Counseling Techniques for Astrologers*:*

> Inexperienced counselors are somewhat overwhelmed by the negative material that flows from their clients. They will be tempted to encourage their clients to be more positive. This is [often] the wrong technique. The client must be encouraged to get all the negative emotions out.

Now whether you can get *all* the negative emotions out is a real question, but at least *clear the air.*

> If they do not, the problem will remain and fester. Sometimes clients do not want to express their negative feelings because they feel guilty about them. All the more reason to gently insist that they do so. This is particularly true with potential suicides. It is frequently anger and hate turned inward that prompts suicidal thoughts.

Especially such clients must be encouraged to ventilate. Whenever you get into such powerful, emotionally-charged situations, of course, you have to evaluate whether you're comfortable dealing with that, and whether you're in over your head. But the fact is that as astrological counselors you can always get in over your head. You can't control your clients. You can't kick the person out the door once he shows up and starts exploding or crying or threatening suicide. You can't kick him out at that point; you have to know how to deal with such emotions effectively. So when you're in over your head, you've got to know how to swim!

After the negative has been expressed, then the positive can begin to flow. However, it won't *always* begin to flow, as some pop psychologists say. But sometimes it will. Sometimes, on the other hand, they have to sit and stew in their negativity for a long time. But when the first positive statements, after the negative ones, begin to emerge, then the counselor can reinforce them gently. Dr. Layman points out that too quick and too strong an agreement might defeat the whole process once again. It might

---

*This book, originally published by Astrological Bureau in New York, is now out of print, although it is perhaps the most practical and concise booklet on the subject I have ever seen. Perhaps some day it can be made available on the Internet, along with other astrological gems that are long out-of-print. I am indebted to Dr. Layman for many valuable ideas and observations used in this chapter.

make the client hesitate, or get paranoid or uptight. At this point, the counseling is a very delicate situation. If the astrologer moves too rapidly, the problem may not be resolved because the client will resist and also just won't return. You can't do massive surgery in a few minutes!

Also, growth of anything, a tree or a person, goes in cycles and phases. Sometimes their growth is in spurts; sometimes there are stagnant or fallow times. Any astrological counselor has to have a sense of rhythm, the rhythm of growth. Of course the chart helps you to get that rhythm just by seeing how things are moving, are they going retrograde now, and so on . . . the transits particularly.

An effective counselor, says Marvin Layman, "must be intuitive" and, I will add, also should be somewhat patient, because of that rhythm of growth I just mentioned. You have to have a sense of the rhythm of human growth, and also not be too egocentric or desire to impress other people too much. If so, your counseling suffers, even if you are trained thoroughly in good "counseling techniques." We all know some good technicians in astrology who are not effective counselors.

On the issue of patience, there's a friend of mine who's an Aries Sun with a Sagittarius Moon, and Aquarius rising, three relatively impatient signs. He has Venus and Mars and Mercury in Pisces natally, and the Pisces was very emphasized in his personality and consciousness in his first 25 years or so. He became a rehabilitation counselor. He got a master's degree in rehabilitation counseling, and was helping the people who had a lot of trouble finding work because they were displaced by some problem or physical handicap. As he grew older and became his Sun more, the Aries came out more. He said to me, "You know, I finally realized that I'd had it with counseling when, as soon as somebody came through the door, my first impulse was that I'd just as soon strangle them as listen to them." There's an Aries for you . . . a little violent and certainly not patient. Fortunately, he had the sense of responsibility to quit. He became a supervisor of other counselors, a real good one, because he knew what was needed in counseling, but he didn't have the patience anymore to do it himself. So he hired all these real sensitive, caring types, and had a whole office full of them for the State Rehabilitation Department.

I mentioned that you've got to have that rhythm of growth. Along the same lines is the question of *timing.* Following your intuition may be great, saying what you think is right may be fine; but timing is really important. You may think of a great "solution." Five minutes after somebody walks in the door, you may think, "Oh, I've got the answer to their problem!" But what about timing? They're not ready yet to hear that. If you suggest a solution or anything like that too soon in the counseling process, it will likely ultimately be rejected. The client usually needs to talk about the problem, and the astrologer usually needs as much detailed background information as possible. The counselor needs time to psychically attune to the client, so that any suggestions he may have are *realistically* related to the person's actual needs and feelings, not mere projections of the counselor's prejudices. After all, you're not doing counseling to prove your cleverness, at least I hope not. Even if the client is temporarily impressed with an apparently clever and quick solution that the astrologer comes up with in record time, my experience is that he or she will almost always find that it isn't really realistic advice after all, even if it takes the client a few hours or days to consider it thoroughly and conclude that it isn't really a useful suggestion. The importance of timing ultimately is that many problems simply have to be outgrown. You can't give the client a "solution" on a silver platter.

There's an old alchemical phrase that Jung often quoted which is *Tertium non datur* ("The third is not given"). Basically what that means is that there's no solution there, except through a third factor, some higher consciousness that transcends the apparent opposites of a conflict. You can outgrow what seemed like an impossible problem by getting to a higher level of understanding. You can also use this principle with a chart, too, for example, if you have an opposition and a third planet is trine and sextile the opposed planets. This phrase means much more than that, too. It has to do with growth of consciousness.

One more quote from Dr. Layman can sum up some of the points we've mentioned so far:

> No amount of psychic ability will enable a counselor to be effective if he ignores the basic principles of counseling. No amount of astrological expertise will enable astrologers to be effective counselors if they ignore sound counseling techniques. The ideal combination is to be a well trained astrologer, firmly grounded in effective counseling principles and having more than average psychic or intuitive ability.

Another thing worth discussing is the question of referrals. As I mentioned in the last talk, there's no way that anybody now days can be an expert in all phases of astrology. If somebody comes to you and says, "Should I invest in the stock market or in a certain stock?" very few of you really have the expertise to advise on that in any more than a general way. Maybe with the natal chart you can say, "Well this transit shows a major time to focus on investments or consolidating your financial situation or improving your earnings." But they probably should go to a financial specialist for specific investment recommendations. You're asking for some very nasty phone calls later if you tell them, "Sure, invest everything in stocks," and the stock market crashes. *Maybe* with the chart you can say, "Well, *if* you've decided to invest in stocks, maybe mining stocks or something would be worth a try, because of your particular chart." But even that kind of advice requires considerable expertise; the old rules often don't work!

What I'm getting at is *acknowledging your expertise and its limits.* Likewise with medical questions. One has to be very careful about any kind of medical advice. I'm not saying to refrain totally from things that will help people to be healthier. Very often, if somebody comes in with a health problem, you can make them feel a lot better right away. A lot of illnesses come on, and the person then gets into a vicious circle and starts worrying about it. (And then they often get into a drug vicious circle, also.) Very often those problems can be outgrown as the transits pass; you can help them change their thought patterns. By that kind of encouragement you can sometimes really be helpful. But you have to be careful, too. You don't want to say, "Stop all the drugs you're taking, immediately." Who knows what they're taking or what that might do? But certainly you can give them a time-frame. "Did this start back here? About when did this start developing?" And so on as you establish a pattern that will help them work with their own cycles and build up their own health as the stressful cycle phases out.

A friend of mine had childhood asthma so severely that he had to be put into the National Jewish Hospital in Denver where terribly severe asthmatics had to live. In those days Denver's air was somewhat breathable. He went on a stringent training program, and mainly through his own *will* (Leo rising with Aquarius Sun) he built up his body tremendously. He did long distance running and rowing. He became the pull-up and push-up and sit-up champion in his high school. He totally outgrew it. Thirty years later, as Saturn got into the same place it was when he first started developing asthma, it all came back and he went back into the hospital. That really worried him, but fortunately, he has some credence in astrology and what particularly impressed him was my saying, "Well, did the asthma start developing when you were about five?" I asked that because of Saturn being in the same place, and indeed it did start then. He sort of gasped in surprise, and now he knows that he can start building himself up again, as the crisis transits pass. It doesn't have to be a chronic illness. And yet the doctors are telling him, "Well, you'll have to have this managed by drugs for the rest of your life. You *are* an asthmatic." They want to label you permanently with a disease that may be only transitory. But he's heard that before and proved them wrong. And no doubt he'll prove them wrong again.

Dr. Layman has some interesting things to say about referrals:

> Refusing to take cases which astrologers are not trained to handle will never harm their reputations. On the contrary, the astrologer will build a reputation as a trustworthy and dependable counselor. [Somebody who's *believable*! Somebody who has some *integrity*. S.A.] The best advertising for any counselor is always word of mouth. Astrologers who take only those cases they are

capable of handling may lose some business in the beginning but will profit in the end. Their satisfied clients will tell others about them and their clientele will slowly build.

Most astrologers focus on the present and the future. That may be fine. But if you're going to build a practice of *ongoing* clients, as well as if you're trying to understand more deeply what's happening now, you'll have more perspective if you can get the background of past trends. As you develop a regular clientele, you'll discover the importance of keeping notes on past experiences that clients had. Something you can probably do only if you initially have at least two successive appointments is focusing on the person's past patterns *as soon as you first see them.* This will take more pre-consultation research into transits and progressions. Ask them, "Well, what happened when Saturn or Uranus was here?" You may not need even to use the astrological language: "What happened around the summer of '49?" If you go back into the past somewhat, you get a sense, so to speak, of *how the chart reacts,* how the various forces and factors in that person (shown in the chart) manifest in real life. You get to know them better. It's not that they'll be the same next time, because we do change. But you'll start to see the past as part of a whole pattern. You'll get a sense of their unique structural pattern and their particular propensities. Then, when they talk about the present, you can oftentimes make it much more meaningful for them. They can relate the present situation to something they've been through before.

This kind of in-depth work does take time, and realistically, with many clients you won't have time to do that. But I think that's the ideal. You could do it in different ways, but if somebody does start coming to you once every six months or so just to see what's happening, to get the astrological perspective, and you know it will be an ongoing type of relationship, it might be worth setting up a separate appointment if they're willing, just to do some of that type of research. It also will often help the client to release old feelings, grudges, or hurts by attaining that perspective.

The Art of Listening

In her counseling training seminars for astrologers, Christina Rose* has found that specific listening skills need to be developed and can to some extent be taught. She writes,

> As astrologers, we are perhaps used to defining our role partly as "communicators". We expect (and indeed are required) to do a great deal of speaking with our clients as we cover with them each area of the birth chart. And yet, as counsellors, we need also to remember that our relationship with the client is shared. Since we are not solo performers to a captive audience of one client, we need the latter's co-operation in discussing his chart so that its meaning can be specifically translated in his individual terms, and related to his individual situation in life. Therefore, we need not only to speak with him, but also listen to him.

In a short article on the art of listening, she gives this example of the same situation done two different ways:

A client comes in, sits down, and then says, "Well, I'm not sure I'm getting very far in my job." The astrologer replies, "Oh, I don't know, with Mercury on your Midheaven and Gemini on the Ascendant and Virgo in the 6th house, I think you're probably doing great and you'd be very good. You're a good secretary. I don't know why you're unhappy."

Then the same situation handled in a different way:

Client: "I'm not sure I'm getting very far in my job."

Astrologer: "Well, you feel it doesn't offer enough opportunity for advancement or enough diversity, or you're dissatisfied, or what?"

Now that's a response to what the client *said*, and it's a clarifying response. Christina Rose writes that "listening is largely a matter of hearing the client's communication on two main levels": what's on top, i.e., the factual content of the client's statement, and what's underneath, the feelings surrounding it. In the second example I read, the astrologer is responding to both levels of

---

*Christina Rose is an English astrologer, one of the first to develop counseling training programs for astrologers, and the author of *Astrological Counseling*, published by Thorsens, Ltd.

communication. There are two levels; it's not just the words, but it's also the tone. Sometimes the tone will contradict the words.

So in this article that she wrote for the Bulletin of the Faculty of Astrologers in England, Christina Rose points out a few things which can impair our ability to listen.

> Factors in the client's chart may be similar to, or the same as, those in our charts, and we may listen for him to say something that we completely identify with, rather than listen to what he is actually saying.

In a sense, I think she's saying that we can project our personal reality onto the client. If we have a certain problem (for example, a certain square or a transit), we may start thinking that our exact problem is his, whereas his may be on a whole different level. Another thing she says:

> Often we may need to remain silent–if we are accustomed to talking a lot, have a great need for control, feel we must give advice, have a great need to display our interpretive expertise and score "hits", we are going to find that just to sit and listen is very hard.

Another issue she raises is if a client's problem is something we feel ought to produce a "solution," we may be too busy thinking things up: "Why don't you do this? Why don't you do that?", while avidly scrutinizing the chart for clues, and miss what they're saying and miss totally the reality of their situation. In other words, then we slip into a mental game, an analytical game, rather than dealing with the person's entire and unique situation. We have then stopped listening. And we may find it difficult to listen to a client who is not doing what we think they should be doing! Especially if we convince ourselves by finding appropriate astrological factors to back up our view. Especially if we're real pushy people, this judgmental attitude can inhibit not only listening but also the client's trusting us! Say we have a whole lot of Leo and Aries: "WHY NOT? YOU'RE NOT DOING IT? WHY DON'T YOU DO IT???? YOU REALLY MUST. YOU DON'T HAVE ANY CHOICE!"

General anxieties, she says, about our own expertise also can get in the way. Or anxieties about our own knowledge or lack of it. One astrologer was aware of money as a "bogey man," which detracted from his listening to his clients. There's often an anxiety for the astrologer which runs along the lines of, "I've got to be seen to be earning the fee that I'm asking." So it makes you feel like "I've got to do something." Thus, in response, we may do a lot of talking to counter our own anxiety, but in the process, diminish what the client is getting out of the whole situation. And if we go on much longer, no one is going to get any more out of this situation, either. Any questions?

Question: I have doubts at times as to what astrology can do as a healing art, and you were talking about the psychic energy being funneled through us. I'm just curious, would you still have doubts about your abilities to really effect a healing or cure on your client?

Stephen: I think it's something that happens or doesn't. You do what you can and then it's in the hands of God, so to speak. I don't think we can tell. Neither can we tell the *ultimate* results from a consultation. Especially when I had lots of clients in the same town, where I'd walk down the street and bump into them, I was always surprised at some of the long-term effects. Sometimes they were *really* much better than I had thought. Even people who seemed to be just like dead logs during the whole appointment, I'd discover later, would actually do something or benefit in a major way. In other cases, somebody would sit there going "Oh yeah! Great!" and seem to be totally positive and enthused, and months later I would see that they hadn't really done anything. I don't think you can really tell, but I don't think we should consider ourselves "healers." I think you just do your best. We can't control or create "healing." That's the thing about defining your philosophy, your purpose, and then you just do it. And that's your work. After that, it's up to them and their fate, I think.

Question: Do you find yourself referring people to different kinds of bodywork therapists?

Stephen: I have referred people to a number of things. I especially refer people to Polarity Therapy,* because I have seen what it can do. I hesitate to refer anyone anywhere unless I know to whom I'm referring them. There are just as many incompetents in psychotherapy and various types of healing as in anything else. I also referred people to gestalt therapy groups quite often, at one time, because at that time I knew some very good people who did that powerful type of group work, but with a lot of sensitivity. I would not ever refer people to a gestalt group in the hands of a triple Aries, like one I went to once, where the guy just wanted to show what a creep he was. But definitely, referrals have a place. Most astrologers are not going to have enough training to get into deep, long-term therapy. Even if you have the training, then you've got to decide if you'll be mainly that or mainly an astrologer. There's hardly ever time for both. One practice has to be the *focus*—the astrology or the therapy. You can mix them, but one has to be the focus, I think. People have to know what they're going to you for. You know, your "label" has to be straight and accurate. But in short, I think most people can benefit from many types of "body-work," including many kinds of massage, and I wouldn't hesitate to recommend it. I personally have seen better results in such therapies than in traditional verbal therapies. They're a good balance for our overly-mental, neurotic culture.

---

*For information on Polarity Therapy books, write CRCS Publications (address on title page of this book). For information on Polarity Therapy training or referrals to practitioners, contact the following professional organizations: In the USA, APTA, 2475 Juniper, Boulder, CO 80304 (Tel:303-545-2080). In the UK, United Kingdom PTA, 27 Old Glouster St, London WC1N 3XX.

4

Setting Up & Structuring a Practice: A Discussion Group

Whatever you can do, or dream you can, begin it. Boldness has genius, power and magic in it.

– Goethe

The highest reward for toil is not what you get for it, but what you become by it.

– John Ruskin

Stephen: As people contribute during this discussion session, I want you to stand up and project so others can hear you easily. If you want, you can come up and talk into the microphone also, as long as you're not too domineering about it! I'll begin by mentioning some issues quite briefly. If any particular issue strikes you as something you'd like to discuss further, jot it down, and then you can bring it up as we go along. You can take over after I introduce these issues, and I'll just try to keep some order during the discussion.

One important issue is *screening clients.* I think this is incredibly important, because you have to *suit the clients to you,* as well as your adapting to the clients. More on this in a moment. That also brings in the question of referrals: knowing other counselors, resources, and so forth in your area to refer people to. Very often you will get clients for whom you can do nothing,

---

*This discussion group took place at the Saturn/Pluto Conference in November, 1982 and was comprised of approximately 30 people who by that time had spent days listening to and talking about professional and philosophical issues in astrology. The original discussion took about 2 hours, but due to the unstructured nature of any such group, some editing has had to be done. We have, however, tried to maintain the tone and essence of all the interchanges that were retained for publication.

or for whom you can do nothing more after you've seen them for a while. Then they have to take charge of their own lives and start doing something for themselves. They may need a jazzercise class. They may need a yoga teacher or an M.D. or some kind of therapist. But they have to initiate something. Encouraging dependency in clients is poor practice; of course I don't have any Cancer influence, but I think it's a very dangerous thing for anyone to encourage too much dependency, even if you rather like mothering people.

This is a slight aside, but it's the philosophical side of this. A polarity therapist who's 65 years old and has worked much of his life as a healer or a doctor of one kind or another has a practical approach. He is a Capricorn. He only does what he feels works. He doesn't even talk much to patients, other than in very short sentences. He says that the most important thing with people who are stuck in a bind or an illness or whatever dilemma is to make them *do something.* Get them moving, get them out of that stagnancy. It hardly matters what they do, in some cases. He often suggests an herb tea or something. But have them go out and do something–run to a health food store and buy Vitamin C. It's symbolic that they are doing something for themselves. They open up a channel then, and their energy will start flowing because of their own effort.

On the question of screening, and this really can't be emphasized enough, first of all is the importance of getting the accurate birth time. As soon as the person calls, that's part of the screening right there. You're wasting your time and theirs if you don't pin down the accurate time. Very often you'll ask them, and they'll give you a *pseudo-accurate* birth time: "Oh, 4:32." What you have to do then is to say, "Ok, what's the *source* of it?" So often they'll say, "That's what my mother said," and you know right away then that you cannot work with that. You've got to get it in writing, if at all possible. I know sometimes they can't find it or some states didn't write it down, or the person is an orphan and the records are sealed. Then you have problems. But in most cases, there is a birth certificate with a time. If there is not, you have *them* call the hospital. It's important to make the client *work* from the beginning. It's a valuable thing you're doing and they should value it. If they're not willing to put a few hours into confirming the birth time or to make a couple long-distance phone calls, then the heck with them. Don't waste your time on an inaccurate chart. If it's not on the birth certificate, they can call the hospital and say, "Do you still have the records from this year and this month?" The hospital will often have it. There are reference books now that give all the Departments of Health and Vital Statistics in all the states where they can write. Make them do it. It's *their* life.

Don't trust Mother's memory, unless it's the only, only source. Mother is often in rather bad shape at that time, and until recently Mother was also usually drugged, sometimes totally unconscious. In fact, after doing charts for over ten years, I thought back over the years, and I could remember only twice that we started into the whole dialogue and *nothing clicked.* Nothing! I had to use only general sign positions of planets, but no houses. In both cases, the time turned out to be wrong, as we only found out later. So you have to trust your intuition. Once you have some experience, if you start dealing with someone and nothing is fitting the chart (and it's not just their resistance, but you *know* it isn't working), you immediately have to suspect the data. There is, for example, the a.m./p.m. misinterpretation that's really a source of a lot of confusion. People say, "Oh, I was born at 12:04 p.m." Clarify it. "Is it right after midnight or right after noon?" Occasionally it's even written down wrong on the birth certificate. Sometimes you have to flip the whole chart over 180 degrees. Then it suddenly comes alive.

Most screening, in my experience, if you're doing actual consultations rather than mail-order work, comes on the phone. What do you want? Why are you calling? Challenge them. You need to establish a focus. It's their desire that's initiating this contact. You're not begging them to come and see you. The more flexible you are, I suppose the more mutable you are, the more variety of clients you might be good with. If you're real fixed you might be good only with a fairly narrow spectrum of clients. But that's ok, as long as you know what kind of people and what kind of problems you can deal with effectively.

If you find that you absolutely hate Leos, or absolutely hate Moon-in-Virgos, don't see them. That's my advice. Sure, you could work on it, and all this. But if you just can't stand certain types of people, don't see them, because how can you give them anything positive? So you have to sit down and screen yourself too. It is important to suit the client to you, not so much their nature, really, as what they want—what kind of problems they're trying to solve. If you get the "I am curious" calls, it's advisable to probe further, right on the telephone, unless you just like the "I am curious" type of consultations, which are often really boring, I think.

Things that I have found useful include a prepared statement of my philosophy and approach, which I mailed to them early. I think for many reasons it is very helpful to make appointments *at least* two or three weeks in advance. For one thing, it gives you a chance to get a deposit from them, through the mail. Then, if they don't show up, it doesn't matter, because you're being paid for the time you put in early. It also gives you a chance to mail to them whatever forms or brochures you want, and it gives *them* a chance to cancel the appointment once they read your philosophy and approach and code of ethics and things like that—whatever you want to send them. If they then realize, "Hey, this person doesn't relate to me at all," they can cancel. The sooner they cancel, the better, before you put a lot of time into preparation.

One thing I send, too, is a very brief "What is Astrology" sheet, two paragraphs saying what I think astrology is. Right then and there, they read it and say, "Oh, is *that* what it is?" or "Hey, that sounds good!" It lets them know you, too. It helps them to define their expectations. Another thing to mail early is an advance questionnaire. (These are things I eventually worked out after a number of years. I wasn't doing this from the beginning.) An advance questionnaire mailed quite early is simply to get their expectations realistic, asking them, "Ok, what are your goals? Think over what your ideals are. What recent experiences have really struck you, impacted you in some powerful way?" It makes people think in advance about what they really want and where they're at.

Of course, the whole question of predictions can be defined early, often right on the telephone, depending on your attitude toward it, of course. But if you're the type who does not predict definite events, tell them right away. You may lose some clients, but at least you'll be working with people that are more attuned to you.

Client problems we won't go into right now in detail, but if anybody wants to, that's fine. A common one is *avoidance*—avoidance of any clear answer, commitment, or revealing statement. Then there's the resistant, or secretive, type of client, especially if they have lots of Scorpio or Taurus, and sometimes Capricorn. Capricorn, you might say, is the typical skeptic. You also get a lot of Cancers. Especially Cancer men often have a kind of over-skepticism, but they really can feel astrology, often in spite of themselves. You get a lot of Cancer men going to astrologers in my experience. The skeptic also is the one who's always testing you; they can really shut down your psychic energy. That's something that you can also screen on the phone sometimes; you can tell by the tone of voice and attitude if the person is just going to put you through the mill. You may not like that kind of experience.

Then there's the insistent, pushy, manipulative person, who—no matter what you say on the phone or in your written material mailed early—is basically going to try to manipulate you into predicting or into saying what they want to hear. They'll try real hard to make you give them definite answers to questions like: "Will this make me a fortune, or won't it?" "When will I die? You really know, don't you?" and this kind of stuff. All I can say about dealing with that type is that you've got to acknowledge your limits and be *extremely firm* and go no further. If they keep hammering on you, you've got to be even firmer. If they still keep hammering, then you have to just hit them or something, or at least invite them to leave quickly!

Regarding fee schedules . . . I already mentioned the deposit. I think a deposit is a good practice for at least the obvious reason that you'll be paid for all your advance work. But it also lets them know that *they're making a commitment.* If they've got to put money down, they've got to think about it. And you give them a deadline, too: "If this deposit is not in one week before the appointment, it is automatically cancelled." Then if the money doesn't arrive, it's cancelled. That gives you that week to work on the chart. You don't even touch their data until the money comes. And they've got to consider, "Ok, do I really want this appointment?" The deposit you can do any way, but I don't think it's a good psychological tact to ask for the whole fee in advance. But just something enough that they'll miss it if they don't show up and to reimburse you for your time invested. There's also the question of a sliding scale, which is a very difficult thing. You basically have to take people's word if you get into a sliding scale type of fee structure. Of course you get the real cheap clients now and then that are always going to tell you they make a lot less, even if they have a $200,000,000 trust fund in their name. So that's really an individual choice. I never use a sliding scale, and never publicized it, but once in a while if I thought somebody was really honestly in need, then I'd cut down the price.

Setting time limits to appointments is something I had to learn from exhausting experience. My earliest appointments were about three and one-half or four hours. Finally, when Saturn squared my Sun, I was forced by lack of energy to cut it down to 90 minutes. Suddenly I just got real practical. Not only my reduced energy though led me to set time limits more strictly; I had also gotten tired of wandering all over their whole life! That's when I started to really focus (Saturn!). I'd say, "Ok, what are you here for? This is a map of your whole being. We cannot talk about every dimension of your being in one appointment, or in a hundred. So we have to focus on one thing or only a couple of things." This makes you focus on essential problems, too, if that person knows that only 90 minutes are available. I personally think an hour is too short, but with much more than 90 minutes, you start getting drained and the client starts losing all attention. If something is going to happen, in my experience, 90 minutes is enough time to allow it to happen. It gives you a chance to attune to the person and to warm up to each other, and also, if the relationship between you and the client is terrible, it's over in only 90 minutes. You don't have to sit with them for three or four hours! If you never want to see them again, you can then refer them as they go out the door.

The question of integrity is something people might want to talk about, integrity on many levels, how rigid you are going to be in adhering to your principles and beliefs. I don't believe in preaching or moralizing to the client, but you do have a certain code of ethics, and having it known by the client in advance is advisable. So it probably should be included on the advance sheets that you mail out. Any code of ethics that you adhere to should include a statement of whether or not you predict, and to what extent you describe future trends. Define it in writing! Then, if the manipulative type of client starts demanding, "I want a prediction on that," you pull out your sheet and say, "Look, you got this in advance. This is what I do. I go through these kinds of trends. I do not tell you what to do and what will and will not happen." Also, getting the prices in writing on the advance sheet is good practice. Very few people ever gave me trouble on prices, but once in a while you'll get a particularly resistant client (real cheap ones, too), and you can just see the pain as they pull out their wallets, you know. That's uncomfortable for both of you. That's another reason for the deposit, because when they pay you the second installment, it's not so painful as paying it all at once.

Another thing to include on the advance sheet is your biographical data. You don't want to take up your whole day on the telephone. So, if you have these prepared sheets to mail out as soon as you talk to people on the phone, they can get all the data later by mail. Biographical data is incredibly important to establish your authority. Because there are no real qualifications, certificates, or degrees in this field, most clients coming to you really won't know how much to trust you. They won't know how qualified you are, how many years of experience you have, whether you've taught in a community college program, whether you have counseling training, or whatever. It's good to have them read that *before* they come to you, because it gives them a sense that they're dealing with someone who might know something. They may even come to you with a lot of confidence in you.

Biographical data includes what you've done, what jobs you've worked at, what degrees you have, what training you have, how many years you've been doing counseling, any articles you've published, anything to establish clearly that this is the major focus of study in your life and that you are, in fact, a specialist in this field.

A business card is not the same. A card with a cute logo of a fish or something does not give the same impression as ten years of data showing that you've actually done something. Somebody at the last conference was handing out beautiful cards, with full-color art and a glossy finish. From talking to her, I realized that she didn't know much about astrology. And she was handing out these lovely cards, saying that she did professional astrological readings. She's a serious student, but she's only a student, an Aquarius. So after listening to her lack of astrological knowledge, I finally said, "Are you actually accepting money for astrological work?" She said, "Oh, yes." I said, "But you don't hardly know anything!" She is a very honest Aquarius and she said, "I know, but I'm learning." I must say, when I was doing classes, I was quite shocked at how rapidly many people (especially the Aquarians!) start charging money and pretending to know everything. They start thinking that they *are* the universal mind! I love Aquarians, really. I get along with them very well. But they are not *patient.* They want to know it all *now* and jump right in. They're fanatics!

Biographical data sheets are also good because those printed sheets may wind up in the hands of somebody else, too, maybe a friend of the person who came to you. And if that person is a little cynical and thinks, "Yes, there are some intelligent astrologers, but how do I discriminate between them and the goons?" that biographical data may really help. Just put down your life experience (if you're just starting out); it doesn't have to be extensive astrological experience. If you have an A.A. in philosophy, put it down. Just show that you are a human being with a little bit of intelligence, and that you've been alive for a few years, doing a few things. Include what jobs you did, and especially if you ever worked in anything related to the healing arts or a hospital or a clinic or with handicapped people–anything where you were involved in the helping professions. That's all related experience.

Very few people will ask how long you've been counseling, but *your fees should reflect how long you've been doing it.* In fact, as an example, I talked to a Swedish lady a few months ago who is now living in the States. She's very practical, a Capricorn with a very strong Pluto also. She has really deep insight, and she is very honest. I was really impressed with her. What she was doing is really good. *You have to learn by doing.* You can't just get it out of books. But don't pretend to know more than you do. *Charge a fee commensurate with your knowledge and experience,* and that's what she is doing. She told me that she tells people when they come, "Here's what I do. I've been studying for so long, and I charge this much because I still really feel like I'm learning." She's really blunt with them–she has a lot of Sagittarius, also. She started out charging $5.00 and said, "Look, that's just to cover my time doing the calculations. I'm not charging you for all the time talking with you, because I'm learning from you as well as you learning from this whole dialogue." Then she went to $10, and I think she's at $15 or $20 now. She still doesn't consider that she is *that* expert yet, but she's being real honest about it and she's getting a lot of clients. Quite a few are coming back over and over. Particularly for those who don't have a lot of friends or relatives or social contacts to practice with, that's a good way to do it. Of course you'll have some rather unpleasant experiences at times, but you'll learn from those too.

Another major question (and I think this would have to wait until you had something of a clientele so you could *afford* to do it) is whether you want to set up a structure of two successive initial appointments. In other words, should you require a commitment to two appointments? Marvin Layman suggests that one should do that and that the first interview with the client should consist mostly of just gathering information, just talking about the person, their life, their concerns. Discuss specific problems and issues. Then, between the appointments, you've got a chance to think it over, to let it settle in, to let your unconscious work on it, as well as to study the chart more; the chart and its progressions and transits will come alive after you've had the initial dialogue with the person. Then you go into things in a much deeper way and focus more at the second appointment; that's also when you deal with their specific questions.

Another way to do it is to make only the natal chart, so to speak, the main focus in the first appointment: "What is your nature? What kind of person are you?" Don't even talk about past or future. Then the second appointment can bring in the transits and/or progressions: "Now what kinds of cycles are you in?" That's one way of dividing it up. That's the way I've done it. For a long time I just did long single appointments, but I divided them in half. We'd focus on the natal chart, so to speak, and just talk but not get into transits or progressions during the first hour. Then I'd take a break and I'd get away from the person, get out of their aura. I'd just walk outside and breathe. Often a lot of things would flood into me then that I needed to know about that person. And then I'd get back to the specific problems and the cycles—transits and progressions. I did that for a long time, but it was one very long session. Eventually, I made it into two shorter 90-minute appointments.

You have to charge for your time in whatever way, but you have to figure it out for yourself. If you're going to demand that they make a commitment to two appointments, that's putting *you* on the spot too, of course. If you don't have a good experience at the first appointment, then, if it's really bad, you can often say, "This does not work; we don't relate. Here's half your money back, and let's cancel the second appointment." You can then refer them to someone else. I suppose you have that option. So there are pros and cons to those kinds of set-ups. The main thing is: what needs to be done with a certain person, and how can you elicit the proper kind of commitment from the client? That's a very individual matter that depends on what kind of work you want to do and on what level you want to do it, and to what extent you want to work on quite serious types of emotional difficulties.

The only other notes I have here are on a few other issues. I'll just read them off and you can jot them down if you want to bring them up later, and then we'll just go from there: *Career planning* (future directions for a profession in astrology); *how to market your services* (That can include teaching, too, in a sense. If you teach, it's a very good way to get clients and it also forces you to articulate your understanding.); *the legal aspects of astrology* and *malpractice questions; becoming an employer.* (If you eventually get a pretty good practice going, it's very efficient to get a secretary or a helper. If you do want to employ a helper to coordinate things and maybe get the charts calculated and so forth, there are certain legal requirements there too.)

The question of recordkeeping and taping. Do you want to tape all or some of the material? I think in many cases you'll want to do this, but when you're taping, you'll often see this worried look come over the client as they think, "What if my husband would hear this?" Very often you can unilaterally turn the tape recorder off, and suddenly a whole bunch of stuff can pour out. So you have to use tapes carefully, because they can limit your free dialogue. But tapes do undoubtedly save you a lot of time and a lot of misquotations. If you don't tape, you often get a lot of calls later, saying, "You said such and such." You'll know that you never said it, but without a taped record you have to go through entire explanations all over again. They heard it because they wanted to. Also, it will save you those calls of "What about this, what did you say?" All that gets very trying when you're a busy person, and no one wants to pay you for your phone time repeating everything again. I don't turn on the recorder right at the beginning, but I always try to get specific time periods onto tape. I almost always give them the tape of the session; I want them to have it. Then you simply tell them to play the tape back if they have questions.

Group practice. That's a really interesting concept. People are so different, and astrologers are so different, and the astrology field is so vast that if you have a partnership you can each have different specialties and you can also each work with the types of clients with whom you're most compatible. There's a practice between two women I know that really works well. One loves teaching, and the other really likes counseling and hates teaching. They have a complementary interaction and a real nice office setup. They've been in business for quite a few years. A group practice is an interesting concept if you can work in harmony with another astrologer. And it frees each of you from some of the burdensomeness and loneliness of private practice, and it allows you to travel or vacation now and then. That's all my notes; now it's up to you to open it up.

Comment: (Inaudible question about the Ascendant.)

Stephen: I don't know about anybody else, but the Ascendant is a very subtle thing. I think it's significant that there are so few good books on the Ascendant. That's because it's not easy to describe it or to see it. In my experience, the Ascendant only came alive, in terms of what it means and how you can see it in people, after about 10 years. It was the hardest thing for me to get at in astrology. Any new subjects?

Comment: I know astrologers who've had the wrong birth date and still done a right reading. It brings in the question of where is it the psychic and where is it astromancy and where is it astrology?

Comment: The synchronicity seems to make a connection.

Stephen: If you use astrology primarily as a mantic art (mantic art means that it's simply a way to focus your psychic attention), you may not even know *any* real, scientific, specific astrology. If you're *that* kind of astrologer, the accuracy of the chart matters much less. It's then like reading the I Ching or the Tarot, or whatever. But if you are more the scientific and practical type of astrologer, then I think it comes out more strikingly when a chart is inaccurate; it also then will be more obvious what kind of astrologer you are, whether or not you suspected that a time was inaccurate that later proves to be so.

Question: If you cannot for some reason get the exact time, how dangerous is it to make a solar chart and then go by that?

Stephen: That's the best you can do, I'd say. I would much rather use a solar chart than many other types of charts that people use. Many people now want to use a relocation chart or an astrocartography chart or this or that. The solar chart is the second best chart we can get, from my point of view, but I would definitely then focus less on the houses and more on sign placement and aspects.

Comment: Well, on the basis of my experience, I had to go by trial and error, to try to find a chart I could work with. I wanted to know how you feel about the solar chart, how accurate one can get, because I prefer the trial-and-error method to the solar chart. . . .

Stephen: Well then you're talking about rectification–trying to figure it out yourself. This is of course different from a solar chart. The solar chart is simply a chart drawn for the exact moment when the Sun is on the Ascendant, and all the cusps are then 30 degrees from the Ascendant. Whereas rectification is an art that only some very experienced people can do. *Rectify* means "to make it right." But very few people are competent at it. It takes sharp perception and discrimination, vast experience with many people, and great patience. It's most possible when you have a birth time within a few hours of the exact time, so you have to guess between only a few possible Ascendants. When you have no idea of the accurate time, it's very difficult. When you have personal contact with the person, it helps, because you *might* be able to guess the Ascendant. Who knows? It is possible and you could do it. I'd never take it on anymore, because you could spend six months trying to find a chart that works. Generally, the only rectifications I ever try to do are if I have to guess between two or three Ascendants and no more. In other words, if a relative said "around sunrise" or "around noon," you can choose the most likely Ascendant from the two or three possibilities and then try to refine that chart down to an area of 2° to 4° of that Ascendant by testing all sorts of transits to those degrees. You can also use Solar Arc Progressions involving the Angles, but I'd give priority to the transits.

Comment: I come from a different field, although all my life I worked in the medical field to start out. But the main thing is this terrible feeling of being unable to be concise and to reach people who have no idea with astrology, because it's so terribly important. I feel totally insecure about it. I feel helpless because I feel like I need to be 150% certain before I say anything to anyone about their chart.

Question: Could I say something about that? So much depends on the person that you're talking to. There's only so much they're ready to hear. And you have to trust that a certain amount of whatever you want to say is in some sense what they need to hear. It's what they're drawing out of you. So you don't really need to worry.

Comment: That's a help. Thank you.

Gavin Carruthers: Some people won't even hear you no matter what you say, or understand it.

Stephen: Right. So why worry?

Question: I have a question that's come up a couple of times today. They come to the consultation and get all these little goodies and they say, "Well, I don't know about my boss, or my boyfriend, or my ex-husband" this, that or the other. Then you ask if they want to have a composite chart and they say, "Oh no, you have to tell me." I have to be very insistent that I can't talk about someone else without them knowing about it. I've made a couple of enemies by being very insistent. I want to know if anyone had a better method.

Stephen: I don't think there's anything wrong with describing the nature of the other person in a sort of token, general way.

Comment: Say, "You can understand that if you were in this position, you might not want someone to get very deeply into your psyche and your life."

Comment: When I'm in that situation, I just ask for their birthdate and take a quick look at the ephemeris, and then I say just a few things that have a connection with the problems they are coming for. Then they are satisfied.

Stephen: Right. You don't have to reveal that much.

Comment: A few esoteric bon-bons.

Stephen: It's an individual thing, and each case is different. Especially if somebody, for example, comes and says they have a great job, but their boss is a drag. You *have* to deal with that relationship. I don't think it's unethical to use the boss's birthday and relate enough of the boss's nature that the person can better understand that relationship. You're not defining or judging the boss or revealing great secrets. You're just clarifying the reality of that life situation and relationship.

Comment: Especially when it turns out that the person's Sun is on their Saturn or something like that.

Comment: I feel a lot depends on how you *define* that relationship. Sometimes you can say just a few things, like if someone comes, and they have a husband who has a lot of air but they're all water. I can say a few basic things without going deeper. I can say, "I really see why you can't stand your husband." Or "Yes, I can see where your natures are different to a certain extent. I can see what difficulties you both might have."

Comment: What would you say if they then ask what they should do about it?

Carruthers: More than anything, it's a matter of sensitivity to the situation. It's always different depending on who it is and what the situation in the relationship is.

Stephen: Ok, who here has not talked yet, who wants to say something?

Comment: I would like to hear some general discussion of marketing techniques.

Stephen: Marketing your practice is what you want to know about, like how to get the word out that you're doing what you're doing. Does anyone have any contributions?

Comment: Most fairly large cities have either neighborhood newspapers that go out weekly, or in some larger cities they even have alternative newspapers that talk about more counterculture and new age things. It depends on where you live. But I run my card in a lot of these.

Stephen: A lady I know does an effective thing. She simply announces in the newspaper that there is a free lecture on astrology. She's a competent lecturer, very intelligent. She also changes the topics now and then. Anybody can come, and she makes it at a convenient time in the evening after dinner, and she gets a lot of people that way.

Comment: Yeah, but you say she's a lecturer.

Stephen: True, and teaching also helps to get the word out.

Comment: Like Stephen said, teaching really helps a lot, and also networking with other people so they know you're a good referral, and talking to different people in the counseling field. I've done a lot of charts for free for people in the counseling field just to let them know what I can do to complement what they do. Then I go to Parents Without Partners and groups and organizations and do speaking engagements. They do the organizing and I just appear. People don't pay much for that, but people will come to me afterwards.

Comment: It's probably appropriate to say right here that I just spent three years traveling around the world. I worked my way around the world with astrology. The way I introduced myself to communities, in every community in the world, and every city in the world . . . there is an international group of some kind, English speaking, and there's usually an American group, either an American club, many times an American Women's Club. Also, there's generally a British group, British Society or British Women's Club, and also Canadians, Swedish groups, etc. Those groups are always available, so I would always offer to give lectures (free). Everyone is looking for speakers, and astrology is a big interest of course, anywhere in the world these days. So that was always my introduction to communities. I would always get one or two appointments from a discussion, so it's a very fine technique anywhere.

Comment (with thick accent): This was one of the main reasons for me to come here (America) because I am lecturing and giving lectures and courses and it's going very good. Last year, I had about 100 students, and I can earn a living from that. I think it's practical advice. I'm working with brochures. (Shows example) I have my own mark on it, a mark that I decided on (like a logo), and then you get known. I make a few thousand of them and spread them all the time in the town where I live. Also in bookshops—I have a connection in bookshops who have astrology books. It works very well. I always have people coming in. When you have students, they always bring clients forward. It works very well.

Comment: We found that with introductory lectures, it is really beneficial to charge a nominal price, even $5.00. People appreciate it more, and the groups are a lot larger.

Comment: Has anyone had any experience with written readings, sending them out?

Comment: What I do with people who are out of town and want a reading is this: instead of sending them a written reading or instead of sitting in front of a tape recorder myself and talking into it, I arrange for them to call me long distance. You can get a little adapter for your phone, and place the recorder on the phone and do the reading over the phone. I've found that you can be sensitive over the phone, and feel the person fairly well. It works fairly well for me. We do try to make it a little more concise; I try to do it within an hour. It costs them $8 or $9 extra for the phone call.

Comment: What I do sometimes is to send a little questionnaire and have them write me a letter, 4 or 5 pages, concerning what they're going through at the time. It greatly amplifies what is going on in the chart. It gives a lot of concrete, gutsy psychological material. You basically know then what it is in the chart.

Stephen: Right, that kind of advance feedback. One thing, also, that relates to the psychic energy dimension that I was mentioning in the last talk, is when you are doing absentee readings, you're using much more psychic energy. I always felt that I was almost going to the person astrally to tune in, and that is very exhausting for most of us. Whereas, if you're going to do something by mail, if you can get some kind of preliminary energy and definition from the person, it will help a great deal and will benefit the person a lot more.

Comment: Also, a lot of those requests are from people who know friends of mine but don't really know me, and requiring advance information is another way of gauging their seriousness. If you can tell from the information that they send how serious they are and how much they want to get into it in a significant way.

Comment: Do most of you write out your reading prior to seeing the client?

Audience: NO!

Comment: Just notes? Not even notes?

Stephen: It's a personal thing. I think the more experience you have, the less you have to do in advance; because you not only focus on the person more effectively in a personal dialogue, but also you just know the astrology much more. You can start seeing it holistically in ways you never could do before. What I've always told my students, especially the advanced ones, is that there are hard work periods of learning astrology and then you'll hit plateaus of astrological competence. Once in a while you'll have this breakthrough, and you'll hit a new plateau of understanding and you'll stay there for quite a while. Then all of a sudden, you'll have another breakthrough and you'll discover a new area of ability, but you'll have to really work at it to reach it. Then you'll hit another plateau; it's basically an endless learning process as you and your experience grow. Also, I think it's totally different with different people; some people get a holistic sense of the chart very quickly. Extremely analytical, non-intuitive people get it last. It takes them the longest to see a chart holistically. But even for them, eventually, they can just start seeing it. It's almost like reading music or perceiving an entire painting. But, I think, it has to happen spontaneously. So, when you start doing work on that level, *and have good rapport with the client,* you usually don't have to do much to prepare, because the clients will elicit what they need. They define what they're there for. And you'll have the ability to "read the chart" and related cycles rather quickly. I've *always* calculated the major transits and progressions in advance, however, *in great detail.*

Comment: It is a personal thing, but I find I'll write five or six pages of notes, and then when the client comes I'll never use them. But writing it down somehow makes it easier to understand. I'm the kind of person who, if I write something down, that it makes it easier to understand. If I write something down, I know it. And you do have the notes then, in case you want them.

Comment: It saves you a lot of time, of course, if you have some kind of preliminary questionnaire such as Stephen mentioned and you write notes concerning the main issues.

Comment: In addition to that, if you do have the notes it is good, because sometimes the client will call up and ask questions. I have a steel file box, full of clients. You'll forget, of course, some of the things you've said to them. So sometimes it's helpful to have the notes. If they're dated and show the transits, you can go right back to it.

Comment: What do you do about repeat visits? I'd like to hear other people's experience. How often do you see somebody?

Stephen: Do you mean should you encourage them to come back at certain times?

Comment: Are you *counseling* or giving a *reading*? Do you see them once a year, or every six months or what?

Comment: I always suggest to a client, even a new client, that they come in every year so they can find out what's going on for them. Some people want to come back after four or five months. It's a personal thing, again. I usually see people whenever they want to come back, and then I charge less.

Stephen: How do you charge for the telephone consultations, like you were talking about?

Comment: I charge the normal price that I charge for a reading, which is $45, and then the people call me and we prearrange a time, when the rates are lower, usually. I tape record with my recorder. You can get this little adapter that costs $2.00 or $3.00 that just has a little rubber thing on the end. You put it on the receiver, and it records the whole conversation.

Stephen: Modern technology transformeth astrology.

Comment: I would like to see everybody go for a solar return once a year. If somebody asks, that's like a doctor's checkup.

Comment: Doesn't it depend on what the client wants? Don't encourage attendance. I don't encourage dependency. I would rather encourage that a person, like Liz said about needing psychotherapy, that we don't become dependent on astrologers to tell us what's going on in our life, but rather that we become more whole and more able to take charge of that ourselves. So I try to encourage the person to know themselves and be more in tune with the patterns. I don't suggest that they come back. I leave that totally up to them.

Stephen: It's an individual thing on the client's part and on the part of the practitioner. Some people may *need* to talk six times, with a whole series of chart comparisons and all sorts of things. Others may need only a boost of encouragement or a jolt of insight.

Comment: I devote all my time to astrology, and the problem I have is that I have another side to my life. These people who hang onto you and ring up for every little thing! I don't have an office, and have to do it where I live. Are there methods to deal with that?

Comment: You just simply tell them that if they would like to discuss it, they can make an appointment with you. You have to be bold about it. Your reputation develops on that basis.

Stephen: Yes. Astrologers are often people who are easily manipulated. You have to be firm.

Comment: I was going to say that when I do a reading for someone, I always offer that if they need any clarification or have any questions, please feel free to call me. However, after the first phone call, I charge $20.00 for every 10 minutes. That has been highly successful. And I want the money in the mail, or they will never get my information or help on the phone again. I've gotten rid of only two clients that way. The rest of them are very happy to send me a check in the mail. I have a very successful practice.

Stephen: So you will accept one call free, just to clarify. Is that it? Then you start charging.

Comment: And that will be pretty quick. In other words, it will be in the next few weeks that they have something that needs clarification.

Stephen: Meanwhile, have they had a chance to listen to a tape or something?

Comment: Oh yes, I tape everything. But there may be something that you fail to mention. And they are perfectly happy to pay. So why not?

Stephen: If you show the confidence that your information is worth something, that's a really key thing. People have to respect it.

Comment: Otherwise, you'll be bugged to death by people who call you and want to know what color toilet paper they should buy!

Stephen: My home phone is unlisted now. I could never eat dinner without interruptions. It became intolerable.

Question (addressed to Stephen): I have a question concerning research and verifying different things in the charts. As far as certain clients that have the same things going on, and what that means over a long period of time, gathering research to support different things. . . . Is that not what you do to some degree, gathering information that you have and put it into your books?

Stephen: If I understand you, what you're calling research is mainly this gathering and observing repeatedly with clients, and in that sense it's research. You see X, Y, and Z all as examples of the same factors.

Comment: How would you do that?

Stephen: Just do it. *A lot of consultations.* Also, I had a very good memory, once.

Comment: Did you write down things after each session?

Stephen: Not usually, but I did keep notebooks, not so much about individual clients but about every astrological factor, aspects particularly. I had just about every major aspect listed with space after it. When something would strike me, I would write it down. Likewise with planets and signs and houses and so on. I have huge notebooks, really, full of stuff. Maybe that's what you're asking.

Comment: As far as supporting what it is you found in counseling people with certain things going on in their charts, for example, one particular transit means generally a certain thing for everyone. . . .

Stephen: I kept a whole notebook on transits, also. First I used Grant Lewi's *Astrology For the Millions* and a few other books. I sort of put together their stuff and then left space for my own observations. I did add a lot of notes about transits over time, so that ultimately it was all there in my notebooks, actually. At that time, astrology was my whole life and my whole mental set. I was so immersed in it that I hardly ever had to look at my notes. But fortunately for me, I accumulated them all so that I could then go back to them for my writing. At that time I retained everything in my mind, somehow, which I can't do anymore. I do recommend keeping notebooks. Especially in the early years, especially with a skeptical client who thought that the astrology really wasn't anything, that I was simply intuiting observations and pretending that astrology showed it, I would grab a book off the shelf or a notebook and say, "This is what some author has said about the very thing you're going through right now." Word for word I'd read it to them. They would often say, "My God, that's perfect, precise!" I remember one engineer, a double Aries (Sun & Moon Aries), Scorpio rising—real suspicious, Taurus Venus—very retentive, engineering background, absolutely didn't really believe in anything beyond the material. He was a mechanical engineer. After a chart comparison with his new girlfriend at the time, he just got this amazing look on his face. Because I saw how skeptical he was, I read the entire thing out of Lois Sargent's book, *How to Handle Your Human Relations.* I told him, "Look, I can see you aren't believing this at all, so I'm not going to say anything myself. I'm just going to show you what this book, written over ten years ago, says about your relationship. Then you can see that it's the astrology saying it, not me." After the appointment, he just said, "Well, all I can say is that no human being could have ever thought this up." Suddenly he got real religious and said, "God must have given astrology to man." His mind was blown! After that he got into meditation and was one of my best students in astrology. God knows what he's doing now; it just opened up his whole life. You've got to relate to the client. If a client is all closed off, there may be only one way to deal with them, and you may have to go right to a book or something.

Comment: I'm so glad you brought this up. It is not in any way undermining the astrologer if you say, "Well, I'll tell you what this author said. I'll read it to you." What was that book?

Stephen: Lois Sargent's book, *How to Handle Your Human Relations.** It's just a little yellow booklet. It is an excellent book on aspects between two people's planets for chart comparisons. In my estimation, it's THE best complete interpretation of all possible *major* aspects between planets. It's only weak in some of the preliminary chapters, and it doesn't have much on the Ascendant or the houses. The actual interpretations of the specific aspects are really, really excellent. She's a little bit old fashioned at times, and you have to take that into consideration. She will tell you that certain things with Mars and Venus mean you should watch out for "unbecoming behavior." But she's really good. The only way she could have written that is that she must have had many years of observation of many rela-

---

*Published by the American Federation of Astrologers, and available from them or the publishers of this book.

tionships. She just couldn't have done that book out of the abstract. It's a very fine book. The title is totally misleading, too, *How to Handle Your Human Relations*; it doesn't say hardly anything about *handling* your human relations. It shows how to *evaluate* various relationships. It's really good on just what the nature of the interchange is between two people, based on specific aspects between the two charts.

Comment: I'd like to ask a few questions about books. I'm interested in cycles and would like to know what book you recommend.

Stephen: What kind of cycles? Transits?

Comment: Ruperti has a book in the bookstores, *Cycles of Becoming.*

Stephen: Yes, a lot of people really like it, so I'd say go in and read some paragraphs and see if you like it. He's very philosophical; he's very broad-visioned, Sagittarius rising.

Comment: Is there another one that you would recommend?

Stephen: There aren't many that treat cycles in a really useful and holistic way. Outside the astrology field, there's important research that's been done on cycles, including a book called *Cycles* by Edward Dewey, who is the head of the Foundation for the Study of Cycles. There's really not much astrology in it and it doesn't deal much with *planetary* cycles, but a researcher could undoubtedly correlate those cycles with many celestial cycles. Within the astrology field, of course Dane Rudhyar goes quite a bit into cycles; it's scattered throughout many of his books. *The Lunation Cycle* is one. That was a breakthrough book, and many people have now followed up on that. He developed certain interpretations of cyclic theory and of the phases of a cycle that are extremely valuable, and now various people have applied that to other planetary cycles, and to progressions also. *The Lunation Cycle* would definitely be worth looking at, and Rudhyar's other work on cycles. Also, *The Transit of Saturn* by Marc Robertson. It's a pretty good book on Saturn's cycle.

Comment: May I just say that, for the people who deal mostly with older persons, I think *Cycles of Becoming** is so very important, because he is talking about how important the different age groups are, which periods have what sort of significance astrologically, and so on.

Stephen: I just want to add to that. I like that book more and more as I get older. Ruperti wrote it when he was about 60, and I think it's only when you pass age 35 or more that you have any developed philosophical dimension.

Comment: It really meets a need for a different approach after age 60.

Stephen: It's very broad. And he has whole sections on the age factor . . . what major dimension of life people are active in at certain ages.

[After some further discussion of books, the following material was read. It was prepared for the discussion group by Dr. Lynn Hawley, an M.D. attending the conference.]

I think all astrologers should be alert to the square of transiting Pluto to its natal position. People at this time will usually be in emotional turmoil and may have many emotional and physical complaints. They need to work at releasing their pent-up emotions in constructive ways. But they also need to pay attention to the physical health.

In my experience and the experience of a friend who uses astrology to work with cancer patients, the issue of cancer may arise at this time. Constructive use of emotions at this time may prevent the seeds of cancer from getting started then. I think that it is wise to suggest physical check-ups to people having this transit and for a while after the transit. Conventional medicine has the most to offer the early cancer which can be cured by surgery.

This transit may occur at any age between 40 and 90. Right now, because of rapid motion of Pluto through the signs, it is

---

*Available from the publishers of this book.

happening to people in their 40's. The factors which seem to create cancer include: radiation, chemical pollutants, and self-destructive emotions. It seems that the body is constantly removing abnormal cells, but that for some reason the person who gets a cancer failed to eliminate abnormal cells. All of this suggests a Plutonian connection with cancer.

5

Ancient Laws — Modern Interpretation: The Rebirth of Simplicity

The mind creates multiplicity everywhere to cover the simplicity in Nature.

– Dr. Randolph Stone

We shall not cease from exploration
And the end of all our exploring
Will be to arrive where we started
And know the place for the first time.

– T.S. Eliot

In the astrology field in the past few years, it has become rather fashionable, and indeed almost a religious tenet for many people, to encourage a great "open-mindedness" among those studying or practicing astrology, as if all theories, speculations, and even remote and tangential ideas have inherently the same value (which is a preposterous assumption). Perhaps this tendency among many astrologers comes from the Uranian need to have continual mental excitement from ideas that at least purport to be new and original, although we know that most of them aren't. Perhaps it comes from astrology's lack of a *recognized* and cogently formulated tradition, which can serve as a *foundation* for astrological theory. I mean to emphasize the word *recognize.* We obviously *have* a tradition, and that's one thing I want to talk about–the ancient laws, the ancient traditions. But it is a widely-recognized tradition that is absent. Almost every person in the field seems to believe in a different tradition.

---

*This chapter consists of a lecture delivered at the Spring Astrology Symposium in Berkeley, California in April, 1983. The theme of the symposium was "Current Views on the State of the Art."

Whatever the reasons for this obsession with "open-mindedness," I am not wildly enthusiastic about opening my mind to any little wind that blows, because it inevitably brings with it a lot of dust and debris. Some years ago I decided that the only reason to have an open mind was to find something extraordinarily valuable to close it around! By that, I don't mean to say that you shouldn't be *broad-minded*; we should not be narrow-minded. We *should* be broad-minded! But broad-mindedness, tolerance of other people's views, is not the same as a naive, almost fanatical open-mindedness with no discrimination. It does seem to me that there is a great need for a strong dose of self-analysis and discrimination in the astrology field today.

Looking at the current "State of the Art," as this entire conference is titled, we have to wonder whether it has really furthered the practice of astrology, the development of astrology, the usefulness of astrology, and the acceptance of astrology by the general public to have done what we seem to have done in the astrology field in the last 15 or 20 years—that is, to have thoroughly devastated, or at least neglected, a lot of the ancient traditions. I'm not narrowly saying, "We should go back to the old," or "We should reject the new." That's not what I'm saying; you have to give me a few minutes to outline the issues I'm raising. But I certainly question at this point the mixture of pop-psychology, Tarot, numerology, hypnosis, and everything else that seems to have been enthusiastically invited into the astrology field. I often feel that in the astrology field today we have reached a point that is similar to the state of mind of the scientifically educated segments of our society: we flatter ourselves that we *know* almost everything, and yet we really don't *understand* anything. That's where the philosophical dimension comes in—to give order and meaning. In our society and in astrology today, the philosophical and holistic principles are neglected and ignored most of the time. That's the fact, in spite of occasional lip-service by many astrologers.

I think it's time for a small group of astrology practitioners, a group whose *primary* focus is acknowledged to be *counseling with astrology* and *helping people towards self-understanding through the use of astrology,* to take a stand, either individually or together in some association. It's time for that group to define astrology *narrowly* for a change, in order to *include* specifically the holistic, artistic, and philosophical factors. It would not be a primary intention of anyone doing this to *exclude* many things that are in fact tangential to astrology itself, but you simply wouldn't bother to include them. It's simply that you would be focusing on the essential valuable things. And just by doing so, you would of course be excluding a lot. It's not that you're *against* what you're excluding, but you don't want to include everything, because then you have no focus and no order. Being *too inclusive* is distracting and ruins the focus and thus the clarity, and this has been a problem for astrologers and astrology for many years. In many fields today, not just astrology, there is this kind of chaotic mixture of things resulting in a witches' brew of incomprehensibility. Defining astrology more precisely is doubly important especially because of the public relations problem with being an astrologer—the "public image" problem. As long as we present to the public a mish-mash of all sorts of things, public acceptance of astrology will be inhibited. The public has a hard enough time swallowing astrology alone, let alone all sorts of other "occult sciences," etc. So, I feel it's time to reconsider our astrological traditions and also to stay closer to them than has been the case in the past two decades. I'll return to the question of *tradition* shortly.

Current Views on the State of the Art

The Conference theme brings to mind a couple of other things. My view is: the use, understanding, and application of astrology is an *art*. Thus, any consideration of astrology leads to various aesthetic questions, such as symmetry, elegance, and simplicity, with which I'll deal in just a few minutes. This is not to say that astrology *itself* is not a science, because I believe it is a cosmic science. But certainly, just about any *use* of it is an art, when applying it to everything from the stock market to human problems.

A variation on the Conference theme might be "current views on the state of the artist," because there's not that much wrong with astrology, really, that a lot of good astrologers couldn't cure! So, current views on "the state of the artist" are at least as important to evaluate as "the state of the art" itself; because once you know the fundamentals, those that are valid and do work reliably, the *astrologer* (the artist) then becomes more important than the astrology. I think we have to ask ourselves: What is our state of mind and being? What are we doing in our lives? Are we beginning to learn the art of living, or do we just reflect our own confusion to clients? Is our mind cluttered with unnecessary fragments of data and useless theories, or have we developed our own simple, personal language for talking with clients and relating the astrological indications to them?

Rescuing the Great Tradition

The whole question of *tradition,* again, needs to be examined further and clarified, and I do not mean to say we should blindly go back to Alan Leo or Ptolemy or to any one older approach. But neither should we blindly reject all of it under the pretense of various kinds of "modern" notions. As Dennis Elwell pointed out this morning, it is unique to this century that an astrology and astrological psychology dealing with *motivation* has started to develop spontaneously. Obviously, that is of considerable value, so I'm not saying, "Oh, let's reject all this modern stuff." But there is a great tradition in astrology, and there are some great truths in that tradition that are today habitually neglected because of the new emphasis on motivation and other "hidden" factors in the human psyche. Unfortunately, that tradition is not only neglected, but also somewhat devastated and corrupted.

Most of us here know that astrology has many valuable traditions. Many of us here feel that a good number of those traditions are either completely inaccurate or basically irrelevant in this era, or perhaps even more often, in need of a reinterpretation in modern language, and with the modern person's psychology in mind. A new way of thinking about and speaking about astrology is needed today. Lest you think that I'm painting too dark a picture, astrology is growing. It is developing. The development it needs is happening. In fact, it is in the slow, painful process of developing just what it needs now, I think. For example, conferences like this, in some ways, are planting seeds for that growth.

I think an incredible amount of progress has been made in the last twenty years in astrology in developing a fairly modern and intelligent sort of astrology, quite an impressive transformation of astrology when you consider what kinds of limitations had to be overcome and when you consider the black and white notions that most of us studied when we first encountered astrology.

As Dennis said this morning, different types of astrology are applicable to different levels of manifestation. So what certainly needs to be asked these days is, "What *kind* of astrology are you doing? What *scope* of application does it have?" So many of the problems in the state of the art today, both as astrologers talk *with each other* and as they try to make clients understand them, stem from a lack of clearly agreed upon definitions. Thus, the ensuing lack of clear communication. You can never have clear communication without commonly understood definitions. So we need to define our terms better and to explain what we mean in more depth. I constantly get letters from people complaining about the shallow and silly kind of astrology that is commonly found in books. The words in the last one I got described the "superficial and irrelevant" kind of astrology that is in most of the literature. As a writer primarily, I can't help but focus, to some extent, on the kind of astrology presented in the literature. It is probably the most inferior of all the kinds of astrology available to the public. There are probably a lot more good astrologers practicing than the literature would imply. It is our responsibility, I think, if we're serious students or especially practitioners of astrology, to learn how to communicate more simply and clearly and on a more practical level. But remember, astrology is a language. With any language, you don't use unnecessarily intricate grammar to communicate what is most effectively communicated in simple language. So our focus should remain effective communication of and with the astrological language, and that usually requires a certain degree of simplicity—a major theme of this talk that we'll return to shortly.

As one grows out of a tradition or beyond a tradition, a problem arises in that growth and change for some reason so often require quantum leaps and radical revisions that leave much of value behind. Often, then, the result is a situation that is worse than that which was just rejected. We see that human tendency a lot in world politics, and in religious movements and the sciences. Look at some of the "wonderful" revolutions that overthrew some nasty dictator or king, and look what replaced the old government. Look at the worldwide currents of "religious" fanaticism. And look at the intolerance of materialistic science. So, we often wind up with this kind of so-called progress in the world. I think this is similar to what's happening with astrology today, or at least what has been happening in the last 15 years. I think this "progress" that leaves behind too much of value from the past describes the "state of the art" today. One writer characterized it like this: "Progress is the exchange of one nuisance for another."*

The old determinism that one finds in a lot of the old astrology books is out of fashion now. It's being slowly replaced; and admittedly, much of it was psychologically crippling in its tendency to instill fear in people. But also, modern people don't like such determinism because it's very offensive to the almighty modern ego that likes to believe that we can control everything. More and more I've come to feel that a great deal of the resentment and the fear of astrology in many people simply comes from the fact that they hate the idea that they can't control everything. Astrology implies that there is something powerful *beyond* them, and that just scares a rigid, egotistical type of person. Such people also often like to feel that they are completely unique, not an amalgamation of archetypal energies!

When the old determinism is rejected or is being replaced, what is it being replaced by? So far, it seems to be replaced by a variety of pseudosystems that have no traditions, or by promising but only half-evolved new sets of terms, or by overly simplistic presentations of limited intellectual quality. (I guess Dennis Elwell this morning called the current situation a "hodgepodge.") And then, of course, you also have the overly complex approaches that borrow haphazardly and overenthusiastically from anything that purports to be "science" or statistics. Let us not throw out the baby with the bath water! I do not think we should trade in a basically solid tradition, a bit corrupt though it may be, a tradition with a core of universal truth. We should not

*The rootlessness of the modern era and its obsession with empty "progress" is pervasive and not limited to just the astrology field. As Pulitzer Prize winning author Robert Penn Warren writes, "The lack of a sense of history is the damnation of the modern world."

trade a solid tradition for a morass of modern mental madness! It would be a poor exchange, and we would lose in the process.

We need to *rescue* that solid tradition and revitalize it, I feel. The great German writer Goethe, the author of *Faust,* said that *one must labor to possess what was inherited.* You have to work hard at making the inheritance *your own.* One of the most philosophical poets in the English language. T. S. Eliot, said much the same thing, when in *The Four Quartets* he wrote,

> We shall not cease from exploration
> And the end of all our exploring
> Will be to arrive where we started
> And know the place for the first time.

At the end of all our exploring, we come back to where we started, but it's only then that we know the place for the first time. So you explore and explore and explore, and suddenly you're right back where you started. But it looks new, because suddenly it's illuminated through your experience.

I think this accurately describes our current situation in astrology, where we are continually exploring *outwardly.* Especially in the last decade there has been incredible expansion, but also fragmentation in the astrology field, checking out all manner of "new" idea and system, only to find ultimately (at least in my case) that so many of the basic ancient laws and *essential* traditions and principles were right in front of us all the time. Those principles could, in fact, have served us quite well if only we had known how to *apply* them, if our consciousness had been developed enough to see the timeless truths in that ancient tradition. In other words, we have to *grow into the tradition,* because the tradition is much vaster than most of our minds are capable of understanding. Especially today, it often seems easier to develop elaborate schemes and theories than to open our eyes to what's right in front of us, because such theorizing enables us to pat ourselves on the back and tell ourselves how clever we are. Then we can brag to other people and it's really fun. The simple and the obvious are not valued by the modern mind. The modern mind wants excitement, not the tranquility of simplicity.

We have to explore as part of the growth process, no doubt. We have to explore and we have to experiment, but we also have to *labor diligently to possess what we've inherited,* and to absorb into ourselves the essence of the tradition. Then astrology can become part of us and can eventually be understood deep "in our bones," rather than stored in the neat little boxes in our minds. I don't know exactly how it happened, and it took a long time, but eventually all the astrology that I had ever studied descended, so to speak. It was almost like it went into my stomach and my bones. Then I could hardly talk about it anymore. It's not so much a mental thing anymore for me as it used to be. In many ways, it seems I've had to outgrow all the cultural and intellectual overlays that actually prevent people from experiencing astrology's reality in an immediate way.

We in astrology love to categorize things, to draw "correlations," and to establish hierarchies of ideas. It's almost a form of worship for us, I think; we get so excited about the infinite applications and implications of astrology's truths, especially in our first few years of studying it. We get so carried away that we just go bananas about it. That's not a bad thing, but it's mental gymnastics. There's a deeper understanding that one has to get to by growing to realize that *life doesn't work in a linear fashion.* All of the clever distinctions ultimately prove to be artificial, especially so in a counseling situation. In any kind of dialogue, even if you don't call it "counseling," it's impossible to make real contact just by using lots of "rules."

For example, the endless arguments over the following things in astrology are what I'm calling artificial distinctions: the arguments between users of transits and users of progressions; which one is right? Or which *one* chart factor rules the profession. In linear thinking, there could only be one, of course. Or does the fourth house stand for the mother and the tenth for the father, or vice versa? That's one of my favorite idiot questions. Human beings are living wholes, and the chart has to be seen that way too.

So along those lines, the image came to me that we can give endless names to the leaves on a tree, but new leaves keep popping out all the time; so it confounds us because we can't control or keep up with life's changes. It makes us feel a little less clever than we'd like to believe we are. WE NEED TO GET TO THE ROOTS, TO UNDERSTAND THE GROUND OF OUR SCIENCE/ ART, AND TO FEEL THE FLOW OF THE SAP. You've got to get to the deeper stuff. If you sit there contemplating the leaves, you'll always be confused. There are no shortcuts to this ideal. It has to be worked for. The roots of the tree of astrology are grounded in life itself and *are* the essentials of the ancient traditions. By laboring to possess this inheritance, the ancient traditions' essentials, we automatically reach into the depths of life's deeper truths. And *then* we arrive at an understanding that is at once profoundly complex and awesomely simple.

By the way, Jupiter is very strong for me in the last few months. I'm much more preachy than normal. But I can't help it! A friend of mine said the following recently. He's a Sun in Cancer with Cancer rising, and Neptune conjunct the Moon in Libra in the 3rd house. I was talking to him about some of these things, and he said:

> Astrology is as complex as life itself is. That's why nobody can make the ultimate statement about its meanings. It is impossible to explain it, to categorize all of its factors and meanings, and to make it simply accessible to lazy minds, *because it so closely reflects life itself.* It's *part of life*; it's not just a mental fabrication or a sterile intellectual construct. Because it cannot be separate from life itself, it's difficult to understand it. No book can ever *sum up* astrology once and for all. It changes as life changes. [One might say, too, that it changes as a society changes. Each society gives birth to its own kind of astrology. S.A.] Because it *is* life, and because it describes the living, moving energies which vitalize creation, all attempts and claims to *rigidly categorize* the factors commonly used in astrology are invariably limited and doomed to fail in most applications.

The more my own studies and experience and research in astrology have progressed, the more I've realized that a great deal of development is needed on the *very basics,* especially in the literature. For example, isn't it amazing that still, now, there is not much good material in print on Jupiter, on the Moon, or on the Ascendant? There isn't one good book, really, on those subjects. There are only little pieces here and there. So much astrological speculation in the past decade strikes me as either premature, presumptuous, or just simply unnecessary, because it's introduced to "explain" (which I am coming to believe is often a pseudo-explanation) what the essentials already show, and what the ancient fundamental laws already illuminate, if only we understand them properly.

I am reminded of what Charles Carter wrote, that he felt that 75% of major life experiences could be illuminated simply by transits, "if properly understood." This was in a discussion of progressions, transits, and various techniques. *If properly understood* is the main phrase there. Note the word "illuminate" too. More and more I see astrology as a lens through which we can see. You keep the same fine lens, ideally, and you polish it through constant use and care. The more you do that, the more fine detail comes into view. Just as the philosopher Gabriel Marcel stated, that existence itself is not "explained" but rather has to be "illuminated" in order to gain real understanding, so astrology is a great *illuminator.* It perhaps is not as great an *explainer* as we'd like to think, but it certainly is a great and profoundly valuable illuminator. It shines a light where before there was darkness. *But it can only illuminate if the astrologer is capable of focusing.* Otherwise, the light is scattered and thus very diffuse and faint.

My overall orientation is probably fairly well known to those of you who have read my books, but I have to define my own bias here before going further. The kind of astrology that is significant for me deals not so much with *information* as with *transformation.* It deals not so much with *knowing* as with *becoming.* Collecting data can be done by a computer, and shoveling collected data into the minds of clients (that is, mere *information*) does not whatsoever encourage *transformation.* When dealing with people, I think you've got to view astrology as an art. The understanding of, or at least a *feeling for,* life's laws, mysteries, and rhythms is what the astrologer needs to convey in order to be a real healer or therapist or counselor. That understanding, or at least that feeling, on the part of the client can encourage their becoming their best–a positive kind of transformation.

Simplicity: A Significant Factor in the Art of Astrology

Before discussing some specific examples of astrological factors and a few specific laws and traditions, I want briefly to outline what I mean by "simplicity" and the importance of the aesthetic and philosophical components of the astrological tradition. Aesthetic and philosophical components in the astrological tradition, as I often mention, are regularly neglected these days, thanks to the tyranny of technology and man's lack of real self-knowledge. And, as both an aesthetic and philosophical principle, *simplicity* is a significant factor. We can only get astrology precisely accurate, and thus reliable, if we keep it simple enough to master. If it becomes just incredibly complex, nobody can master it. What practical use can you make with something that's entirely beyond your grasp? We can keep it simple only by acknowledging its proper applications, limits, and the scope of its *reliable* use. We need not prematurely reach out in desperation to embrace things that will needlessly complicate it. I'm not saying we should close off totally to every new idea or every new technique. But know when you *need* a new technique, if you can!

If we want more people to understand what astrology is, rather than rejecting it outright, for that reason also it is incumbent upon us to develop a way of defining astrology which is ultimately simple. By keeping it simple, we not only make it intellectually accessible to other people, but we also bring it down to earth, so that many, many people can experience its value and benefit from it. And yet, I see little indication that the general public's respect for astrology or understanding of it is being augmented by the TV appearances of astrologers, the books, the radio shows. (We no longer speak in our society or in its educational institutions of studying something merely because it is good or true or noble, a valid reason for studying astrology.) So, it appears to me that so far we have failed to achieve the simple clear definition and language needed to communicate astrology's value effectively.

Evidently it's a symptom of our era, and not at all limited to the astrology field, that all these little disciplines are speaking their own highly specialized language and they never speak with each other anymore. The Chairman for the National Endowment for the Humanities, William J. Bennett, just published an essay recently in which he said, "Increasingly, we read or try to read self-isolating vocabularies that abound within sub-disciplines. There seems to be a competition for complete unintelligibility." I thought that was a good remark. You must admit that many people would feel the same way about astrologers' jargon.

This simplicity is something to strive for. We should emphasize that it's not at all the same as simple-mindedness, nor is it the same as being simplistic. It's an aesthetic quality, like elegance and symmetry, that has a powerful, practical impact in the field of astrology itself as an evolving science and in communicating about astrology with the public. I have two quotes here from L. L. Whyte from his book *Accent on Form,* which is quite a brilliant book by a physicist who is also a philosopher. I quoted it quite a bit in *Astrology, Psychology and the Four Elements:*

> The task of science is not merely to identify the changing structural pattern in everything, but *to see it as simple.* Science starts with the assumption which is always present, though it may be unconscious, may be forgotten, or may sometimes even be denied: *There exists a simple order in nature; a simple way of representing experience is possible; the task of science is to discover it.*
>
> The deepest aesthetic and scientific principle lies in a tendency toward simplicity, order, elegance, form.

Astrology reveals the overall pattern of simplicity, order, and elegance that operates throughout the universe and within every individual. The following explains why retaining astrology's simplicity is *especially* important for beginning and intermediate students, and for their teachers.

The worst thing you can do when you're learning astrology, especially if you're an impressionable, sensitive sort of person, is to listen to everybody, to every idea, every theory, every speculation or "new" concept. It's the worst thing you can do because it will thoroughly confuse you. It will produce irritated ripples in your mind that then prevent you from seeing clearly or from reflecting the reality of life in your own way in your astrological studies. It is much better to find one approach to astrology and to follow it to its depths and logical conclusions. If it is valuable, if that approach that you started out with is basically true, then it will automatically unfold and flower. If the approach that you adopted is essentially sterile, you can then go on to another approach when you discover that fact. It doesn't matter, in a very broad sense, whether you start with a very modern sort of person teaching, with all sorts of psychological stuff, or maybe with a very traditional but solid and competent practitioner, as long as you learn that system and take it to its conclusions and see what it will do for you in your life. It's difficult to navigate a river in two boats. You've got to see what one system can do, I feel, before you know whether you want to study another system, or adapt it or change it to something new. After you have built a foundation of the procedures and ideas that you find through experience work in your life and provide you with clarity and understanding, then you can experiment with various refinements or expansions of the basics. I just tell people, beginners especially, that at the beginning of astrological studies they should look for something that's true and revealing and accurate and workable *for you personally.* If it doesn't feel right to you and make you feel elevated in some way, forget it. Then learn it, develop it, use it for a long time, and then you'll know what was there, because you will have made it your own.

Ancient Laws & Astrological Laws

Astrology will eventually need a systematic statement of its laws, definitions, and postulates.* (Everybody take a deep breath now!) The title of this talk is "Ancient Laws–Modern Interpretations." Unfortunately, it's hard to relate to that subject today because a lot of the ancient astrological laws aren't stated very clearly. They're found here and there, or they're found in fragments here and there. I think we are a long way from being ready for the birth of a systematic statement of modern astrology's laws and basic definitions. But it is slowly happening, and you never know when an astrological Newton or Einstein might show up and tie it all together.

*As stated earlier, such a statement is doomed to failure if done too rigidly. However, formulating astrology's basic laws, definitions, and postulates can be done both systematically *and* in a flexible, open-ended manner; and I submit that much of this work has already been done, but that few people recognize it.

If such a systematic statement of the laws and definitions of astrology can be achieved, it will have to be based on observation rather than speculation. Since astrology deals most effectively and immediately with inner life and thus with a domain of life that is not easily measured, such a systematic statement will not come from statistics but from extraordinarily penetrating and perceptive observation of the subtleties of life, combined with disciplined logic and sharp discrimination. Then some real-life equations might come into being. Many of us know a lot of real-life astrological equations that are extremely accurate and that we can rely on. But the twenty-five equations that you know and the thirty-six that I know aren't even the same, in many cases! So these astrological laws and this vast observational experience are widely scattered and not synthesized nor systematically accumulated.

I have to borrow a couple of things from Euclid's *Elements* to give you an example of what I mean by a systematic statement of astrological laws. Many of you will remember Euclid's name and propositions from studying geometry years ago. Many years after I studied geometry, I began to feel especially thankful that I had studied it when I got into astrology. Euclid's *Elements* is the foundation of a great deal of modern mathematics, as well as logic. It's made up of hundreds of "propositions" which are then mathematically proven out. But preceding all those hundreds of propositions are 23 "definitions," 5 "postulates," and 5 "common notions." So you have a total of 33 fundamental statements upon which all the rest of his work is based. Now astrology needs that, I think. Astrology needs to develop that. We need an astrological Euclid. Only after Euclid set forth those basics could he go on with the propositions. Astrology is swarming with propositions, thousands of them. Various equations, correlations, and statements that such-and-such in a certain sign in a certain house or aspecting such-and-such, means such-and-such. We all know that many of those propositions are true and others are false, and others need to be rephrased to be more broadly accurate. But the definitions and the basic postulates and assumptions need to be clarified. That's one reason that, at the risk of boring audiences for the last two years, I keep talking about all these kinds of fundamental issues in astrology.

By the way, Archimedes, another famous mathematician, before setting forth his mathematical propositions, first set forth "definitions" and then a series of what he called his "assumptions." Only after that did he go on with his propositions. When reading the works of Euclid and Archimedes recently, it occurred to me that in 1936, when Dane Rudhyar published a truly "break-through" book, *The Astrology of Personality,* he wrote, "astrology is an *algebra of life.*" I think that's true. It's a funny algebra, though. It has developed sort of backwards, I guess mainly through observation, with propositions being accumulated by the thousands before the definitions and postulates and assumptions were ever clearly stated. Now let's get the definitions and the assumptions in astrology; that will help weed out the erroneous propositions.

I want to borrow two of Euclid's so-called "common notions," which are basic assumptions upon which a great deal of mathematics is based. These may sound very familiar to you.

> Common Notion #4: Things which coincide with one another are equal to one another.

That's so simple that the modern mind can't handle it. Think about that: "Things which coincide with one another are equal to one another." You see, our modern mentality is schizoid. It's dissociated—subject-object. Everything is scattered. But if it's true, that things which coincide with one another are equal to one another, then we can go back to a lot of traditional astrological language. This statement parallels the microcosm-macrocosm idea that astrologers have used for years: "as above, so below." More specifically, if the movement of the planets in the signs and in the houses, and their various alignments with each other, coincide invariably with certain archetypal sorts of experiences and with certain qualities of experience, then they are equal to one another. In other words, if those movements of the planets coincide with the functioning of your mind (i.e., your absolute experience of life), then *the planets are your mind,* or at least—to use less archaic perception—the planetary pattern is equal to the psychological state.

With the modern mentality, we don't like to talk like that; we don't want to talk about "Jupiter made me do it," and we like to believe that we can control our lives to some extent. But we're part of the same cosmic fabric as those planets, whether you think of it causally as the planets "influencing" us, or synchronistically and acausally: we experience this while Jupiter moves like this–it really doesn't matter. But we're part of the same thing. More and more I ask myself, "Why put in all these intermediary concepts?" Why not just accept the planets as part of life and talk about them directly? Have them live once again in an immediate sort of way! After all our exploring, we come back to where we started but only then do we know the place for the first time. If things coincide with one another, they're equal to one another. So if Saturn invariably correlates (or coincides) with a certain sort of experience, it's simply a Saturnine experience, just like the ancients have told us. The modern mind's state of total dissociation is unfortunate and separates us from the cosmos and robs us of all simplicity.

Common Notion #5: The whole is greater than the part.

Now this idea is not very popular today either, especially among technocrats. This little gem explains why no one is succeeding in isolating one astrological factor and then subjecting it to statistical analysis and getting any meaningful results. We're isolating the part from the whole. This Euclidian notion, "the whole is greater than the part," also acknowledges the aesthetic and holistic dimension of life itself as well as the holistic dimension of astrological practice and hence the need to see the whole person and the whole chart, to read the music of life as it vibrates in reality.

It's my feeling that it's much better for us to work at developing *the ability to read that music,* to apprehend the whole, than to introduce more isolated factors into the picture. My own aesthetic bias is getting more dominant over time–the whole *is* greater than the part–simplicity and aesthetic qualities like that are becoming more and more important to me, mainly because *they work!* They *reveal.* If you can focus on things through a simple system, you begin to *see.* You begin to have things revealed that cannot be revealed in any other way—certainly not through analysis. The whole *is* greater than the part. I was fortunate in that the first intelligent astrological books I read were Rudhyar's; and he, of course, many years ago was talking in terms of holism, and I immediately liked the idea. But it was many, many years before I could feel what that meant with a chart and with the person. There were many years of wading through the isolated factors before the whole began to reveal itself.

Retaining the Simplicity in Modern Interpretation

Now let's look at a few basic factors in astrology, and let's see if the cosmic language can speak to us *on its own terms* and *illuminate* life in its own way without us intruding too much. We do have to speak English, unfortunately. In fact, it occurred to me this morning when I reviewed these notes, that it would be such an advantage if we could grow up using the astrological language and thereby learn it instantly and naturally. It wouldn't then require so many stages of translation in our own minds before we understood it. As things are, we have to learn so much, and then *unlearn* it. So it's a long, long process.

First of all, the elements are a good example of the simplest and yet most useful, things: only four factors, and you can just do infinite things with them. You could, in many cases, do an extremely good counseling session just based on the elements emphasized in the person's chart. At a talk I gave in 1976, a man in the audience spoke up and said that he was actually "embarrassed" at how much he could do with the elements alone. It made him feel like he had wasted a lot of time on a lot of other, less essential things. The term he used was "embarrassed." He said he could find out all sorts of things just with the four elements. He was tuning in real well on the elements. The four elements are a beautiful example of the most ancient and universal of concepts. The four elements (in some cases five elements in the Orient) are such a fundamental feature of many different cultural systems, and healing and astrological systems. To me, they're not just symbols; they're actually "stuff."

Jupiter

I mentioned before that Jupiter, the Moon, and the Ascendant are three factors that are not emphasized or explained enough in the literature; and it's really almost shocking, certainly disappointing. There are so many books on Saturn, for example. Don't you think we should emphasize Jupiter more? Not just Saturn and Pluto and Neptune and problems and crises and all that creates difficulty! We've got to have some Jupiter. But Jupiter is too simple, and no one likes simple things these days. Jupiter represents philosophy, too. And we don't live in a philosophical age; we live in a relativistic age. Everybody's *thinking* all the time. They don't *believe* anything! Or they change their beliefs every few days. Jupiter has so much to do with the simple principle of *expansion,* and in many cases, I think, the word "improvement" is valid. Of course, not every Jupiterian expansion is an improvement. But so often, people feel that there's been an improvement in their lives in the area expanded by transiting Jupiter.

One thing I've noticed just in the last year (maybe it's because I've become more Jupiterian, with transiting Jupiter trining my Ascendant and Saturn) is that the Jupiter sign of any person is always a powerful personality "tone." That sign's qualities seem to be invariably very strong, although not always obvious at first. Even if the person has nothing else in that sign, no other planet in Jupiter's sign, still that sign's quality is pervasive throughout the individual's personality and character. The way I wrote it in my notes is that "the person has a *strong dose* of those qualities, and *usually* the more positive aspects of that sign's qualities." I will not go out on a limb and say that everyone *always* expresses the most positive qualities of the Jupiter sign, but in many cases they seem to have that sign's energy and qualities and abilities together in quite a highly developed state. Those qualities and abilities are so natural for them that they'll often take them for granted.

It seems to be extremely common to see a very well developed example of a certain sign in a person whose Jupiter is in that sign—especially common if they're strongly Piscean or

Sagittarian people. That is, if major factors in the birth chart are in Pisces or Sagittarius, then the Jupiter sign is particularly powerful, even if no other planet is in that sign. A good example is someone I know who has a Pisces Sun and Sagittarius Moon. That person has Jupiter in Virgo but no other planets there. Virgo is astoundingly powerful for that person in many ways that I won't go into now. But the Virgoan qualities are very well developed, and generally in positive ways, without being a particularly over-critical person.

Jupiter can also explain a lot about relationships, especially about relationships that work well, which is not emphasized much in the literature of synastry. Most chart comparison books seem to dwell on problematical features of relationships. In fact, one might ask, "Isn't Jupiter a planet of love, even more than Venus?" Venus weighs everything and is very self-oriented, pleasure-oriented, and limited to a narrow field of action.* You think of Taurus' keyword, "I have," which is so valid. Then you think of Libra, which can handle one person, but no more. They want relationships to be fairly exclusive. But Jupiter is impersonal. It's not limited to the personal. It's broader, more generous, less judgmental, more tolerant than Venus. So when you talk about relationships, for example, you look at Venus and very often you see *demands*—emotional demands. With Jupiter, you don't see demands very often. You may see disappointment from expecting too much, or maybe promising too much, or sometimes from wanting to give too much or trying too much.

I have a good quote here that reminds me of Jupiter, by Eleanor Bertine, a Jungian analyst. Writing about relationships in her book *Jung's Contribution to Our Time,* she said:

> Certainly mutual acceptance and trust are the two cornerstones of psychological relatedness. [Acceptance, trust, means Jupiter. S.A.] Acceptance means taking the other person as he is, without reservation. People often say, "I like this about so-and-so, but I don't like that side of him at all." Such an attitude is not love. Its concern is with the assets and liabilities of the other person, not with the person himself. When one loves, one accepts the other in his

*This is true of Venus in *most* signs. In fact, it's mainly when Venus is in the two signs ruled by Jupiter (Pisces and Sagittarius) that you most often find Venus' more generous and noble qualities. The above comments on Jupiter refer to its *essential principle;* this does not deny the fact that it is distorted in some people, thus becoming preachy intolerance.

> entirety as a human being, with faults as well as virtues. [That's the Jupiter experience! S.A.] One sees the whole person, and his very faults are part of his beloved humanness. . . . So we see that full acceptance requires and presupposes the presence of the other cornerstone, namely trust. (page 162)

She's talking about Jupiter there, not Venus. That's just one aspect of Jupiter that you don't get from most books. Jupiter is much more than an abstract principle of expansion. It's very much in your everyday life. In relationships, people rarely want or love or like or accept the other person in his or her totality, and that of course often leads to misunderstandings. Jupiter gives you the key to developing tolerance and acceptance, and you can consciously cultivate that impersonal type of love that Venus only rarely attains.

The Moon

The astrological literature on the Moon (outside of the Orient) is pathetic, especially considering that probably 85% of the people active in astrology are women. Some of you women are going to eventually have to get together and write something on the Moon! But I must admit that the Moon naturally doesn't lend itself to being written about. It's so much feelings and nuances and moods. Still I'd like to make just a couple observations about the importance of the *lunar principle.* We could get into a whole workshop just on that subject and about the re-emergence of the lunar principle in the Western world. We do have to acknowledge that it's a powerful re-emergence. The Western world's emphasis for so long has been on the individualized ego, the Sun. We emphasize the Sun signs. Whereas if you look to a more collective culture, for example India, the individualized ego is much less developed in most people than in the Western world, and the astrology of such cultures is always more lunar than ours.

The Hindu definition of *mind* includes the Moon, emphasizing it much more than Mercury. That tells us something too. In the West we confuse Mercury with mind. We think, "Oh, I'm so smart, I got A's or a high score on my IQ test." But that's just the tiny, narrow calculator-dimension of the mind. The Moon is the mind in the broadest sense of the word: the collective mentality, the family, memory . . . you can perhaps even take memory to mean more of the past than just in this life. The Moon is also the feelings. In the West, we don't like to admit (or we're taught not to acknowledge) that most of us think mainly with our feelings, and then we quickly ask Mercury to provide us with a "logical" rationalization for how we feel. We don't think so much with our heads as we'd like to believe.

Although the Moon is strongest in less individualistic cultures than ours, the Moon in all human beings shows a *persistent collective feeling or mood.* One could write a whole book on the Moon and say many things about it, and this is just one approach to understanding the Moon. It shows a persistent collective feeling or mood, or both, that's *always there* in a person. But it is a predisposition that comes out especially in social situations, in any collective situation, any family situation, any domestic situation. The Moon's "collective" qualities are activated any time you are seeking some sense of *belonging.* It's a feeling in every person of "Let *us* do or be or feel something"–a collective feeling. If one can't express that urge and that feeling, if one can't express and satisfy those emotions in a social situation, in a close relationship, or–especially–in a domestic or family situation, then one can't feel comfortable, accepted, at ease, secure, and nourished. (You also notice the Moon's collective feeling states even in a small office where the *atmosphere* is immediately influenced by everyone's *moods.*) The Moon reveals your reaction to and sensitivity to the environment–especially the social environment.

In a social situation, for example, the Moon starts to stir. At the party tonight, therefore, a lot of people's Moons will be real active. People will want to feel *comfortable* in the environment, and the needs and emotions of the Moon have to start coming out or you just won't feel very good. So how might the various Moon signs react in social situations in terms of the Moon showing this environmental sensitivity and this subliminal feeling of "Let us do or be something." So, partly for fun, let's play "fill in the blanks." So we'll quickly go through the Moon signs, and experiment with how each one *feels* in a social situation.

Moon in Aries: Let's *activate* and *energize* the environment. Dynamize your immediate surroundings so you feel comfortable. Let's activate the environment, let's energize it. Doing anything is better than doing nothing. Certainly doing anything is better than silence! So there's that quality, that feeling, in an Aries Moon, and it's there all the time. But certain situations elicit it.

Moon in Taurus: Let's *control* the environment, put it in my order, and keep it that way! Then I'll feel secure. People must ask permission if they want to change anything in my area of control. No spontaneity will be allowed unless I plan it in advance and proceed with it slowly.

Moon in Gemini: There's a deep, deep feeling that says, "Let's *communicate.* Let's make connections with the environment." Let's get out there and wire in to all that stuff!

Moon in Cancer: Let's *merge* in the environment. Of course if the environment is at all unfamiliar or threatening, you don't want to merge. So then it's *let's retreat!* Or let's go back home because this isn't my kind of atmosphere.

Moon in Leo: Let's *vitalize* the environment. Let's *encourage* everybody to feel *great!* And then they'll love me for it.

Moon in Virgo: Let's be *proper* and *restrained* and intelligent in this environment, and we'll analyze it in a logical fashion and decide exactly how it measures up. Or it could be "Let's criticize this environment" if the person is super-sensitive and high-strung, as is often the case.

Moon in Libra: Let's establish *harmony* with the environment. We don't want to rock too many boats at once here. Occasionally a Libra Moon (and some of you have seen this, I'm sure) goes off the deep end and decides it's not worth the effort to try to be liked anymore. Then they seem to intentionally irritate everybody. Then their feeling is, "All right, let's *oppose* the environment just on principle!"

Moon in Scorpio: Let's *hide* from the environment, or let's *understand* its hidden workings. Even if there *aren't* any hidden workings, they'll still try to understand them anyway and may well imagine all sorts of secret goings-on, some of which might be directed against them. So Scorpio Moon also feels, "You better keep a close watch on the environment. Be wary!"

Moon in Sagittarius: This is a quote from somebody with a Sagittarius Moon: "I always feel, let's *jolly up* the environment." (She is English.) Or let's *inspire* the environment, let's *uplift* the people by teaching them. Keep in mind that this is a subliminal thing. It's not that you consciously think, "Oh, yes, I must uplift the environment." It's the Moon's urge in you.

Moon in Capricorn: Let's *structure* the environment, which implies a degree of control over it. So it's also sometimes, let's assume responsibility for this entire environment, or let's become boss of the entire environment. It's also at times, let's *defend* ourselves from the environment.

Moon in Aquarius: Let's *electrify* the environment. Or even more so, let's *disrupt* it. I can't stand this orderliness, or this predictability and tranquility. Let's disrupt it, let's revolutionize the environment, just for the fun of it.

Moon in Pisces: Let's *imagine* what we want the environment to be, let's create our own environment in our minds. Let's *escape* from the environment, or let's be sympathetic toward anything out there. Let's love and help the whole environment.

Similarities Between Virgo & Scorpio

The following is another example of how a very basic factor, *if understood properly,* explains all sorts of things without the need to introduce some secondary minor factor. A great deal of confusion stems from not recognizing the full spectrum of a basic factor's nature and thus looking for something minor in the chart to explain it. Over a period of time I happened to deal with a series of people, all of whom acted as editors and agents in the publishing field. Their similarity of personality really struck me. I eventually found that they all had Sun in Leo and strong Pluto and/or Scorpio emphasis in their birth charts. This started me paying attention to aspects of Pluto and Scorpio that are often dominant, but rarely mentioned.

Especially the two that I had extensive dealings with were extremely analytical and extremely sharp at sizing up all sorts of things—business decisions, manuscripts, and so on. And yet there was no trace of Virgo in either person. Mercury was quite strong in both of them, but not enough to be that sharp. And their Mercury signs were Leo in both cases, which tends toward an enthusiastic and often dynamic mind, creative and broad, but not particularly analytical. When you look at the whole chart, in each case you find a tremendous emphasis on Scorpio and/or Pluto. One has Scorpio rising and Pluto in her Sun sign, Leo; and the other has Sun, Ascendant, and Pluto all in Leo. The Sun and Pluto were clustered right at the Ascendant, too.

These two people and a number of others with strong Scorpio but no Virgo led me to a further realization of the analytical and "shrewd" qualities of Pluto and Scorpio. Pluto and Scorpio are very analytical. They seem very much like Virgo at times, especially in their thorough attention to detail. They like to really pin things down and at times are just as finicky as Virgo is. *Thorough* is the word to emphasize. Scorpio is more thorough than Virgo, often compulsively so. But their analysis of a situation, thing, or person is so impressive, because it's not purely a mental analysis. It's a shrewd, gut-level perception. It's an analysis of the situation by the subconscious, you might say. It's not just a narrow mental exercise. They seem to get to the core of things. They somehow penetrate to the core of an idea or person or situation through their emotions; in their perceptions, they get there differently than Virgo. But the final result often looks quite similar! They have shrewd and often extraordinarily *precise* judgment. But it comes from the feelings and intuitions, not from the head. You see the shrewd, analytical deductive abilities of Scorpio also in their traditional affinity for detective work and research.

Another similarity between these two principles, Virgo and Scorpio, is that both signs very often turn negative—not only toward others, but toward themselves. They often hold themselves back a great deal; self-repression and excessive self-control leading often to personality problems are common. Virgo and Scorpio, probably more than any other signs, can cut themselves down, undermine themselves, hold themselves back. Also, Pluto and Scorpio—like Virgo—have the quality of worrying, fretfulness, and fearfulness. Vague anxieties in them often underlie a lack of self-confidence very reminiscent of Virgo. So the reason I point this out is simply to demonstrate that, if you understand the wide ramifications of only the basics, this tremendous world opens up, and you don't have to "account for" everything by inventing a new theory.*

Applying vs. Separating Aspects

The next example here is one of an old tradition that may need some revising. It's commonly held that aspects are more powerful when forming (or applying) than when separating. In fact, in DeVore's *Encyclopedia of Astrology,* which is generally a very good book, it says, "Aspects are more powerful when forming than when separating." Many people hold that to be true natally and in transits, too.† However, this idea may need to be revised. I'm pointing this out, not only because it's an interesting possibility that you may want to consider, but also because if in fact the opposite of the tradition is true—that separating aspects are more powerful by far—then that gives you another insight into a chart and its energy flow using just the basic factors, without adding more secondary "stuff."

Now in modern cyclic thinking, the conjunction of two planets marks the most intense phase of a cycle—the initial release of energy, the beginning of a new cycle. The separating conjunction, therefore, is still reverberating from the intensity of the conjunction. How can it therefore be weak? Likewise, the separating square or opposition aspects indicate a state of energy flow wherein the reverberation is still extremely powerful from the intensity of the exact aspects just past. Again, how

*There are many other similarities between Virgo and Scorpio that could be discussed, such as their common liking for health and healing work, military service, and anything having to do with "cleansing."

†This tradition is not without some justification, e.g., the argument that applying aspects in the natal chart are strong because they come into focus by progression. Still, it is a confusing tradition because of its ambiguity and the lack of definitions for "powerful," "strong," etc.

can such "separating" aspects be regarded as weak? Rudhyar, by the way, has done detailed explorations of the different phases of a cycle—for example, how the square aspect occurring *before* the opposition differs from the one occurring after it. To explore this idea briefly, first of all here's a quote from Barry Lynes, author of numerous books and pamphlets on new uses of astrology, including *Astro-Economics, The Next 20 Years,* and *Secret Astrology,* which is about Russia and the psychology of that nation.

> I have long believed that the last planetary alignment the Sun makes *before* birth [i.e., the last *exact aspect* formed before birth] is the major determinant of a person's or a nation's prime "orientation" or "way of being." I have long been irritated by astrologers failing to distinguish between applying and separating aspects. It is absurd to tell people that they are a particular Sun/Planet combination when that combination occurs *after* they were born. What they *breathe in* with their first breath is what counts—what energy is in the air! (has already been released by Sun, Moon, or planetary alignment)

Many other astrologers have noticed *through observation,* not just through speculation, that the most powerful results of an aspect often happen after it's exact. If you look at transits, Charles Jayne observed many years ago that Saturn transits often manifest some time later than the exact aspect. Students of astrology will sometimes await with foreboding the exact Saturn transits and when they get precisely aligned, they say with great relief, "Hey, I'm home free, nothing's happening!" Maybe even months later, the whole Saturnian development will ensue.

Those of you who have had transiting Pluto conjunct, for example, a natal planet have observed deep, profoundly thorough Plutonian changes that take place for *years* afterwards. Sometimes that transit aligns five times, and the transformation in your life can go on for years and years. During and after that period, you'll often find that your personality became more Plutonian. Those who have had a Uranus transit, especially by the "hard" angles, have experienced, no doubt, more revolutionary and radical life changes in the *next* couple years *after* the aspect aligns than in the previous couple years. That's been my experience. This is not to deny that some people are more sensitive than others to specific planetary energies and thus do feel the impact and corresponding changes of a planetary transit *before* the exact alignment. The main point I'm trying to make is that the energy release unfolds and manifests over time.

Physiologically, the ailments that reflect a particular transiting aspect often linger on for many years *after* the aspect is over. There is other evidence for considering separating aspects to be stronger than applying. (This is what I mean by redefining an old astrological law with a modern interpretation.) Some of you may not agree with this, but I think it's accurate, just based on observation, although pressure toward change does build up during the time the aspect is forming. Stock prices and the precious metals markets tend to go up or down fairly sharply right *after* exact aspects (and also right after planetary "stations," too–the turning direct or retrograde of the planets in the sky). One could give many more examples of this, the most noticeable of which is how the New Moon (a conjunction) *begins* a new period that is characterized by the New Moon's placement and aspects in relation to each individual's natal chart. In other words, as the Sun–Moon conjunction unfolds (or separates), the energy expands and develops.

Final Comments

I can't emphasize enough how much our particular cultural milieu and historical period imprison our thought. Astrology *should* be a way of transcending such limitations, so that we can achieve a cultural and historical overview of life itself. But instead we are often completely entrapped by relatively transitory biases and fashions. In closing, I want to mention two examples of this phenomenon and how we are thereby prevented from acknowledging or understanding some of the very ancient traditions in astrology: one example is *exaltations* and the other is the issue of *character* in relation to the birth chart.

The concept of exaltation is older than recorded history. For example, the ancient seven planets already had assigned "exaltations" in the Greek astrology of over 2,000 years ago, and we still use those exaltations today. In the idea of exaltation (as well as its corollary concept, *fall,* and I should add also the concepts of *dignity, detriment, dispositor,* and most rulerships), I think we have some valid astrological facts and laws and traditions. They just need to be defined more tightly, and then they are quite reliable. But just to keep to the subject of exaltation for now, the dictionary tells us that the word *exaltation* has the connotation of "elation and intensification," and also "noble, elevated, lofty, sublime, and of high station." Why is it that today we often take issue with such ancient concepts as exaltation, thinking them outmoded or irrelevant to our "enlightened" age? I submit that the idea of exaltation is itself too lofty for the relativistic modern mind, which can accept no greater level of potential development than its current state and which abhors the idea of sublime cosmic or divine principles that may in fact be *absolutes* in the ultimate assessment of human nature. In other words, it is difficult for most people today to accept the truths of life which exaltations imply, due mainly to our contemporary rationalistic way of perceiving. I maintain that one needs to understand and accept the reality of certain truths of life and human nature before exaltations can be acknowledged to symbolically describe valid ideals–i.e., the highest possible manifestation of the planetary principles.*

Exaltations therefore point toward character development and the possibility of improving different parts of ourselves. A materialistic culture ignores this growth of character, and a type of astrology that expresses only the cultural bias ignores the deeper values implicit in astrological traditions. You see the simple basics of a birth chart come alive most dynamically in those who have developed not only their talent potential but also their character. Everyone is born with potential, but few really develop it, and even fewer develop their character to the utmost. As the poet Goethe wrote, "Genius is formed in stillness, character in the stream of human life." Nowadays, however, people don't talk much about character, but some of the old astrology books do. That's another old tradition that I think we should

---

*Examples of the ideals symbolized by exaltations are: Venus' compassionate, impersonal love in Pisces, Saturn's rigid commitment to law and fairness in Libra, and Mars' strength of purpose and capacity for achievement when disciplined in Capricorn.

retain. Although I admit that character was often mentioned rather judgmentally in these old books, at least people then had a definition of character and a sense of human nobility.

We live today in a rationalistic, nihilistic, materialistic culture in a relativistic age, and much of our astrology reflects that, although we may like to deny it. This rationalism and nihilism is why few people in astrology today have the courage to speak of character. However, when Isabelle Pagan and Charles Carter and others were writing in the earlier years of this century, the question of character was always a major focus of any attempt to understand a person and his chart. It is not fashionable to speak of character today, nor of absolute good and bad, nor of "old-fashioned" ideas like nobility, courage, generosity, integrity, altruism, and so forth. I cannot help but feel that our contemporary alienation from the old standards and ideals (such as character) is a prime reason that we are uprooted from astrological tradition.

In today's astrology, the lack of simplicity and clear definitions is a direct result of the lack of sharply defined values in our society. Since today it is difficult to speak of good or bad character, we are often left with a formless puddle of vapid generalizations and rationalisms, often posing as "clever insights" or "shrewd advice"—especially in the astrological cookbooks. Astrology is an individual art, and we cannot separate it from the development of our own character if we want to practice it with others; nor can we speak clearly with a client without our having defined our values and beliefs for ourselves. In summary, astrology's current chaotic, transitional state today is a reflection of our society's collective mental state. That is part of the problem, a large part of it. We simply live in a chaotic age.

6

Key Issues in Astrology Today: Summaries of Small-Group Brainstorming Sessions

Who dares nothing, need hope for nothing.
— Johann Schiller

Where is the wisdom
we have lost in knowledge?
Where is the knowledge
we have lost in information?
— T. S. Eliot

During the Saturn/Pluto Conference in November of 1982, a gathering devoted especially to the "Purpose, Practice & Profession of Astrology," a series of unorthodox small-group sessions were held, culminating in the following reports. A variety of topics (printed in italics in the following transcript) were randomly assigned to different groups, and the groups were assembled by all participants drawing numbers. Various procedural guidelines were explained to the groups, after which they each followed their own initiatives and elected their own "secretaries" to record their findings. After initial "brainstorming" on the topics at hand, the principle issues, conclusions, and suggestions had to be put into some kind of order and finally into the brief reports that follow. All this was done within limited time periods.

The following material represents the spontaneous findings and key issues that over seventy people contributed toward defining. The transcript from tape recordings has been edited in order to eliminate totally extraneous comments, exchanges with the moderator, and so on. Otherwise, this material represents the "grass roots" expressions of dozens of people from around the world who are among the most active in the professional astrology field. Considerable discord and disagreement surfaced in some of the groups, which is to be expected and in fact welcomed in any spontaneous confrontation with serious and controversial issues. Yet, in spite of occasional friction, some excellent observations and suggestions were defined, many of which should be taken into consideration in any steps toward increasing organization or professionalization of astrology. I should also emphasize that no conference speaker or staff member, including myself, participated in any of these groups. Hence, there was no input from anyone except conference registrants to direct the findings toward any specific conclusions, and the only group leadership present developed spontaneously from within the group. This material is being included in the hope that it will stimulate further dialogue, communication, and effective long-range planning within the astrology field. S.A.

GROUP I (Halva)

How to build self-esteem and confidence for people for whom astrology is presently a primary vocation or for those who would like to make it their primary vocation.

1. Creating organizations and groups for people who are interested in astrology, which means that if you are interested in astrology, it can be very supporting if you know how to reach other people who are interested in astrology and if you know how to buy books and get information on the subject. I think that's a very good thing for your development, and I thought all the members of the group were thinking about the same.
2. Availability of information and education, which are almost the same, but not quite.
3. Asking money for your service.
4. Establishing good rapport with clients. By this we mean making a comfortable environment, giving people coffee and things like that, you know what I mean?

5. Self-knowledge. Knowing your own self, and also self-acceptance is also important. It's not necessary to be a "perfect" Jungian, or a perfect astrologist. That was one important point in our opinion.

6. Realistic and quality publicity in the media about astrology. That was another point which might enlarge your self-confidence.

7. Try to be open to new developments in the field. In fact, I have called this point "vesatility."

8. Make confidence through experience, and then the typical American expression (which I don't understand, but I think you will) just "plug away." Perhaps somebody will explain it to me, but it's not important to know it right away.

9. Study of astrology. Ask people who are critical of astrology if they have studied astrology. I think that's a good question when people have criticism, because most people who have criticisms haven't studied astrology. I think that's a very fundamental thing. You can get self-confidence by asking such a question.

10. If necessary, confidence-building courses. For instance, assertiveness training and things like that.

GROUP II (Barbara)

[*Same topic as Group I.*]

I think we were in essential agreement on most of the major points. But we framed it a little differently. We were dealing with the same question of *how to build up confidence amongst people who are studying astrology, or practicing it.* However, we did try to rank it in some kind of order of priority.

1. We felt, most importantly, *know and accept all aspects of yourself.*

2. Utilize techniques to become fully aware of your own dynamics: physical, mental, emotional and astrological framework.

3. Realize that you do not have to be a high priest or priestess, and that mistakes are part of the learning process.

4. Forgive yourself and learn from your mistakes.
5. Techniques of self-knowledge include:

a) Meditation and visualization of every aspect of your own chart–planets, signs, houses, and aspect patterns. Yoga and various kinds of bodywork, T.A. and various kinds of therapy.

b) Do many charts and be receptive to learning from charts. Ask for feedback from clients, and don't feel that you know or have to know everything about them. Ask them to tell you. Watch transits in friends' charts. We had one group member who encourages getting feedback from clients by offering a very reduced rate consultation within six months after the original consultation, which I think is a good idea.

c) Network with other astrologers and attend conferences, workshops, etc.

d) Trust your own intuitions and instincts. (I said that because I'm a Virgo, and I think it helps a lot to know basic techniques, you know, *before* you begin to jump off to interpreting on a strictly intuitive level.)

e) In teaching, help students to recognize various elements within their own charts with techniques such as "guided feedback" and games such as one group member uses where he has a pile of photographs of people by ages and sexes and he has students pick from those photographs the ones they are most attracted to. Then learning to recognize that these attractions reflect certain energies in their own charts.

f) Set goals for yourself in life and give yourself contracts, for instance, that you can let yourself fully explore and experience various negative emotions or aspects in your charts within a limited time frame.

6. Don't be afraid to charge a fair price for your labors.

GROUP III (Robert)

As an astrologer, what is authentic healing and what can you do to promote it? What are the authentic, therapeutic benefits of astrology?

We divided the question into two parts, basically. We've managed to get it together to come up with some pretty good ideas. For the first part, "As an astrologer, what is authentic healing and what can you do to promote it?", we came up with seven recommendations, sort of in a more process-type nature. It was hard to get a complete separation between what a good counselor would be doing, and also working on the question of authentic healing.

1. Developing a sense of rapport and an authentic feeling of presence with the client, the sense that the client feels that you're there for them, that you know what you're doing and that they can feel confident with your work.

2. Being non-judgmental and having an atmosphere of detachment surrounding the interaction–in the sense of not setting them up or putting out any information for them to be working off of; in the sense of not necessarily role-modeling, but at least not telling them what to do. Letting them tell themselves what to do.

3. Wholism in terms of cyclic patterns. Getting back to their own cycles and the balance of those cycles that are working within them and within all of us.

4. Insight into what is happening or about to happen, and the resources to refer the client to members of the helping professions if need be. Like if you find that you have a lack of rapport or if you needed to refer them to a stronger type of therapy or else someone that might be better suited to handle what was coming up.

5. Empowering the client–encouraging the client to own or re-own his own power.

6. For the astrologer, displaying a sense of competency or professionalism in his work. A lot of integrity.

7. Development of skills, or training of both counselors and clients in self-help abilities. In a sense, self-development as the process goes on, on a day-to-day basis, both for the client or the astrologer himself.

What are the authentic therapeutic benefits of astrology?

1. The process of individuation, or the client becoming aware of his own uniqueness, or self-validation. Self-understanding leading to understanding of others.

2. Getting the person in touch with unconscious "advertising."

3. Understanding of projections and awareness of how to deal with them.

4. Developing an overview, seeing the larger drama of life, the cosmic interconnections, or clearing their own personal perspective so they have a better viewpoint both on what's operating within them and also what they're doing in interactions with other people.

5. Pattern perception, increasing awareness of cycles and timing, beginnings and endings, upward and downward spirals—getting back to that idea of cyclic patterns that are operating in all of these different situations. For astrology itself, the flexibility that we mentioned about referrals and networking; it can be used so well with other disciplines or types of therapy, since it's of a sort of structural nature and it is so wide open that it can absorb so many different things and still maintain its own integrity, so you can also let the other therapy operate.

6. As a universal language embodying both symbolic and mythologic belief systems, operating from and leading to the archetypes.

GROUP IV (Dorothy)

[*Same topics as Group III.*]

I thought we did pretty well. It's not that easy to work in a group where everybody talks at once. I'll just tell you what we wrote down.

1. We wanted to be active in our own communities, promoting networking, developing connections, and supporting various astrology groups that are in our city. Also being conscious of people that we can refer our clients to. Being aware of the resources within the city. Educating the public and public relations. Actually doing group work—"the Age of Aquarius."

2. The primary prerequisite is the education of astrologers: continually working on yourself, becoming more conscious so you are more able to create an environment so that anyone else can grow or improve just because of your "beingness." Learning counseling skills.

Then we had a big discussion as to whether astrology was actually healing or not. We decided that astrologers cannot heal and we can only heal ourselves, although the chart can be used as a diagnostic tool. The primary consensus was that healing is anything that improves the client's condition. So it's basically towards individual growth, and healing is growth.

3. Becoming in touch with what or who your client is—what your client is doing. A lot of it depends on the counselor's attitude. Being able to listen, being able to emphathize (very different from sympathize), and being able to empathize without judgment. Being able to create an alternative perspective so that your client can objectify his situation.

GROUP V (Rose)

What kind of relationship should be fostered between client and astrologer? What kind do you want to build? What are the differences between doing "readings" and a dialogue format in a consultation?

"What kind of relationship should be fostered between the client and the astrologer?" We decided it should be *flexible*—it should be that of a client and counselor, or professional with the patient, or teacher with student. It should be detached, intimate, but non-Plutonian. It should be mutually respectful. There should be emotional exchange. There should be trust. It should be pleasant, friendly, and there should be conditions at times or no conditions set when they come to you.

"What kind of relationship do you want to build with your client?" It should be the kind that will serve the client best. It should be adaptable to the immediate situation and needs of the client, depending on the reasons for the client being there. It should not be cut and dried. There should be no set methods. All avenues for relationship and interchange should be available and open.

"What are the differences between doing 'readings' and a dialogue format in a consultation?" Readings are talking *at,* not *with.* It's giving *your* interpretation, your association, your perspective of what is, which is one man's opinion, which can be right or wrong, depending on how tuned in you are to the client's vibrations and expressions. Dialogue is sharing, interaction, feedback, listening, healing, helpful, offers insight, food for thought, creates different perspective. Consultation is giving advice, recommendations, alternatives, remedies and prescriptions.

GROUP VI (Bill)

What are some of the ways of integrating the astrologer's profession into the mainstream of the culture? What are some possible links and bridges that can be developed to the outside world?

1. The first idea to integrate astrology into the mainstream of the culture was through the media. Under that heading is advertising, pamphlets, articles, workshops, and especially writing bibliographies for all the articles that are put out—responsible bibliographies. Television, videotapes, etc.

2. A second idea was to have personal contact, personal communication, with professionals in other fields so that it could be spread on a professional level throughout the mainstream of society.

3. A third idea was to be in support of the VIPs throughout the world by contacting them, doing their charts, and soliciting them to speak for astrology.

4. The fourth idea we had about integrating into our society was to de-mystify astrology. Under that was knowing the biblical history of astrology; to make that language of *The Bible* and astrology to blend more so that they could come together instead of opposing one another.

5. Another one was to speak the language of the client, whether the client was a Navy man, or a shipworker. Direct your language to the culture from which the client comes, instead of just staying in our own language that we can derive from the books that we read.

6. Another idea is enhancing professionalism in the field. We have to form a respected and accredited organization that we could all support, and to distinguish astrology from other intuitive sciences. To really have astrology stand out, but not be related to Tarot cards, healing, or other related intuitive science fields. We would like to see it proud to stand alone.

7. The next idea was to have community participation as a way of integrating astrology into the society. That was through lectures, classes, parties, and fairs (astrological fairs).

GROUP VII (Carolyn)

Should astrology be considered a complete psychology in and of itself? What are the advantages and disadvantages of mixing it with the many other types of psychological techniques presently in vogue?

Our group was full of Aquarians and Pisces, so we didn't stick to the rules. We talked about the question, eventually. But we did it our way.

The basic question of whether astrology is a psychology in its own, we decided was true. It predates psychology and it is a framework for studying the structure of the mind, just like all psychologies are. It can stand on its own. But we can all benefit from techniques that psychologists have learned. In mixing the two of them, we felt the advantages of using the techniques of psychology were that since the goal is healing (client = goal) any of the techniques we could steal from psychology would be great.

The disadvantage we were most concerned about is that we didn't want astrology to get lost. For if psychology is to absorb astrology, then there isn't an astrology anymore. So we came up with these recommendations:

1. Astrologers need to work on developing counseling techniques.

2. We don't need to follow any one psychological framework. We just need to learn to be better counselors, not strict Jungians or strict psychosynthesis. But we could be using the different techniques from all these different forms of psychologies.

3. It may be a large advantage to have a working vocabulary in the various systems of psychology so you can make referrals for clients, i.e., a Pluto person might want to work with a Gestaltist, and a Neptune person may want to do dream work. This would be an advantage.

4. We felt that astrologers needed to learn communication techniques so any kind of workshops on communication techniques would be helpful.

5. We really need some more books on counseling techniques for astrologers. We felt that was a high priority.

GROUP VIII (Brigetta)

[*Same topics as Group VII.*]

(With German accent . . .) We dealt with the same questions. In the beginning we had a statement that went, "Astrology cannot be integrated into psychology, but psychology can be integrated into astrology." Like Carolyn said, astrology predated psychology and is so much bigger; psychology is just a part of it. Actually, we made one statement that everyone agreed to: "Astrology is the most complete model of psychology that we know of." We could all say "yes" to that one.

We got into a discussion about whether astrology should be integrated at the university level or not. I myself studied psychology in this college and found it very limited and really sort of boring to sit in the classroom and learn the things that I'm normally really very excited about. They get so boring in the institution because it's so rigid. We're talking about Germany too, and not the United States. Maybe there is a big difference, but I doubt it!

On the other hand, we disagreed. One woman said, "We really need some more esteem, reputation, recognition from the outside. It would help a lot to have a piece of paper that says 'I studied astrology and got a degree and can really do it.' Some people would listen to you more." Also, research is needed. People really go for numbers. We had different opinions about this.

7

Thirty Years of Working with Astrology

(Presented at a Conference in San Francisco
During a Jupiter-Uranus Conjunction)
[Revised for Publication]

> *True art is creation, and creation is beyond all theories. That is why I say to any beginner: Learn your theories as well as you can, but put them aside when you touch the miracle of the living soul. Not theories but your own creative individuality alone must decide.*
>
> —C.G. Jung

> *Astrology, a discipline rejected and ridiculed by Newtonian-Cartesian science, can prove of unusual value as a source of information about personality development and transformation....For an approach that sees consciousness as a primary element of the universe that is woven into the very fabric of existence, and that recognizes archetypal structures as something that precedes and determines phenomena in the material world, the function of astrology would appear quite logical."*
>
> —Dr. Stanislav Grof

This talk is a distillation of some essential observations that I keep coming back to over and over. It is a distillation of many years' research, reflection, discovery, and—I should emphasize—experimentation. The brilliant German astrologer Reinhold Ebertin, who is unfortunately still too little known in the North American astrology world, relates the Saturn-Pluto combinations to "in-depth research". I was born with that conjunction, and in-depth research has been one of my strong points. Combined with my Aquarius Moon and strong Uranus inclinations toward constant *experimentation*, I have for years attempted to *distill* the essence of various astrological truths, if they were validated by my experimentation and experience. It has not always made me popular that I could not in my experience validate many astrological theories, fads, and superstitions, but I have preferred to emphasize the positive applications and the reliable laws of astrology that seemed to be useful and of benefit to human beings.

I am also obsessed with simplicity, possibly because of my strong Libra aesthetic sense. And I was glad to see Einstein's statement that, if one really understands something, one should be able to explain it to a young child. If this group of people is going to transmit the wisdom of astrology to younger generations, we are definitely faced with the challenge of keeping it simple and devising a language that expresses the wisdom, the insights, and the inspiration that astrology can provide in a way that *anybody* can understand. Astrologers do not need to be esotericists. We can be esoteric with ourselves and colleagues if we want, but we need to use a clear, simple language if we want to reach more people—especially the younger people, many of whom are very open to the astrological language, but they don't really do the in-depth study, in my observation, that many previous generations did. After all, they have become used to immediate information being available on any subject they want, through computers, the internet, etc.. (Unfortunately, the quality of that information is often not questioned.) So, it's quite a challenge, I think, to find a way to reach people today that combines clear communication skills with the essential truths of astrology that are unchanging.

After more than thirty years of involvement with astrology, I am so often reminded of that famous quote from T.S. Elliot (see page 146) that, after all our exploring, we arrive where we started and can perhaps know the place for the first time. After years of experimenting with all sorts of theories and methods and reading so many things, including for years almost all the major astrological journals, I keep coming back to the same reliable things, along with a few new discoveries now and then. Recently, I did two years of intense research on Jupiter in preparation for my book *Exploring Jupiter,* and it just amazed me how I kept coming back to the simple, basic principles that I learned from Ronald Davison's textbook thirty years ago. [Now published as *Astrology: The Classic Guide*.] And I kept seeing remarkable evidence for what I learned from Margaret Hone and Charles Carter and from others who emphasize the classic meanings of the planets and also the four elements. So, in this era of ever-changing fads and claims of "NEW, NEW", I think it will benefit all practitioners of astrology to *deepen* their understanding of the basic laws and principles rather than constantly adopting ideas and theories that are supposedly new. No matter how clever or intriguing the new overlays may be, if the foundation upon which they are placed is not strong, the entire structure will collapse.

The futurist philosopher and architect Buckminster Fuller said, "Unfortunately in this world we were not given an operating manual for Spaceship Earth." That may be so for the planet as a whole, but it occurs to me that astrology can be seen as an operating manual for navigating through life. It gives us various gauges; it provides a type of radar, a compass, and it presents us with a cosmic gyroscope that indicates when we're out of balance or when we are likely to be especially stressed, to the extent that we will need to compensate by paying more attention to ourselves in some way—psychologically, spiritually, physically. So, it's an apt image: astrology as an operating manual for living, if properly understood and aligned with positive values.

There is another image that I heard recently which can be useful when we are confronted with the common criticism of astrology that it cannot be proven, measured, or scientifically validated. Well, scientists today use computers and disks all the time these days. But if you take a disk and grind it up and scientifically analyze it, can you find any information there? No. No information that you can ascertain through any materialistic analysis—none whatsoever. But does that disprove that there was information coded onto that disk? Of course not. Likewise, if you envision the cosmic mind as a sort of celestial or universal "disk", you can take the next step of allowing for the possibility, at least, that there is information coded into this cosmic (or archetypal) mind that can be accessed in various ways. And astrology, I think, is one of the more reliable and precise ways of accessing that information. I like this analogy. The fact that you cannot analyze everything materially or statistically is irrelevant. The question is: what is it good for? What can it show you? Can it inspire you? Can it help you understand other human beings and what you yourself are going through in your life?

Soon after imagining this analogy, I came across a supportive notion from the field of physics. The environmental scientist and astrological researcher William Keepin, Ph.D. has pointed out that the physicist David Bohm proposed that the universe is a *holomovement*: a single unbroken entity in flowing motion, in which each part replicates the whole. The three basic manifestations of this entity are matter, energy, and meaning, and each enfolds the other two. To Keepin, Bohm's vision was presaged by astrology's ancient principle: *As above, so below*. "It's not that Saturn sends rays to my brain and makes me do Saturnian things," Keepin said in an article in *Life* magazine. Rather, planets and people are part of a single process, bound together by patterns of meaning. Astrologers merely attempt to chart those patterns. But since meaning cannot be quantified, astrology cannot be proven scientifically. "It's like trying to prove the beauty of Mozart's music using chemistry," Keepin said. "Music is beautiful to those who hear."

So, this beautiful music of astrology needs to be reflected in the language that astrologers use in communicating their understanding of life's meaningful patterns. Admittedly, simplicity and clarity are an obsession with me, partly because of my Libran desire for elegance and symmetry. But my focus on clarity also came out of my experience with lots of counseling. I had to do what people needed, and it was obvious when I was communicating well and when they were not getting it, when they weren't really understanding me. So I had to adapt my astrology as it evolved to what suited people's needs. I did not really start with a rigid, pre-ordained approach. My approach evolved from what worked with clients. And from the years of teaching I did, I could see what sorts of ideas and methods of presentation excited students and which didn't. The teaching and counseling, in other words, were a constant "reality test" of the theories and interpretive phrases I was developing, Without that experience, my writings would never have been as well received as they have been.

Over the years, one thing I concluded firmly was the need to use a minimum of reliable factors in birth charts, at least with people who are not extremely advanced in astrology. I've seen so many computer print-outs in recent years that are so crowded with symbols and lines that it just looks chaotic. Especially when every minor aspect is drawn in as well, the chart no longer looks like a mandala of individual order but rather just like a huge mess of confusion and congestion! How can you get a sense of order and clarity out of that? Just from a statistical probability standpoint, you can find an infinite number of "reasons" for anything. So you have to find what is *reliable*. Just like in any scientific field, you've got to test and test and test it again, trying it in many different circumstances. And then use it if it tests out. Sure, there's an endless number of theories and factors out there we can use, but we better be careful. And there's an endless number of measurements we can do. But don't lose sight of the fact that when people go to astrologers, they are not going to find confusion or to collect a million petty details on a tape. They aren't going just to hear a lot of speculation, although admittedly some people do go mostly for sensationalistic predictions. But even if they seem to be asking for prediction, it may be their way of asking for clarity and direction. So, if you just throw a lot of data at them, they are going to walk out of there having gained what? Perhaps enthralled with their own greatness for a few minutes if you flattered them, or maybe all excited about some coming event that may or may not happen, but two weeks later what will the effect be of that interchange?

There are so many ways of looking at astrology. You can see the Cosmos as a giant system of ideas. You can see it as a weaving of archetypes. Dane Rudhyar said that astrology reveals the *structural patterns of life*. He didn't say that all the *contents* were shown, but the structural patterns themselves are revealed very well through astrology. Then all the details of all the events of life fill in those patterns. So, after studying Rudhyar in depth, I went on to study Polarity Therapy, which emphasizes the energetic reality of the four elements, and it quickly became apparent that astrology revealed the energy patterns of human life, of experience, of the cycles of life, and of your body. And you can work with those energies through various healing arts. Speaking of working with the energies, I found a great quote the other day from Dr. Deepak Chopra: "At the same time, the body is monitoring movement of stars. Biological movements are a function of planetary movements—circadian, seasonal, etc.... There is an underlying intelligence that organizes the infinity of things happening in the universe and connects all things with each other." (Interview in the *San Francisco Chronicle* January 11, 1997.) That's quite a profound summation of astrology, really, and very well put. So astrology is our way of *monitoring that pattern of order* that's pervading the stars, the planets, the body, our minds, our emotions.

One story I was reminded of when I read the Deepak Chopra quote is one of hundreds that all of us discover over many years if we've got our eyes wide open while we're using the astrological language, watching transits, and so on. Sometimes it's just amazing how literally this monitoring system and language describes what's happening in life. Many years ago when my son had transiting Neptune opposite his natal Mercury, he developed an incredible case of eczema. His was the worst eruptive case the doctors had ever seen. I took him to a homeopathic clinic where the most experienced doctors consulted for about two hours before they gave him one dose of one remedy. There was incredible improvement within one hour. Within ten hours he was 60% cured. Within twenty-four hours the moist rash was all dried up, and within seventy-two hours all that was left was scabs and scars; all the itching and pain were gone. And what remedy did they come up with? (I did not tell them about astrology or transits at all.) They gave him a dose of *Mercurius*. His Mercury was being "afflicted" by Neptune. His nervous system and skin, etc. were being disordered by the Neptune transit. It's a remarkable thing to study, and it should put you in awe, not about how much WE know, but of how little we know, as we watch the parallels and patterns unfold from the cosmic mind level right down to the event level.

The energy reality of astrology deserves a few more comments. I believe astrology can be characterized as a science of energy that can give you a blueprint of the individual's attunement of the soul in this lifetime. To me, the elements are the real energy substance of astrology, personality, and even types of consciousness; they can show your attunement, where you're coming from, where your awareness is rooted. A striking example of the energy reality of astrology is the following: I recently came across a quotation I had never noticed before in Ronald Davison's book *Synastry*—a very perceptive and worthwhile book. He basically said that "a relationship, when you are physically near a person on an ongoing basis, is like a permanent transit." I will never forget that quote! When we have transits, as slow as some are, at least they eventually change. But in an involved relationship, no matter how much those people are changing over time themselves, there are certain things present that stay forever. That, I think, is a reflection of the interaction of the two energy fields.

One of the reasons I was pulled into astrology is that I was always puzzled and confused by the vast differences in human nature, and I was especially fascinated by the question of *motivation*: what is motivating that person to do this, to think this way, or to seek a certain goal in life? Of course you can find out a lot about motivation from the traditional basic factors in a chart, especially specific planets' positions. But there are a couple things that are very important but are, I feel, slighted in astrological literature. Everyone says the Ascendant is so important, even though there are remarkably few useful things written about it in the available books. But even more ignored is the subject of *aspects* to the Ascendant. *If your birth time is reliable*, close aspects to the Ascendant should be considered as strong as anything in the chart, and especially powerful in revealing the motivation of one's personal expression. (And if one's birth time is not known with much certainty, looking at various close aspect to the Ascendant possibilities may help in rectification.) During the two years research for *Exploring Jupiter*, we repeatedly found incredibly famous Jupiterian people with Jupiter aspects to the Ascendant. When my daughter asked me to do her boyfriend's chart, when I first saw primary emphasis on the conservative sign Capricorn and no apparent indication of the rebellious behavior he was always expressing, I thought, "This kid has got to have some Uranus influence." Before getting his birth time, I couldn't see much Uranus influence in the overall patterns in the basic chart, so I said to myself, "He must have a Uranus aspect to the Ascendant."

And sure enough, he has Uranus trine the Ascendant exactly in his natal chart, and there's this rebellious streak, but also an innovative and creative streak and a growing interest in politics. So, I'd recommend that one keep an eye on these aspects, for they'll often clearly symbolize a dimension of the personality that perhaps nothing else explains so directly.

Another motivation factor, which can be overlooked in some charts, is related to the old idea of "dispositors": i.e., where are the ruling planets of the most emphasized signs in your natal chart? If you have a lot of planets—especially personal planets and the Ascendant—in a certain sign, always ask yourself, "Where is the ruler of this sign?" And, even more important than that ruler's house position, the *sign position* is crucial in an energy analysis of a chart. I eventually devised an entire system which I called "sub-tones" once the importance of these rulers' sign positions became clear to me. We can't get into the details of it here, but it is explained in some detail in *New Insights in Modern Astrology* (co-authored with Liz Greene), and it actually comes in handy in chart comparisons also where a strongly emphasized sub-tone links up well with dominant factors in the other person's chart. But the main value of the "sub-tone" idea is that it further explains people's motivations, and in fact it adds another level of sophisticated psychological insight that no orthodox system of psychology can provide. When I started looking at people's major sub-tones, it often explained a whole new dimension that I was overlooking before. I now think that its value lies not only in the way it makes you focus on the *energy* of a particular sign or combination of signs (and thus their elements), but also that such placements *tone the way the mind works* in each person—often unconsciously. In other words, once again this is a way of understanding human motivation more deeply. I believe that we still need to define many astrological factors in a more modern, dynamic, and practical way; and this sub-tone idea, I think, contributes something valuable by blending ancient traditions, psychological insight, and the simplicity of using the astrological fundamentals.

So you can say that each one of these interpretive guidelines that you discover is like a new lens that you try on your cosmic "macroscope". If it leads you somewhere and you see more clearly with it, then you continue to work with it and you refine it If it doesn't prove useful, you can throw it in the dust bin and forget it Most of the techniques I ever tried I have completely abandoned because I didn't find them useful. But what you find useful will depend on what kind of astrology you are seeking to practice, and what level of life you are dealing with. In a professional practice, however, the client's needs come first, and Jung's advice would be good to keep in mind: "We can never know in advance what course a given case will take, for which reason it is better…to abandon all preconceived opinions….[one] should use them merely as hypotheses for a possible explanation." "The enormous variation among individuals… has set before me the ideal of approaching each case with a minimum of prior assumptions." I might add that approaching things in this open way will also enable you to learn a great deal that will sometimes be quite surprising.

I myself have never viewed astrology as merely a symbolic study or a "mantic" art through which your psyche projects what it wants to, like the reading of tea leaves. Although practicing good astrology requires a lot of psychic energy, I have never viewed it as a way of channeling psychic work. I view it as a definite science, and I can illustrate what I mean by a few examples. When writing my book *Exploring Jupiter*, I wanted to include Churchill's chart. I had studied Churchill and his life intensely for a number of years, not astrologically but historically. I had in my files four different charts for Churchill, but I knew his life well enough that I felt that all four were wrong. Needless to say, if one chart is as good as another merely to trip off one's intuition or psychic powers through its archetypal symbolism, as some have suggested, there would be no way to distinguish an accurate chart based on true birth data from an inaccurate one. And there would be no need to bother obtaining an accurate chart. Well, I wrote Paul Wright in Scotland, the astrologer/author who is a Virgoan researcher, and he sent me back a chart I had not yet seen; and sure enough, everything clicked immediately with that chart and what I knew of Churchill's personality and talents. The new chart had Libra rising, whereas the others had Scorpio, Leo, Capricorn, and Virgo ascendants.

Likewise, there are a number of wrong charts published for John Lennon, which I had long felt could not be right. When, however, I saw the Aries rising chart published in Paul Wright's book *Astrology in Action*, with the Aquarius Moon, I knew that this was finally the right one. If you analyze that chart (also published in my book on Jupiter), you'll find—for example—an incredible number of factors in his chart which show a *sharpness*, starting with Aries rising, all the Virgo, Mars in his Sun sign and so on. Shortly after I had written the Lennon biography in my Jupiter book (in which I said, "He was always at the cutting edge of everything he did."), I was watching a TV interview with Elton John who had known Lennon and had worked with him quite a bit. And I was amused and pleasantly surprised to hear Elton John say that Lennon "was always at the cutting edge of everything he did!" So, you see, if you get a sense when you are working with someone's chart that something isn't right, trust your intuition. Maybe the chart is not right. If the client's resistance to what you are saying is noticeable and, in spite of their openness, he or she cannot honestly accept your statements, pay attention to that resistance! Either the chart is wrong, or your theories or interpretations may be misguided.

C. G. Jung repeatedly counseled therapists and psychologists to pay close attention to resistance. What he says in the following quotation is 100% applicable to the practice of astrology.

> ...it is more important for the patient to understand than for the analyst's theoretical expectations to be satisfied. The patient's resistance... is not necessarily wrong; it is rather a sign that something does not 'click.' Either the patient is not yet at a point where he would be able to understand or the interpretation does not fit.

Similarly, we should be careful not to hold our cherished astrological theories too rigidly or to get so wrapped up in our own monologue of interpretation that we fail even to notice such resistance. As Jung said,

> The patient is there to be treated, not to verify a theory. For that matter, there is no single theory in the whole field of practical psychology that cannot on occasion be proved to be basically wrong...The resistance might very well prove that the treatment rests on false assumptions.

There are various trends in society and in the world of astrology that we should look at carefully as a new millenium dawns. The pervasiveness of technology, and its handmaiden—a feeling of never having enough time—are obviously complicated issues, and we can only touch on a few practical implications here. Astrology, if it has any hope of being recognized as the valuable tool that it is during the 21st Century, cannot afford to ignore technological developments. It is undeniable that astrology practitioners today can save thousands of hours per year compared to the tedious calculations and research methods they used to employ. However, we should ask ourselves frankly, since we no longer draw up the chart by hand, thus allowing the subconscious mind to dwell on it and absorb it during that time, do we take the time to reflect on that chart before talking with a client? Practicing astrology well takes time, and no computerization will change that. If you're going to do good astrology work, you can't sell people a computerized print-out, spend ten minutes with them, spit out a few glib comments, and show them the door. It takes time for the magical, healing potential of astrology to manifest. For the deeper wisdom to surface, you have to have a dialogue; and that is lost in "internet astrology" and selling print-outs from a program written by someone you don't know that reads like a machine wrote it. (In my own work, we tested dozens of products that were being sold, and we could not in good conscience recommend one of the computerized "reports" to the people who contact us for referrals.) I was especially shocked some years ago when ads started to appear in magazines with the headline: MAKE MONEY WITH ASTROLOGY. These ads, placed by one of the largest astrology software companies, were directed at anyone, regardless of whether they had any astrological knowledge. All you have to do is buy the program and sell the multi-page "product". A parallel might be: "Send in blood samples. Make money with medicine (even if you don't know anything about what you are giving the people)." To me, that was a completely unethical business practice.

Data transmission has little to do with real *communication*. And words transmitted through an internet "horoscope reading" or through a print-out that is sold truly convey a superficial impression of astrology's potential for understanding, in most cases. In one study of communication skills, only 7% of in-person communication was judged to be based on the words exchanged. The other 93% was discovered to be tone of voice, body language, attitudes, vibrations/compatibility, empathy, etc. So, if YOU are not there, the vast majority of the potential communication will be missing as well. You are, in effect, the *translator* of the cosmic language who can give some guidance as to what the cosmos is saying for each individual in a focused way that relates directly to the individual's current situation. *Time* is also required to encourage the client to relax and reflect on what is being discussed, so that "free association" can take place… sometimes leading to one of those "Aha!" insightful flashes that could never come about from a standardized print-out of generic abstractions. In fact, one of astrology's greatest values is that it can reveal a higher order in the apparent chaos of life. But it must reveal it in its own time; you cannot push a revelation!

Although many people celebrate the democratization of knowledge that the internet brings, there is another side to this global development. One reservation I have is that there is a generalized degradation of standards in virtually every field that is widely promoted on the internet. One metaphor I read was that it is like having a museum with no curator; Picassos are hung right next to finger paintings by four-year-olds. That is nice and cute and democratic, but astrology as a field already has very low standards and respectability. The proliferation of astrology-related sites on the internet will probably have the result of astrology's being reduced to the level of a game, rather than a valid and valuable study/science that people can rely upon. I do not mean to infer that people should ignore this communication revolution. It does have the capacity to reach far more people globally than ever before. But perhaps those astrologers who utilize it should emphasize the standards of knowledge, experience, and expertise that those contributing to their web sites have, to distinguish them from the hundreds of "get-rich-quick" and superficial sites that are developing and will probably continue to proliferate.

Another aspect of the computerization of astrological work that I have to mention results from repeated experiences of important chart factors not being reflected in a computer-generated chart.

When you do a chart by hand and have to run your finger down the column of the ephemeris, you notice which planets are speeding up, slowing down to turn direct or retrograde, and so on. On the other hand, when a chart is printed out by computer, you merely see it labeled as "retrograde" or not. And far too often, all sorts of old-fashioned generalizations about retrogrades being bad or weak are then applied. I personally have come to conclude, after three decades of experimentation, that the speed of the planet is infinitely more important than is commonly emphasized—both by transit and in the natal chart. A number of other astrologers have come to the same conclusion. For example, Tracy Marks independently came to a similar view, which she wrote about in her book *The Astrology of Self-Discovery.* The *slower* a planet is moving, the more powerful it is. A stationary planet is perhaps ten times more powerful than a planet moving at normal speed through the ecliptic. And my own view is that the planet's speed is far more important than whether or not it is going retrograde. So, if you use a computer-produced chart, I think it is advisable to look at the ephemeris and see if any planet is slowing down, speeding up, about to turn retrograde or direct. It is another overlooked factor in astrological work, and an important one which I think should not be neglected even as this field becomes more and more computerized. If astrologers can employ the new technology intelligently, combined with solid standards and intelligent presentations to the general public, the Neptune in Aquarius period may be able to extend the reach of modern astrology in a way that benefits people world wide.

8

In Conversation with Stephen Arroyo

An Interview Conducted in England by Dona Spano
(Slightly edited by the author for this edition)

Dona: The focus of your work is changing and expanding. What is your sense of your evolving role in astrology?

Stephen: I'd like to promote certain kinds of astrology. I have connections in business and publishing, some astrological knowledge, international connections, etc., plus my moon in Aquarius, so it's relatively easy for me to promote new visions and concepts, in a number of ways. It's not that I'm against all other approaches to astrology; I want to push the most positive approaches to modern astrology, those approaches that deal with the real essentials that are often neglected.

Dona: What kind of astrology would you like to promote?

Stephen: Intelligent astrological psychology; a simple, clear language of experience that any intelligent person can understand.

Dona: You have spoken of questions needing to be raised, waiting to be asked, by serious astrologers. I want to hear your questions.

Stephen: I think of them as key issues, each of which raises many questions. Certainly one of the key issues is professionalism. The data of astrology is there. Astrology has a great tradition. There are intelligent people active in the field; excellent books are available. It has all been said, and now astrologers are running around in circles in their own world. It would be better if they could learn to relate their knowledge to the public. Many intelligent astrologers who would be practicing if it were a viable profession, providing a decent living, have been forced out of their field, out of astrological counseling. So much of astrology is alien to this culture that it takes a great deal of effort to integrate astrology into society, but it must be done. Astrology has made great strides in the last 15 years, particularly in becoming more acceptable to the public. But the intelligent application is the next step.

Another major issue is interpretation versus understanding. Using the chart for *understanding* is more important than convincing the client of the astrologer's cleverness in a brilliant chart interpretation.

Dona: How can we make astrology more credible, integrate it into our society?

Stephen: A lot of the astrologer's time is wasted by the general public's silly expectations. This won't change quickly. An astrologer must educate his/her clients ahead of time, telling them what he/she does and doesn't do with astrology, whether by phone or an information sheet.

The credibility of *astrology* has increased in recent years. That of *astrologers* needs to be established by each person in his/her own work.

To establish the credibility of astrology, we shouldn't try to convince the skeptics. Some astrologers may enjoy preaching—but if you're a good counselor, then counsel.

Dona: What signifies a good astrological counselor?

Stephen: All astrologers should ask, "what is the client's state of mind when he/she leaves my office?" If there is a superficial mental excitement that distracts for awhile or an anxiety about the future, then the astrologer is not very good. If the client leaves with restored self-confidence *and* increased self-acceptance, then the astrologer may have done effective work.

The client doesn't have to *like* what's in his/her chart; but he/she may need to accept it. One of astrology's greatest strengths is that it encourages the recognition of the warring factions within every person, so that a sort of psychological Geneva Convention can be established for dealing with the struggle within. It doesn't end the struggle, but it does clarify it.

Dona: In your lecture today, you spoke of the way some clients dig themselves into a hole, and then want the astrologer to climb down into the hole with them, and about the challenge to astrological counselors to use the clients' level of awareness to bring them out of their holes. How is this done?

Stephen: Establish communication with the person. Throw the person a rope however you can. Sometimes it's right to climb down into the hole for a few minutes to be there with the client, and then show him/her how to get out. But in general, the astrologer has the advantage of a much wider perspective if he stays out of the hole. Clear expression of a broader perspective might motivate the person to help him/herself.

It is essential to establish a *real connection with the person.* Words can do that, if used simply at the client's own level. Not all astrologers can do that. If you want to counsel, you need that natural capacity. It's a very demanding role. You need to *see* the other person. Somebody with a strong Leo energy may give a good "reading", but might not be very good as a counselor (that is, the self-centered, non-receptive kind of Leo). [But the Leo may make a greatly encouraging personal coach!]

Dona: Is there a future for the astrological counselor?

Stephen: The individual trying to make a living from astrological counseling has to fight. He/she needs to be very dedicated. It is such a psychically exhausting job; he can't see too many clients, and financially he often needs to teach also, and so ends up working long and varied hours.

Practitioners need to organize and professionalize. We need codes of ethics, an international understanding of the goals and purposes of astrological practice, and that needs to be widely publicized so that the general public thinks twice before going to an unqualified astrologer. But real professionalism starts on the individual level.

Dona: What is your sense of the value, importance and ethical responsibility of prediction in astrology? If, as astrologers, we have precise tools of awareness and an understanding of future trends, do we have a responsibility to communicate this? Can depth astrological psychology be integrated with prediction?

Stephen: Prediction in an individual's life is a delicate issue. If a prediction is *elicited by the client*, if the whole picture fits, if the whole chart points to something the client is asking about, then the astrologer may decide to give his stamp of approval, which may then feel like a prediction to the client. But it really came from the client himself; it would then not be an alien overlay superimposed on the person's life by an outsider. It is an art. Every case is unique. We can't make rules.

Dona: As astrology appears to be getting more and more complex, you are espousing simplicity. Where are you going with this revolutionary and cleansing concept?

Stephen: Simplicity is a significant factor. *It is premature for astrology to branch out excessively and desperately* until the fundamental traditions and principles are thoroughly understood and *put into modern language*. Astrologers can't even agree on the meaning of the houses or what the Midheaven signifies! In increasing complexity, we're dissipating energy that should be going into essential questions and definitions. Otherwise, astrology is building the new system on sand instead of on a rock.

Dane Rudhyar said, "The chart is a grid that is connected to the cosmos." In astrology we are translating the planets as symbols of the cosmic order, using spoken language as our medium. There is a need for care, discipline and simplicity so that the higher truth is not lost in the translation from the cosmos, through the astrological symbology, into English.

Dona: You have spoken of astrology as "an abstract study that needs to be brought to earth". Can you explain that?

Stephen: Astrology is geometrical, mathematical, basically measurement. Your question bring s up the issue of language once again: can the astrologer speak so as to bring this cosmic power and perspective down to earth? We have so many theoreticians speculating about astrology today. It is amazing how little of the human element of *experience* is in the astrological literature. The literature of psychology has constant references to real people, case studies, surveys, etc.; you have to go to real people to find the truth of how these abstractions manifest in life. And yet, when an astrology book is published that focuses on case histories and personal experiences that reveal and validate astrological principles, it *never* sells well and invariably goes out of print after the first edition. Astrologers, evidently, just aren't interested in reality. That is one of astrology's next steps—to acknowledge the individual's experience and variety.

Excerpt from an Interview in Chicago

Question: You've written a lot about counseling with astrology and many astrologers use transits as a basis for prediction of various kinds. How does predicting fit in with counseling?

SA: Generally it only does in a *structural* sort of sense. In other words, the transit can give an outline, but doesn't fill in the details. The person has to fill in the details. One thing emphasized in my books is that the individual client, you might say, has to *elicit* a prediction that is specific. In other words, they have to give enough information to the astrologer about their lives and their choices and what is coming up for them, as well as what their past has been. The astrologer then says, "Well, here is the cosmos' message," and "What do you think it is saying to you in this case?"

Sometimes it's so crystal clear, there's no doubt about what the answer is. But still, it is the individual that elicits the answer, from the cosmos; the astrologer is the medium for the answer. They are not the great all-knowing sage. They help the discovery process along by helping to interpret the cosmic language for the person who doesn't know the language or who needs an objective perspective. When most people go to astrologers, what are they asking? They're asking, "What is the cosmos saying?" This is a very important point that astrologers might want to think about. When people go to them, they don't need to get sensational predictions. Some clients pretend to want sensational predictions, but most of them essentially want help, guidance. They really want to know, "What is the universe doing with me? I want some order in my life." You, the astrologer, claim to know this cosmic language, and they want it interpreted. "Give me the translation. What is it?" Unfortunately, often what they hear is more gibberish than they can ever imagine, with a lot of foreign jargon. "Your square, your trine, your sextiles, your Chiron, your asteroids." That is not going to help them at all, if that's what they hear. They have to hear clear language that says, "Well, here are the basic messages that the cosmic pattern seems to be communicating to you."

A good astrologer has to be somewhat nurturing, somewhat caring, and able to have some patience to go through it. If they just make predictions, they will never be good counselors. Most of their predictions will be wrong if they try to be too specific. The specific, right-on, amazing things I've come up with have always been because it was elicited by my intimate knowledge of the person's situation. Then, I sometimes got feedback months later where they'd say, "You sure were right-on in your predictions." Why was that? It wasn't because I plugged in many little variables in the astrological equation and came up with some brilliant conclusion. It was because I knew their life, or because they gave me a lot of feedback about what was meaningful to them. I don't think predictions, *per se*, out of the blue, ever fit into counseling. But definitely, you have to look at the cyclic aspect of astrology as one of its strongest assets that recommends it to the general public. It's not really "predictions." It is and it isn't; you have to be careful with that word. I've seen probably 90% of astrological predictions in my experience prove to be wrong.

Many people came to me or wrote me because of erroneous and frightening predictions from "astrologers." That makes me especially conservative on this issue, because I see the bad psychological effects, as did Dane Rudhyar before me. He really made a big deal of warning people about misusing the trust that people place in them, the ego trips, the predictions. The old fashioned fortune-telling approach benefits no one and may make a lot of bad karma, in fact, as well as a poor reputation for astrology. Definitely, you can predict certain cycles very accurately, certain structural patterns, but you don't know what's going to happen. You don't even really know if it's going to be hard for them or easy, or anything like that. A Capricorn may enjoy a Saturn transit. But you can know that the universe is impacting you with a foreign energy, or your energy field is being altered by a new attunement. You have to define this and work hard at it and know what your priorities are. If the universe is hitting you with some Neptune energy, "You're going to be more spaced out. You're going to have maybe less ambition and be more free floating; your imagination will be wilder. You're going to be more sensitive to everything." Those aren't pluses or minuses; those are just facts. They aren't fearful predictions or overly optimistic predictions. You can talk in a language that deals with the actual energy that people can understand. They can respond, "Yes, I've wanted to drink more lately," or "I've really tuned into music lately." Maybe they have Neptune transiting. "All these things that used to be meaningful suddenly have no meaning and I'm disillusioned." Great. Then you can talk to them more about Neptune. What does it mean? "Ok, it dissolves this, etc. It sensitizes you to every subtle influence." Then they can start tuning in on dimensions of life that they have never known or have forgotten for decades.

The overall question of communication in any counseling art is a question of one person to another. You've got to be able to make that connection and listen as well as talk. You have to develop listening skills as well as communication skills in a simple language. Therefore, that eliminates many people from the field. Many people are not very good listeners or not very good at speaking clearly. It's a demanding art to do well. There's no doubt.

Appendix: The Media Blackout on Astrology

For anyone who has read the preceding chapters of this book or who has been active in the astrology field for the past decade, there is no need to belabor the *fact* that there is an almost complete media blackout on any form of intelligent, modern astrology. (This is most true of the *mass* media; an occasional book publisher *has* promoted an intelligent book on astrology now and then, but only a very small percentage of the population are book readers.) The mere possibility that there might be some validity to astrological tenets and the implications of that possibility are so frightening to so many established groups and powers in our society that the media regularly joins hands with most "scientists" and academics in a conspiracy of silence, and—in some cases—even a cover-up of fraud, as I will mention below. When not sensationalizing astrology or naively promoting "scientific" misrepresentations of true astrology, the media portrays sun-sign columns as real astrology and inevitably ignores all pro-astrology research and statements by competent professional people, both within and without the scientific world. The media remains strangely silent when positive findings are produced by competent researchers, or when intelligent, capable people of proven expertise acknowledge the value of astrology and encourage its study. And the media, most strangely of all since ordinarily it loves a scandal and the possibility of destroying a reputation, also remains silent when the critics of astrology are proven to be liars, deceivers, perpetrators of scientific fraud, or at least completely ignorant of the subject that they are publicly condemning.

Hence, lest I indulge in the same type of baseless condemnations that astrology's perpetual critics are guilty of, in this appendix I simply want to set forth briefly some of the facts that prove my assertions regarding the vast media blackout on real astrology. Part of the problem derives from the fact that the media is afraid of rocking too many boats. Their primary aim is not to express truth but to make money, and therefore they do not want to alienate too many power groups or too large a segment of the public. How television views this taboo on astrology is explained in this quote from the August 13, 1983 issue of *TV Guide* magazine:

> The one absolute ban is anything to do with the subject of astrology: "It is the No. 1 taboo," says Garry Marshall (top Hollywood producer). "The big one. It's never been broken." Marshall offers this explanation: "Half the people in this country totally believe in astrology. The other half think it's crazy. So either way, if it goes on television, it is sure to offend half the people in this country. No network wants that." (Mary Murphy, "Hollywood's Forbidden Subjects")

As noted journalist Ben Bagdikian outlined in detail in his book *Media Monopoly*, huge news chains now control a great deal of what is reported, and deliberate censorship of vast areas of legitimate (and usually controversial) news is now *institutionalized* and thus commonplace. Various rationalizations are used for this type of censorship; many of the media believe that they know what is "real news" and what people are truly "authoritative sources." Others in the media believe that many subjects are beneath their exalted, skeptical, narrow, fashionable mind-set. But, no matter how the censorship (or blackout) is rationalized, whether it is done unconsciously or intentionally, the fact remains that it is happening in what is supposed to be the freest country in the world. Ben Bagdikian writes:

> Authorities have always recognized that to control the public they must control information. . . . By the 1980s, the majority of all major American media . . . were controlled by fifty giant corpo-

> rations. These corporations were interlocked in common financial interest with other massive industries and with a few dominant international banks. . . . The fifty men and women who head these corporations . . . constitute a new Private Ministry of Information and Culture.
>
> Twenty corporations control more than half the 61 million daily newspapers sold every day. . . . This is more than an industrial statistic. It goes to the heart of American democracy.
>
> More than any other single private source and often more than any governmental source, the fifty dominant media corporations can set the national agenda. . . . There is, in the output of the dominant fifty, a rich mixture of news and ideas. But there are also limits, limits that do not exist in most other democratic countries with private enterprise media. The limits are felt on open discussion of the system that supports giantism in corporate life and of other values that have been enshrined under the inaccurate label "free enterprise."

Open discussion of astrology is likewise limited in all the mass media because it threatens the enshrined values of the materialistic science establishment and the cultural religion of scientism, as previously explained in this volume at some length. In addition, astrology has now been declared "a tool of the devil" by many religious fundamentalists, who have – like the media and some "scientists"–neglected to find out anything about the subject before loudly voicing their strongly-held opinions. (It would certainly shock them to know that much evidence points to Jesus having been a member of an Esssene or similar sect, a group which actively studied astrology. It has also been convenient for them to ignore all of the astrological references throughout the Bible and the fact that one of the most recent and authoritative translations of the Bible describes the Magi from the East who came to visit the baby Jesus as "the three astrologers"!)

So, this taboo against any realistic, intelligent discussion of modern astrology persists, supported by a strange and not very friendly alliance of media, church groups, academics, and pseudoscientists, as well as various other authoritarian types in other fields. (You might say that these groups are united by their hatred of the common enemy–astrology.) Perhaps the most frustrating obstacle of all for any person or group which seeks a more fair and objective treatment of the subject of astrology is the limitless arrogance of the media. As former Press Secretary to President Carter Jody Powell describes at length in his recent book, *The Other Side of the Story*, the media often *doesn't care to know the facts* and will *never* admit that it is wrong. This was his considered opinion after intimate dealings with hundreds of media people for many years. The sensational story is what they are after—all the better to sell the product, as well as to further their careers.

A good example of the media's not wanting to know the facts and maintaining its perpetual neglect of all positive stories on modern astrology is the following. In April of 1983, an extremely impressive 4-day conference was held in Berkeley, California devoted to modern, intelligent astrology. The theme of the event was "Current Views on the State of the Art"—what could be more newsworthy? The event was sponsored by an established publishing company and was held in one of the finest hotels in the area, a hotel where many large corporations and universities hold conferences. As in any other professional conference, the speakers included quite a number of "authorities" in the astrology field, many of whom have credentials and degrees in other "respectable" fields: Dr. Bernard Rosenblum, M.D. (a practicing psychiatrist and author of a book on counseling for astrologers); Dr. Ralph Metzner, Ph.D. (former Harvard professor, author of numerous books and articles in the psychology field, and currently the dean of a college); Dennis Elwell (one of England's most respected thinkers and speakers on astrology, a professional journalist, and author of dozens of articles in magazines and professional journals); Leyla Rael-Rudhyar, author, and wife of the greatest pioneer in modern astrology, Dane Rudhyar, a man now also being recognized internationally for his extraordinary achievements in art, music, and philosophy; Barry Lynes (author of a number of books coordinating astrological research with history, economics, and international relations in a scholarly way never done before); Robert Kimball (an international lecturer on astrology who had also been involved with one of the earliest computerized studies of astrological factors); and Stephen Arroyo, M.A. [Psychology]

(State Licensed in Marriage, Family & Child Counseling, former university professor, experienced in many areas of the healing arts, and author of internationally acclaimed books that have been translated into nine languages).

One would have to assume that there would be at least some media interest in a major international conference in any other field if the event had a comparable lineup of speakers. The entire 4-day event had a total of fourteen lectures, and information on all the talks as well as complete biographical information on the speakers was assembled into a media kit announcing the event. All the information was sent, along with a letter inviting their reporters to a press conference, to over 100 San Francisco Bay area media, including *every* major TV station, radio station, and newspaper. The press conference was scheduled at a convenient time on the day before the conference started, to give them plenty of time to plan their coverage. In addition, all the media were notified more than three weeks before the event, in the hope that some reporter could be scheduled in advance to attend at least the press conference, if not the event itself. The media were also informed in the letter that they could call the conference coordinator collect to find out more information if they could not send anyone to the press conference. In short, every effort was made to make this professional event accessible to media coverage, and the organizers encouraged any type of announcement of the event, any story about the event, or any interview with one of the speakers.

The result of this effort demonstrates the media's disdain for any news about serious astrology and how the media intentionally ignores positive astrology stories and even consciously covers up such news: Not one reporter attended the press conference! Not one reporter called to clarify any facts about the conference, because they did not want to know the facts and did not intend to report the event as genuine news, in spite of the fact that it certainly was "news" for such a professional caliber conference to be held on the subject of modern astrology. Not even one newspaper or radio station announced the event briefly as a short news item or public service announcement. These are the same media that regularly and predictably run after any story that trivializes, sensationalizes, criticizes, or attempts to discredit astrology.

Is There Really a Free Press in America?

There is no doubt that many of the media who were notified in advance of the April, 1983 Conference and chose not to cover it quite enthusiastically printed and broadcasted the story in 1975/1976 of the 186 "scientists" who signed an attack on astrology. Among those 186 people were many well-known figures in the world of science, but unfortunately virtually none of them knew anything about the subject they were attacking. Their abuse of authority and their scientific responsibilities has *never* been reported by the establishment press, *even when many signatories admitted later that they knew nothing about astrology and had never researched it.* The 186 "scientists" were completely uninformed about the object of their scorn, and yet the national news which played up the original anti-astrology attack for many consecutive days refused to publicize the scientific fraud implicit in the statement. As Malcolm Dean later reported in his book *The Astrology Game,*

> Two separate investigations revealed that practically all of the scientists who signed the anti-astrology statement had not researched the subject.

However, the national media's complete irresponsibility and disregard for accuracy or fairness did not stop there. A counter-statement acknowledging astrology's great value and myriad applications was prepared by a group in New York, and it was signed by hundreds of people, including many with advanced academic degrees and "respectable" titles. It was certainly an impressive list of highly intelligent people, which is evidently why it was all the more important that it be buried by the media as quickly as possible . . . which is exactly what happened. Although submitted to many national media, to my knowledge no trace of it ever publicly surfaced. Hence, in the mind of the general public, astrology's reputation was severely damaged, and no responsible reply to the attack was ever formulated. One often sees, in "letters to the editor" columns in magazines, a spokesman for some group or profession being given the space and consideration to reply to criticism that was published in an earlier issue of that magazine. It appears, however, that such courtesy does not extend to anyone defending astrology. This is, unfortunately, a reflection of the mass media's attitude toward astrology. They will not hesitate to publicize any sort of hearsay that discredits astrology, and yet they tenaciously refuse even to admit the existence of intelligent replies to such attacks by competent professional people. This can hardly be called a "free press." All journalistic ethics are put aside so that the media can remain *fashionable* by automatically sneering at astrology whenever the opportunity arises.

Another example of this media bias, this preference to publicize anti-astrology propaganda (often posing as official scientific opinion) rather than anything that even remotely supports astrological traditions, is the complete lack of honest mass media coverage of a recently published book. Entitled *Astrology: Science or Superstition?*, this book was written by two associates at the London University Institute of Psychiatry, H. J. Eysenck and D. K. B. Nias. This book, while critical of some aspects of traditional astrology, also acknowledges that there are facts that support astrology and that a new theory might be necessary to "explain" these facts. They acknowledge that, "If there is truth in any of this, then its significance for science, let alone life, is obviously enormous." Perhaps most importantly, they expose the "scientific" pretensions of various anti-astrology propagandists who pose as objective authorities but use deceit to reach the conclusions that they want to find: "Much of the conduct of the critics [of astrology] has been less than ethical. . . ." However, not only have this book's most important points been conveniently neglected by the media, but also various publications that have a professional responsibility to review such books objectively have fallen far short of their obligations. *Psychology Today* must be the worst failure to live up to the "scientific" standards that it pretends to uphold, for it assigned the review of the book to one of the anti-astrology "scientists" *who is himself personally criticized in the book for unethical professional behavior!* Talk about a media cover-up!!

OTHER CRCS BEST-SELLERS